TO THE DARK TOWER

After leaving Balliol (where he was a classics scholar) and after the publication of his first three novels, Francis King joined the British Council and worked for them in Florence, Greece, Egypt, Finland and Japan – the reason, no doubt, that so many of his books deal with the problems of the expatriate and are set against a foreign background. In 1964 he resigned from the Council to devote himself entirely to writing.

Francis King has received many awards for the strength and sensitivity of his writing. He is regarded by both his fellow authors and by leading critics as one of the finest writers working in England today.

Also in Arrow by Francis King

A Domestic Animal
The Man on the Rock
The Waves Behind the Boat

Francis King

TO THE DARK TOWER

ARROW BOOKS

ARROW BOOKS LTD
3 Fitzroy Square, London W1

An imprint of the Hutchinson Publishing Group

London Melbourne Sydney Auckland
Wellington Johannesburg Cape Town
and agencies throughout the world

First published by Home & Van Thal Ltd 1946
Arrow edition 1975
© Francis King 1946

Made and printed in Great Britain
by The Anchor Press Ltd
Tiptree, Essex

ISBN 0 09 910540 3

CONTENTS

PART I

PART II

PART III

PART IV

TO
MY SISTER
ELIZABETH

PART I

FIGURES

From General Sir HUGH WEIGH, Dartmouth, *to*
Miss SHIRLEY FORSDIKE, St. Jocelyn's School

May 2nd, 1936

DEAR MISS FORSDIKE,—I return your copy of *South American Generals*, signed as you requested. To be frank, I do not remember you from my visit to the school—probably because I met so many people, and felt so nervous at having to make a speech before my daughter and her school-fellows. One's own children are so critical.—Yours truly,

HUGH WEIGH.

From the Diary of General Sir HUGH WEIGH

May 2nd, 1936

A mistress at Judith's school sends me a copy of *South American Generals* to sign for her. She talks of her *great* admiration, her *deep* respect, her *real* love for my books. Everything is underlined, the writing is perfect. Do I remember her? Perhaps she was the old maid who lisped and called me " General," and then knocked over the cake-stand in her anxiety to see me fed.

I have begun to re-read *A Farewell to Arms.* That is a virile book.

Mark Croft is back ; there is a picture in *The Times.* Incredible to think of this freckled boy returning from the Amazon with specimens I would give my eyes for. I should have spent longer there than I did. Shall I write to him and ask him to

meet me ? Those letters beginning, "You will be surprised
at hearing from a complete stranger . . .", how odious they
are !

Yet I should like to meet him.

Have put on another two pounds in weight. Must spend
more time on exercise.

From JUDITH WEIGH, St. Jocelyn's School, *to*
Sir HUGH WEIGH

July 22nd, 1936

MY DEAR FATHER,—You mustn't complain of my not writing
to you often. I am really very busy. Exams began yesterday,
and to-day we have the swimming sports. I think I might win
the swallow-dive, if only I can get over that giddy feeling when
I get on to the board. I wish I could dive like you.

A mistress here, Miss Forsdike, wants me to go and spend
a week of the holidays at her home in France. She is much the
nicest mistress here, I think. She teaches art. I've told her I
will go.

I'm bottom of my form again.—Love,

JUDITH.

July 24th, 1936

MY DEAR FATHER,—. . . But why shouldn't I go ? It's only
for a week, and you know you won't miss me. Miss Forsdike
will be so disappointed. I've already told her yes. And she
said we should bathe and go sailing and bird-nesting. And it's
so long since I've been out of England. Please . . . Father !

July 26th, 1936

. . . This is just to tell you that I *am* going to France—even
if it means running away from home. I don't see why you
should fuss so. Miss Forsdike is quite all right. I wish you
could meet her. . . .

From Sir Hugh Weigh *to* Miss Shirley Forsdike

July 27th, 1936

Dear Miss Forsdike,—A few days ago my daughter Judith wrote and asked me whether she might spend a week with you in France. Having given the matter a great deal of thought, I decided against it. To be quite frank with you, I disapprove, *on principle*, of any intimacy being struck up between a mistress and one of her pupils outside the ordinary contacts of the school. This is not a personal matter—please believe that. I am not hinting at anything undesirable in your relations with Judith. But I do really believe—and I should say this whoever made the invitation—that it is better for all concerned if the feeling of reverence that a pupil feels for her teacher should be left untroubled by any closer intimacy. You will, I am sure, appreciate this point of view, and not be offended.

Unfortunately Judith is a very strong-willed child : it is a fault which she inherits from both her parents. And in her last letter she has given me to understand that if she cannot go to France with my permission she will go without it. I am reluctant to put the matter into the hands of the headmistress, feeling as I do that we can arrange the matter between ourselves. Would you please cancel your invitation to Judith ? I am sure that some excuse could be found. And this would both save her face and release me from the unpleasant task of asking the headmistress to intervene.

Again, do please believe me when I say that I have no personal animosity against you.—Sincerely,

Hugh Weigh.

From Miss Shirley Forsdike *to* Sir Hugh Weigh

July 29th, 1936

My dear Sir Hugh,—I have done what you asked me. The invitation has been cancelled.

It has taken me a long time to decide to write this letter : and

now that I have decided, it is impossible to know how to begin.
For us English there is something ridiculous in making confessions. We feel ashamed, or uncomfortable. And at the
moment, even as I take my pen in my hands, I feel as embarrassed
as if you were here, beside me, instead of so far away.

But the thing must be said. You see—I love you. Oh, yes,
I know : I have only spoken to you once, I do not know you,
you are old enough to be my father. But there it is. When
I was fourteen, I saw your picture in a weekly newspaper :
you were then leading the guerrillas in South America. I have
that picture now, with many others. It is here before me, as
I write—the picture of a middle-aged man with closely cropped
grey hair, and the face of a god. That is no exaggeration. You
are a god, a superman : and we live in times when supermen
are rare.

Ever since I saw that photograph I have loved you. I have
thought about you incessantly. My life here has been dull,
intolerably dull, but there has always been this one thing,
this compensation. I have read your three books over and over
again, until I know every word of them by heart. And all the
things that I have found in them—the things that have irritated
or disgusted others : your brutality, your single-mindedness,
your obsession with discipline, your asceticism—I have loved
you the more for them. You are, as I have said, a god, because
only a god can do this—can exert some sort of supernatural
sympathy, transforming the humdrum stupidities of life. This
is not simply a matter of hero-worship : you possess my soul
entirely; I am yours, entirely yours, whether you want me or not.

There ! It has been said. And I am weeping, from the relief
and the happiness of the thing. I say it again—I am yours,
yours. For thine is the kingdom.

But what next ? That is for you to decide. I have acknow-
ledged your possession.

So you see, when I asked Judith to come and stay with me in
France it was not for the reason that you suspected. It was in

order that I might get her to talk about you. And of course your natures are so alike. It is difficult not to love her for that.

I am twenty-six. This is my photograph.

SHIRLEY FORSDIKE.

He did not answer.

The photograph was of a girl with large, almost bulging eyes, lustreless hair, and a faint, finicky smile. But the forehead was noble, the structure of the bones clean and clear.

As he looked at the photograph he felt a brief shock, such as one experiences when suddenly immersing one's hands in cold water. " She might almost be my daughter or my sister," he thought. There seemed to be a family resemblance—in the defiant carriage, the clenched fists, the deep lines running from nose to chin. It made him feel that her love was incestuous.

But then he thought : " She has imitated me—my stance, everything." The realisation gave him a childish feeling of pleasure.

From Sir HUGH WEIGH to MARK CROFT

August 15th, 1936

DEAR MR. CROFT,—How enjoyable it was meeting you last Saturday and talking about South America ! You seem to have achieved all the things that I should like to have achieved in my travels out there. I am afraid that I have been too much a Jack-of-all-trades ; and in any case, my military career has prevented me from giving all the time that I should to plants. But it is a rare pleasure to talk to an expert.

I have read that chapter you gave me of your book. Of course, my opinion on it as *literature* is absolutely valueless, but it does seem to me to avoid the defect of most classics written by men of action—I mean the tendency to be heavily " literary." Neither Lawrence nor Doughty (whom I admire as much as I do any man) avoided it. But you have. As for the subject matter : it is refreshing to read of such adventures in our unadventurous times.

But this letter was not intended to be a eulogy—though you deserve one. What I intended to say was : it would give an old fogey a great deal of pleasure if you would come and spend a week-end here. I can offer you bathing, sailing, and an excellent chef (my old batman).

Let me know.—Cordially yours,

HUGH WEIGH.

From the Diary of Sir HUGH WEIGH

August 22nd, 1936

Croft accepts my invitation, but asks if he may bring his fiancée. I had not realised that he was engaged—though I do remember now that when we left the Club he was met in Piccadilly by a gauche creature in flat-heeled shoes. I make the excuse that I am expecting Judith home with a friend, and the house will be full. He swallows it.

. . . Down in the cove this morning a Dartmouth naval cadet climbed on to the rock which Judith calls her Tower, and dived off it. I immediately felt I must emulate this—and did so. Really, I am too old for this sort of vanity. But his admiration made it seem worthwhile. Young, with the sort of hands which dangle too much at the wrists.

August 26th, 1936

Croft arrives. After dinner, he talked of his fiancée, the daughter of a gentleman farmer. I go to bed early, leaving him drowsing in the garden over a cheroot. He is incredibly young.

August 27th, 1936

Croft and I go bathing. The naval cadet is again in the cove, reading a novel by Taffrail. We begin by talking, and end up by racing each other out to the buoy and back. " I say, sir !

You *are* a swimmer ! " This from the naval cadet, half in admiration, half in protest. But I notice again that I am getting fat.

August 28th, 1936

Up at six, cold bath, two hours with the dumb-bells. Horror of getting old.

At breakfast I make a cynical generalisation about women : " Men love women for what they may receive in the future ; women love men for what they have received in the past. Man is for the possible, women for accomplished fact." A stupid remark—but true. . . . Croft, however, regards it as a personal insult to his fiancée. He sulks all through the morning. What it is to be young !

Pouting suits that snub nose and freckled face.

He is a Socialist. At dinner he tells me that he went to Eton and the House. But he is a Socialist. He is a little shocked at my heresies : " Man has a craving for hierarchies, pageantries, inequalities. Man must suffer, or make others suffer." He regards me as a reactionary : and of course he is right. I react against his flat-heeled farmer's daughter who went to Girton on a county scholarship, against the Left Book Club twaddle that I find by his bedside, against his breathless enthusiasm over the People.

If this were all that there is to him I should refuse to see him again. But he has found two new genera of cactus. He has starved, and been bitten by a snake, and almost died of amoebic dysentery.

This makes him a man.

August 29th, 1936

A sultry, suffocating day. I have a migraine which neither an early morning bathe nor a game of tennis can dispel.

Croft leaves. A queer feeling of bereavement, personal loss. Restlessness. The naval cadet is not in the cove. I lie on my bed. trying to read Borkenau's *The Spanish Cockpit*, and sweating.

If I were not so old I should go to Spain. But emotionally I should be drawn to the Republicans. And my intellect says " No."

Thunder to-night. Sheets of notepaper in Croft's waste-paper basket covered with unfinished love-letters. What nonsense one writes about that particular expenditure of energy !

My nose bleeds in the night.

Sept. 2nd, 1936

Judith is home after a week with the aunts. " How did you enjoy yourself ? " I ask. She wrinkles up her nose and then throws an arm round me. " It's much nicer being with you." Later she sits on my knee and tells me that I shall soon be bald. I have spoiled her horribly. But she is one of the few people for whom I can feel any tenderness.

We do not mention the funny little Miss Forsdike. But the letter and that appalling photograph are still in my bureau. My first impulse was to write to the headmistress, but I decided against that. Pity ? I hardly think so. Rather this vanity of mine. Of course I know that it is ridiculous for the creature to worship me in this way. The woman is obviously un-balanced. But—the letter gives me an odd shock of pleasure whenever I read it.

I feel as I did when that boy in South America threw himself in front of me and was shot by the snipers. It was an incredible action. But moving.

Sept. 3rd, 1936

Judith takes an unconscious delight in touch. On the beach she begins to bury me under sand. Then she scrabbles it away and begins to wrestle with me. There is certainly pleasure in this lazy contest under a hot sun. She is strong and lithe, and makes me feel that my muscles are softening. Later she curls up beside me and goes to sleep, her head pillowed on my chest. Her close-cropped hair smells salt.

The cadet from Dartmouth watches her incessantly. When she looks his way he grins. A healthy animal. But she doesn't like it, turns away pouting.

Sept. 5th, 1936

The cadet has a friend with him. The friend does not bathe—remains in flannels and an alpaca coat. He is about twenty-five, with a severe, analytical face and glasses. He glances up at me continually.

Sept. 6th, 1936

I am beginning to resent this scrutiny from the young man on the beach. How I hate his intellectual vanity. I should like to duck him and then give him a hard game of tennis. All head and no body.

Sept. 7th, 1936

The young man lies on the beach reading a book called *Passion and Society*. He has a physique if he would only cease to swaddle it in all those clothes. Judith and the naval cadet (Eric) splash each other and then race across the estuary.

Can there be any doubt where one's choice should lie? *Passion and Society*, or that delightful splashing?

Sept. 8th, 1936

The naval cadet joins us, bringing his friend with him. The friend stares for a while, then turns away from us and continues reading his book.

He is too self-consciously aloof. Judith begins wrestling with me and we roll into him. He moves away with a disdainful smile.

Sept. 10th, 1936

The young man makes me talk. I keep on feeling that I want to impress him. He is very intelligent. But that analytical gaze frightens me.

Sept. 11th, 1936

Again I talk to the young man. He shows interest, of a frigid kind. But I would rather have enthusiasm. Vanity, vanity! Why should I wish to impress him! Why, why?

Sept. 12th, 1936

The young man works in a bank in Cardiff. But he wants to write. He has a way of nodding his head at everything I say. It is as if he were accepting each fact and then pigeon-holing it for further reference.

He is one of those people who give the impression that they know more about one than one does oneself.

Sept. 14th, 1936

The naval cadet and his friend leave to-day.

" I am sorry Eric is going. I like him."

" Yes." This from the friend.

There is something in the inflection of that " Yes " that disquietens me.

" Why do you never bathe? " I ask.

" Because I don't like to."

" Can't you swim? "

" To be frank—no."

" It's time you learnt."

He shrugs his shoulders.

" Don't you feel you're missing something by always sitting here reading. When you're young, and have the chance, it seems a pity to neglect the other side."

" *Mens sana in corpore sano?* "

Is he laughing at me? But this sort of antagonism gives me a surreptitious pleasure. I have an impulse to pull off all those ridiculous clothes and drive him into the sea. *Passion and Society*!

At dinner Judith is thoughtful. Is she in love with the naval cadet?

A night of insomnia. The old dreams.

From General Sir HUGH WEIGH *to*
S. N. GEORGE, Oxford

Nov. 15th, 1936

MY DEAR S. N. G.,—Thank you for your new book of poems. But first I must congratulate you on your honorary degree. I get a certain cynical satisfaction out of your receiving this mark of esteem after that long-forgotten disgrace in Mods. Why couldn't they have realised then that you were one of the masters of the English language? Still, yesterday's compliments from the Public Orator must have made some sort of amends. And I know how much you must have enjoyed the dinner given to you by the Milton Club. You are at your ripest, and wisest, and most artful among undergraduates.

As for the poems: I do not have to say how fine they are. I think of the Beethoven Quartets: they will stand in the same relation to your work. You say you're a little troubled by adverse criticism from some of your contemporaries. But why? These poet-reviewers remind me of that old story of the Jesuits and Pizarro's men. The Jesuits told the ignorant *conquistadores* that the only emeralds which were genuine were those which could not be destroyed by fire. This was, of course, untrue; but the men believed them—and threw away the stones that they had amassed. Later, the Jesuits picked them up. This is what the reviewers do to your poems. They say that they are not the genuine thing—and then appropriate from them.

I have been asked to go to Germany in December as a guest of the government. What would you say to accompanying me? I know that you, the Liberal Humanist, will find much to disagree with. But perhaps I shall convert you.

Let me know.—Affectionately, H. W.

From S. N. GEORGE, Oxford, *to*
Sir HUGH WEIGH, Dartmouth

Nov. 18*th,* 1936

MY DEAR H. W.,—Thank you for the nice things that you say
about the book. It is the last that I shall ever write—which
makes your appreciation all the more valuable. I feel now that
I have nothing more to say—the rest is silence. It is not an
unpleasant feeling : rather akin to that lethargy, that sluggish-
ness which affects one after an exam or a strenuous love-affair.
I have thought this before—that there is nothing left in me—
after every book that I have written : but this time there is
something final—my positively last appearance. Of course,
I shall continue to write essays and give those talks for the
B.B.C. which you so much despise. But " the infirm glory of
the positive hour "—that is over.

The meeting of the Milton Club was a great success. By
the end everyone was a little drunk—except myself. As you
know, I am always sober. They sang " He's a Jolly Good
Fellow " and carried me up to my rooms at the end : which
was charming of them.

I have now returned to the country, and have staying with
me a Rhodes Scholar (American) and Rice, that soldier who
wrote to me about *The Effigy.* They are both full of enthusiasm
—a change from Oxford. At Oxford it is simply not done to
become excited over anything. But for these two *Tristram
Shandy* is a discovery : they'd never even heard of it before.
It is delightful to introduce them to a library—to read :

> Thou hast conquered, O pale Galilean.
> The world has grown grey at thy breath. . . .

and find that the words have a *physical* effect on them. But
imagine my reading Swinburne to the Milton Club !

In the evenings I translate Homer to them : and such is
their enthusiasm—such is their fanaticism for the *Iliad*—that
when I came to that famous parting between Hector and

Andromache I found the tears streaming down my cheeks. (You will laugh at this : it is unmanly.) But I didn't feel ashamed, as I might have done if I had been with any other young men. I knew that they were equally moved.

All right, H.W., all right : I am a sentimentalist !

I think you would like them, though. The American is large and seems lazy (but isn't) : he wears an enormous ring on his middle finger and is reading law. Rice is just a little Cockney with no idea of hygiene. But—well—I feel less *old* with them about. That enthusiasm is infectious.

I have just realised that I have said nothing about your invitation. As I now feel that there is nothing left for me to do— there are the three volumes of poetry, complete, before me—I should be delighted to accompany you. I have not been to Germany since 1926 : and no doubt it will be much changed. You, I imagine, were last there at the end of the Great War.

I wish you would pay me a visit. The chrysanthemums are superb.—With love,   S. N. G.

From the Diary of Sir HUGH WEIGH

January 2nd, 1937

It is only now—on the journey home, as I am rocked about in this deck-chair—that I have the time to record some of my impressions of our German visit. I am the only person left on the deck : a few souls are drinking and telling smutty stories in the bar, the rest have retired. This gives me a feeling of superiority. I can't say how pleased I felt when the only survivor apart from myself—a woman, who was pacing the deck in tweeds and a Henry Heath hat—suddenly made an inarticulate noise and scurried away. And I wasn't even feeling queasy !

S. N. G. left me long ago, looking unhappy and rather apologetic. He is a wretched sailor : even a glimpse of the sea from our carriage window made him swallow hard. I have

just visited him, where he lies supine, his charm evaporating
with each new paroxysm. He looks old, old-maidish, querulous.
But the heavily pomaded steward who whistles " The Lambeth
Walk " drearily, as a sort of *marche funèbre*, still gives him most
of his attention. I notice that people always *do* give S. N. G.
most of their attention. I think they know instinctively that he
is someone to protect. It is as if they could see all the years of
mother-love that have been expended on him.

For me Germany has been a success—a definite success :
to ask me out was an inspired piece of propaganda. Believing
all the un-English things I do, I suddenly found other people
who thought as I did. This doesn't mean that I have become a
traitor : if there is a war I shall, of course, muddle along with
old England, simply because I am English. But for no other
reason. *Germany is right.*

I knew it when we saw those peaceful, cow-like women,
and the virile youth goose-stepping through the streets of Berlin.
Those were fine faces—pitiless, strong, terrible. I felt I was
going to choke—with admiration, love perhaps. I had thought
this spirit had gone out of the world—had evaporated in the
stale exhalations of culture and higher education. A virile
barbarism, pagan, not effete, strong, ruthlessly strong, ascetic—
I had found what I had imagined no longer existed.

But at the same time, as I watched those youths marching,
arrogantly, superbly, as I caught my breath, longing to command them, to lead them, I saw the certainty of war. It was
inevitable. It was the destiny for which these supermen had
been begotten. Yet the realisation did not trouble me : rather
it filled me with a curious exaltation. I think I was glad.

I had felt that exaltation before. In the trenches : seeing our
dead or their dead (it did not matter)—the young bodies littered
in excruciating attitudes, with the smells of tainted flesh and
smoke and wet clothes—it had seemed to me that here was a
brotherhood to be proud of—the brotherhood of Slayer and
Slain. Those soldiers were nearer than lovers, their hate was

more noble than any love. I saw then the need for suffering and death.

Yes; as those German youths passed us, S. N. G.'s eyes closing in distaste, I think I was wishing for a war so that that communion could be achieved. I *was* wishing for it.

Of course I have told S. N. G. nothing of all this. He would think me mad, it would shock him profoundly. But even he was impressed by some of the things that impressed me. When we visited the camp in the Tyrol and saw the school children—healthy and happy at winter sports, young savages, many of them stripped to the waist, sunburned to the colour of biscuit, muscular—I think, then, that the Platonist in him was stirred to admiration. One cannot be a lover of Ancient Greece without seeing that such things are right and natural and worthy of the dignity of man.

But with S. N. G. it was a perpetual struggle. He was always divided. Of course this healthy virility was admirable—but what of the concentration camps? Instinctively, he accepted those cow-like women—but had he not been an ardent feminist? There was beauty in the athletics that we witnessed—but what of the exhibition of degenerate art? Was that not beautiful also? The human body; the human mind; instinct; reason; virility; culture; these things tore him apart. He wore a perpetually puzzled air. Of course the dilemma had always existed for him, he had always been aware of it: but now it was real, insuperable.

For me there was no such dilemma. I accepted it. If suffering was the price of that regeneration—so be it! I accepted suffering.

I think it is possible to be too civilised.

January 5th, 1937

Spending two days in town at the Club. I have just been to dinner with Croft. He has a flat overlooking Hampstead Heath—everything neat and a little fussy. An original Derain on one wall and a pietà reproduction on the other. An E.M.G. gramophone and several albums of chamber music. A silk doll lolls on the mantelpiece with some shells and china ornaments. Croft explains : " Cynthia—my fiancée—saw about the furniture. She chose the flat, really." An absence of books. Art and music seem to be his interests.

I feel more at my ease in the study, not because of the untidiness but because there is a smell of tobacco instead of scent, and the chairs are worn and covered in leather. Some rooms have a definite female smell. I think all rooms have sexes.

Croft is charming, but quick tempered. I praise Germany, which makes him blush and contradict me. I begin arguing in a friendly fashion, when I suddenly realise that he is in deadly earnest. He begins pacing the room, hands deep in his pockets, head bent forward, lecturing me about the evils of Nazism. This seriousness is delightful : I find myself egging him on, making interruptions, countering his arguments, just as one barracks an orator in the hope that he will be witty. And—yes—there is a pleasure in the antagonism.

He tells me that he wants to go back to the Amazon. He is full of projects—pulls out maps, shows me his notebooks, produces photographs. I exclaim about one of the photographs : " Oh, those hideous protuberances ! . . . " It is of a native woman, stripped to the waist, with great swelling breasts. Croft stares at it, blushing, then snaps the album together and pushes it back into the cupboard. I have shocked him.

After this incident conversation becomes rather strained. Strange that someone who has travelled so widely should, after all, turn out to be as prudish as your stay-at-home bank clerk. Does travel really broaden the mind ? Yet at dinner he had talked without any self-consciousness of circumcision rites among the Mazequals ; we had even discussed polyandry, and the orgiastic marriage ceremonies of the Koryaks. Why should my remark have displeased him ? From that moment his manner changed ; I could see that he wanted me to leave.

An odd thing happened when at last I decided to go. He saw me to the door of his flat, and offered to accompany me down to the street ; but I said that I could manage. As I descended, in the semi-darkness, I saw a figure mounting beneath me, one hand resting on the banisters ; but before we met it had slipped down a short corridor leading to another flat. I heard no sound of a key ; it was too dark to see if the person were hiding in the shadows.

Puzzled by this I continued my descent to the bottom of the stairs, pretended to open and shut the front door, and then waited. Footsteps running. The click of the door of Croft's flat. A whispered : " Darling ! You're earlier than I thought."
" I passed someone on my way up. I don't think he saw me."

The door clicked shut again, obliterating their intimate voices.

Was this his fiancée ? Or another woman ? And were they living together ?

For some reason the question filled me with curiosity. I almost went back. And all the way across the Heath I pondered. Why, why ? Why this curiosity ? Why a sort of baffled anger ?

When I got home I could not resist a cigarette. My first for four months.

January 8th, 1937

Meet Croft for lunch at Simpson's. Gather that he doesn't like the place. Almost his first remark is : " I hate to see them trundle these carcases about."

I try to get him talking about botany. But he is full of a question that some M.P. has asked in Parliament. Is he a bore ? I am beginning to think it.

As we walk in Green Park he tells me about his plans for a new expedition—back to the Amazon, perhaps, or to the Congo. This is his real self—the self I admire.

I think I should like to accompany him. Should I offer myself ? Why not ?

Feb. 2nd, 1937

Return to Dartmouth. This morning I go down to the cove to bathe—for the first time this year. I feel proud in the certainty that I shall be the only person in. But when I get there three youths and a girl are splashing about, rather unhappily ! It's as if the enemy had ambushed me.

How ugly people look in the cold—running noses, bodies amorphous in overcoats, chilblains, a blue pallor of the skin. Horrible !

Feb. 5th, 1937

Judith writes : " Miss Forsdike has left here. She has given me a locket which belonged to her grandmother—as a leaving present. Was it all right for me to accept it ? "

Feb. 6th, 1937

I tell Judith to return the locket.

Succeed in staying in the water five minutes longer than the three youths and the girl. Beginnings of a chill—in spite of a tumbler of whisky and lemon.

I grow old, I grow old !

Feb. 9th, 1937

Miss Forsdike has become a *waitress* Judith tells me. Apparently she talked of the narrowness of school life, the need for experience, etc., etc., when Judith said good-bye to her.

The woman is mad.

It is always schoolmistresses who talk of the narrowness of their life. It must be the most disappointed of professions.

Feb. 14th, 1937

Something of the old manner survives ! This morning Clark wakes me ten minutes late. I reprimand him. " I'm sorry, sir." He makes for the bathroom to get my bath.

" Well—what's the meaning of it ? "

He limps back. " Everything's rather muddled this morning, sir. My wife's had to go to hospital, sir."

" Oh, I'm sorry. Let me know what I can do."

That's all. He limps out. He expects this severity from me—would be surprised at anything else.

But, of course, he knows that I shall give him an afternoon off—and send something from the hot-house. We understand each other.

March 1st, 1937

A sudden interest in chess. Will now study every book on the subject for the next six months, become an expert, and then drop it. Bridge, polo, music, botany—they have all gone the same way.

I notice a nun buying sock-suspenders in Woolworth's. What delicious and tantalising images are conjured up by the sight.

March 16th, 1937

Clark's wife has died. She was a fierce old slattern who caught him by having a baby (which I do not believe was his) : I remember when he came back from leave and told me about it—half proudly, half apologetically. For some reason I flew into a rage—told him he was a fool (which, considering what followed, was prescient of me). And now she is dead. . . .

Clark asks for a *week's* leave. But when I look flabbergasted he modifies this to a day. Funeral arrangements, etc. A week would have meant having his daughter, Ethel ; and women servants are intolerable. They always like to put themselves in the position of (*a*) your wife, or (*b*) your mother. Subconsciously, of course. But I hate it.

April 2nd, 1937

Judith home. The child is growing up, rather disturbingly. I feel inadequate—for the first time. Finicky over food ;

sudden tears ; keeps a diary which I am not allowed to look at. Sad that she should have left that neutral state which makes all young people companionable.

April 4th, 1937

Last night Judith had a nightmare and woke me by screaming. I went in to find her sitting bolt upright in bed clutching the blankets. Her pupils were oddly dilated, like a cat's.

" Anything the matter ? "

" Only a dream." Her teeth began chattering.

" What happened ? "

" Nothing."

" Don't you want to tell me ? "

She turned away, her eyes slowly filling with tears. The electric light made deep shadows under them.

" Will you be all right ? "

" I think so."

" Not sure ? " I took her hands, with their stumpy fingers, like a boy's. " Would you like to come to my room ? "

" May I ? . . . Please."

At first she lay down on the divan in my room ; but soon after I had turned out the light she crept into my bed beside me, cold, still shivering, her body curled against mine. Soon she was asleep, her shoulders rising and falling beneath my hand.

I brushed my fingers against her cheeks. They were still wet with tears.

April 5th, 1937

S. N. G. once said in exasperation : " You are incapable of tenderness." That is not true. The other night—with Judith beside me—it was tenderness that kept me awake, watchfully, fearing another nightmare. Youth has this effect on me. The epileptic boy in the theatre, when everyone was filled with revulsion. . . .

April 7th, 1937

Up to London for a big function at the Guildhall. Public faces in public places—how I hate them. This is the last invitation that I shall accept. Judith says : " May I come with you ? " I wish she could. But perhaps it is as well for her to keep her illusions. This, to my mind, is the pathos of youth : all the dull events that beset us when we grow up—dinners, love-affairs, committee meetings—seem so romantic, so desirable. What a shock it is to discover the truth ! " But there *must* be something more to it," one thinks. " This can't be all. I must have missed something." One day Judith will learn that it is more interesting to swim in the cove than to stuff oneself at a public banquet.

From SHIRLEY FORSDIKE

April 12th, 1937

MY DEAREST,—I have put off writing to you from one month to another, always hoping for some answer to that letter of mine in which I told you that I loved you. Anything would have been better than your silence—anger, a letter to the headmistress, anything. To feel that I am simply beneath contempt—that is intolerable.

As you may have heard from Judith, I have left the school for this restaurant. I imagined that it might help—might make me forget you among faces and noise and bustle. But it hasn't. I am still where I started from. I wonder if you realise what this obsession means : to treasure a newspaper paragraph in which you are mentioned—only your name perhaps ; to read over and over again one of your articles, until I know each trick of style, the exact way in which you will say a thing ; and then, when I get back to this horrible boarding-house and sit down to dinner, to try and turn the conversation in such a way that you will be mentioned—the last war, generalship, South America. Hearing two people discuss you on a bus I stayed on long past my stop. I think I would have joined in if they had not left before I could reach them. And the newsreel : you only appeared for a moment, watching an interservices football match, but I went again and again. And always I felt the same intolerable excitement—the dryness of the mouth, the singing in the ears—when the camera flashed to you, in an old macintosh, your hands deep in your pockets.

Can you understand this ? Can you see what I suffer ? Can you see that anything that does not concern you does not exist ? What happened yesterday, what will happen to-morrow—nothing matters, unless someone mentions your name, or I read about you, or I see you come out of your Club and get into a taxi, or you have an article in one of the papers. I live only at these moments. These moments are my life. There is nothing else.

Oh, I know what you think. " A repressed spinster. Crazed. Man-starved." But it isn't as simple as that. When I was still at the school it might have been so. It might simply have been that I needed someone to sleep with. But it can't be that now— or I should have cured myself by coming here. Certainly, I hoped to cure myself. But it hasn't made any difference.

I could have any of these men if I wanted them. But I don't. After Danaë had been visited by Zeus in a shower of gold, do you imagine that she could then tolerate the caresses of mere mortals ? I am for you, and of you. If you will not have me, then no one shall.

I was so happy yesterday ; and even to-day the glow has not left me. Yesterday I *saw you*, the first time for so many weeks. I read in the papers that you were a guest at a banquet at the Guildhall. So I overstayed my lunch-hour and joined the little crowd who were waiting outside. I thought I should faint from the anticipation. One man looked at me and said : " Aren't you feeling well ? " But I nodded my head and moved on.

Then the moment when the doors were thrown open, and between the slouching, apathetic crowds, all waiting for some sort of revelation, there moved the smiling public figures—the privy councillors and their wives, the ministers of this and that—all strutting and chatting and nodding, all seeking for acknowledgment of their own importance. Stupid, smiling faces, mildly cheered as they vanished into their cars.

Then you, striding erect, your forehead creased as though in perplexity, your eyes preoccupied. Can you see the contrast? Are you surprised that the crowd which had cheered half-heartedly at its ministers of State should now roar at you in a frenzy of enthusiasm? Yet few of them knew who you were.

That is a proof of your power. Those people knew the falsity, the emptiness of all the figures that had preceded you. They knew that the smiles and nods were a frank request for honour. They could see the smallness beneath.

But you—they could see that you were real. There was no fraud with you. They knew that their love or hate meant nothing to you. You did not want their respect. You did not care about them. The day-to-day popularity of alderman and M.P.—you rejected it. You were grand in your self-sufficiency.

I saw then what you could achieve if you wished. Those apathetic faces—sickly, worried, perplexed; the City clerks, the women out shopping—you were the figure they had been subconsciously waiting for. They were tired of the demagogues and the yes-men. If you had stopped then on the steps of the Guildhall you could have told us to do anything and we would have done it.

Do you doubt your power now? Do you wonder why I called you a god?

Oh, you can save us, all of us. You can take away the ordinariness and the stupidity and the meanness of life. You can make men and women out of us. You can give us a direction, an aim. You can lead us.

Believe me when I say this. In my last letter I wrote, " For thine is the kingdom. . . ." That is true.

Use me, do what you want with me. I know that I cannot hope for your love—if I had it, it might perhaps kill me or drive me out of my mind ; it would be tremendous, super-human—but let me come and be your servant, let me be near you. I would expect nothing. I need nothing. You would not have to pay me. This is all that I ask. And if not this, then find something else for me to do for you—anything, anything at all. If it is for you then it will be sufficient. At the moment life is a matter of aimless waiting—a preparation, perhaps. When will the tongues of fire descend ? When will you reveal yourself ?

Answer this letter, I beg of you. Acknowledge my existence. If I do not exist for you, then I do not exist at all. I exist only in your eyes.

This letter gives me a sad feeling of peace. I have said so little of what I should like to say : but the thought that you will read it is enough. Will you forgive me ?—Always, always yours,

SHIRLEY.

Of this letter he wrote in his diary : " She is mad. How can I answer her ? " But several days later there is a further entry :

I have been re-reading that letter from Miss Forsdike. For some reason it disturbs me. I have brooded on it all this evening. She is unbalanced, of course—it would be wrong to make too much of it. And yet . . . I go back to it again and again.

It is as if she were the devil, taking me up into a high moun-tain and showing me all the kingdoms of the world in a moment of time.

She talks of my power. " You can lead us. You can give us a direction, an aim." I have felt that myself. I have thought that, and put away the thought.

Often I have felt that if I wanted to I could do anything with men. But I am afraid of this power. It is something that I dare not, must not use. Often I have felt what she describes in her letter—that people are waiting for some divine intervention from me. Perhaps I should give it to them. Perhaps it is wrong of me to hold back.

"The smiling public figures." How well I know what she means by that. But is their deceit any worse than mine ? Are they greater impostors ? The difference is that they are satisfied with the esteem of the many, while I want the esteem of the few. Mine is the larger ambition.

The few—S. N. G., for example—are not taken in by public speeches, and honours, and decorations. They see these things for what they are—a pretence. But is not the "integrity" which they admire in me also a pretence ? In their fear of being imposed on by politicians—in their reaction towards someone like me, apparently without ambition—are they not being imposed on by a force more subtle ? I am cleverer than the public figures ; I want more. That is the only difference.

This woman reads my thoughts. She is prompting me—crudely, ludicrously—but prompting me, always prompting me.

I will not give in.

A letter from S. N. George (*extract*)

May 6th, 1937

. . . Two women bicycled over from Somerville to-day to see me. I gave them tea in the garden. How I love sitting behind my silver teapot, civilised, comfortable, with my roses around me and a cat on my lap ! I know you despise this ; and I myself feel furtively ashamed about it all. But old ladies, and Kensington hotels, and the Army and Navy Stores—these have for me the same romance, the same nostalgia that *you* find in the Aztecs. This world of Daimlers and modesty-vests and Queen Mary toques—as I grow older, I feel more and more that I belong to it.

The two women were intelligent but rather dreary. Of course they asked the expected questions : Is it necessary to have a knowledge of Orphic rites to appreciate *The Effigy* ? What are you working on now ? Would you please explain that line ? . . . etc., etc.

Then we somehow moved on to politics, and one of the women began talking of the equality of the sexes. H.W., why do they do it ? Do they really believe that such a thing exists ? I didn't give my opinion because I was afraid of shocking them. But what I should like to have said was that so far from Nature creating the sexes equal, she seems to have taken a perverse, an almost fiendish, delight in their inequalities.

On the physical side man has it all his own way—pragmatically, æsthetically. Nature has given him abundant energy, the pleasures of concupiscence, health ; but woman is a sickly creature, slave to a monthly ritual, incapable of true orgiastic frenzy (she would like to think she is ; in this she imitates man). Then the æsthetics of the question. Women artfully conceal their deficiencies under clothes, and corsets, and paint, and jewellery. But compare the sexes naked. . . .

Is this equality ? But take the spiritual side. Here women have it all *their* way. Men are for the most part brutes : savouring their physical sensations, making money, acquiring possessions—wives, children, houses, honours. You must turn to women if you want true Christian virtues. It is women who are weak, and humble, and selfless, and loving. (That, incidentally, is why so many of my best friends are women.)

The equality of sexes ! Nonsense !

Of this letter the General wrote in his Diary :

Certainly ! There is no equality of the sexes. Thus far I agree with S. N. G. But when he talks of men lacking the Christian virtues, then I say, " Thank God ! " This does not seem a deficiency to me : rather it is the glory of our sex. I hate these Christian virtues which S. N. G. talks about. They are fit only for women. Why do men covet them?

April 22nd, 1937

Judith has been out to a dance with the cadet we met in the cove. I ask her when she is going to see him again. She blushes: " Never—I hope."

" Good heavens! . . . What's happened? Have you had a quarrel? "

" No. I think he's rather a cad, that's all."

She won't be more explicit. But one guesses. She reminds me of her mother in this. And Judith, too, will be passionate once she overcomes her revulsion.

May 2nd, 1937

The disturbance still goes on—ever since that letter from Miss Forsdike. I seem to be losing self-discipline. I say, ' I will not think of this ': and then my mind reverts. ' If I have this power. . . . Shouldn't I use it? Am I not destined to be a leader? etc., etc.'

I am trying to curb my ambition. In every way I try to humble myself. I have refused the invitation to lecture at Oxford, the presidency of two societies, birthday honours. This sort of renunciation is the *proof* of merit. It is better than the achievement.

How I sympathise with Lawrence, hiding away in the Air Force! It is self-discipline that counts. But we are in a dilemma. Each renunciation of power brings power. The more we humble ourselves the more others respect us. There is no escape from our destinies. Our ambition works through each relinquishment of ambition. That is the tragedy. . . .

May 5th, 1937

When I go down to the cove this morning, who should I see reading under the shadow of a rock but the analytical friend

2

of the cadet—alone ! He is still in the alpaca coat, and he reclines in exactly the same way, humped forward, head tilted on to his shoulder. I greet him with a mixture of repugnance, affection, and surprise. But he looks up calmly, slipping an envelope between the pages of his book to mark the place. " Hullo."

I feel rather foolish at this drawled greeting. "I didn't expect you here so soon. It's only a few months since you went. They give you good holidays."

" I've left."

" Left the bank ? "

He turns over on to his stomach, and then looks sideways up at me. " Yes. I've saved twenty pounds. That will keep me for about six weeks. By that time I hope to have finished my book."

" Was that why you left—to finish it ? "

" Partly. I'd got stuck. In any case, I doubt if I could ever produce anything worthwhile if I stayed on."

" Are you staying with your friend—the cadet ? "

He gives me an odd smile, knowing, almost patronising. " No. He's away. Didn't you know ? "

" I haven't seen him for months." It is as though I want to defend myself. Hurriedly I ask : " Where are you staying ? "

" I have a room the other side of the river."

" And you decided this was the best place to write in ? "

" I came here to study my subject."

" Your subject ? "

" The subject of my novel. I felt I was losing its essence. It was leaking away. So I came here to recapture it—to get its full force, so to speak." He rises to his feet, stretching, yawning, and moves away. " And now I must go."

" Good-bye."

" Good-bye."

He slouches as he walks, his book under his arm. He is still smiling.

I feel vaguely uneasy. I am used to summing people up : but I can't do it with him. Each time I meet him it is as if I were exploring a different level of his character. But there is nothing to grasp. He is everything—and nothing. . . .

May 6th, 1937

The analytical friend is called Frank Cauldwell. At first he takes no notice of me. But then he puts down his book suddenly and begins asking questions. Not even amusement behind the glasses. Impossible to tell what he is thinking. But I answer him as best I can.

At last, rather crossly : " You seem very interested in me."

" I am. I am interested."

" But why ? "

" I'm sorry. Do you mind all these questions ? Am I being rude ? "

" No. But it puzzles me. Why should you bother yourself with what I think ? "

" You're—a—Person who Matters."

(Is there mockery in the words ? It is difficult to tell. I must be careful.)

" I see."

" To be frank, your personality obsesses me. I feel I must try to understand it. There's some sort of answer there."

" Answer ? I don't understand you."

" It's difficult to explain myself. But often I feel this with people. I am obsessed with their personalities for weeks or months or years on end." (Why do I instinctively think of Miss Forsdike ?) " I suppose that's why I want to be a novelist."

" But why my personality ? Is it so very strange ? "

" No—o." He is doubtful. " I really can't tell you why one personality should obsess me and another not interest me at all. There was a man at the bank who was had up for kleptomania and self-exposure. I suppose the majority of people would consider him an ' interesting ' personality. But no

—I couldn't interest myself at all in him. And yet I had known him better than anyone else there."

"That's hardly flattering to me."

He laughs, then looks serious. "You see, I *know* that your character is vitally important. I know that, I am certain about it. It has an enormous, a profound interest, for me. But why this should be so I can't say. And this ignorance in its turn intensifies my obsession. I want to find out. Curiosity. Nothing is stronger."

"But you really cannot see why I interest you ? "

"Partly, yes. You're a military genius—one reads that in the papers and one believes it to be true. I think you're a great man. But that doesn't entirely explain it. Your life is a sort of myth. If one could see the implications of the myth, one would understand much. But the myth is powerful whether one understands it or not."

I think : "He is talking nonsense." I feel suddenly irritated. Myth, personality ! He is worse than Miss Forsdike !

I say : "Yes, I think I see what you mean."

"Do you ? Do you really ? I didn't imagine that you would. . . . Take the Oedipus myth. That story has obsessed generations of poets—and not poets only. It has had a universal application. But it is only in the last forty years that Freud has come along to explain it to us."

"And I am a myth ? "

"I think so—yes. One can't be sure."

I rise to my feet : "Can you swim yet ? "

He shakes his head, smiling : "Not yet."

"Well, I'm going in again."

Sting of water, washing all his nonsensical theories out of my head.

May 26th, 1937

Cauldwell has been here for three weeks now, and still I feel that I do not know him. He will never betray himself—while

I have been stupidly indiscreet. Why, why ? He is the only person to whom I have told so much—apart from S. N. G.

He never comments : perhaps this accounts for my candour.

May 27th, 1937

We take the little steamer up to Stoke Gabriel and then walk back. Another lengthy conversation. I am talking to him about the visit to Germany when, suddenly conscious that he is staring at me, I ask : " Do my views shock you very much ? "

" I try not to be shocked by them."

" But not very successfully ? "

" As a novelist, I tell myself that I must not be shocked by them—and I think I succeed. But as an individual . . ." He shrugs his shoulders. " It's very difficult, you know—this separating of the novelist from the individual. But it must be done. Sometimes I feel that I am two people—the commentator and the participant."

" You have strong views about your functions as a novelist ? "

" Certainly I have strong views as to what my personality as a novelist should be. The trouble is that my creative ideal can seldom be reconciled with what I actually am. Hence this feeling of being two people. Ideally, the novelist should be shocked by nothing : he should examine, he should explain ; he should never pass judgment. But as an individual I continually want to pass judgment. Ideally, the novelist should be a depersonalised beholder—an eye for seeing, and nothing else. But as an individual I cannot depersonalise myself ; I have strong prejudices ; I have likes and dislikes ; I have certain traits of character—physical cowardice, a horror of sex, great ambition. The whole problem is not to let all these individual obstacles get in the way of the artist. This is the double life. When I am in the rôle of participant I give full rein to my idiosyncrasies ; I pass judgment, I am egotistic, I am bigoted. But when I am in the rôle of novelist—when I am faced with my subject—then all these idiosyncrasies are bundled away :

I try to depersonalise myself ; I will only behold, never criticise ;
I will be entirely frigid ; I will only see things as they are—
not as I would like them to be ; I will become an eye for
seeing—nothing else. . . ."

Saying this much he stops short, blushing. We walk on in
silence. For the first time he has given himself away.

May 28th, 1937

To-day I give Cauldwell his first swimming lesson. He is
(as he admitted yesterday) a physical coward. Water terrifies
him. He won't duck, he won't go out of his depth. I get him
to float with my hand under his stomach. " One—two—
three ! " Jerkily he goes through the motions of the breast-
stroke. "I shall never learn," he says gloomily when he
splashes out of the water and shakes himself like a dog. Drying
and dressing is an elaborate business with him ; he dislikes being
seen naked. His skin is a transparent white, like lard—the
unhealthy colour of nearly all sedentary workers. He has a
blue-green mark on his throat where his stud has pressed.

June 2nd, 1937

" How is the novel going ? " I ask.

" I think it's shaping well."

" I didn't see you yesterday."

" No. I spent the day writing. I wrote for fifteen hours on
end. Then I went to sleep. I've only just woken up."

He certainly looks tired : his eyes are red, with a sty beginning
in one of them.

June 5th, 1937

For the first time he asks me to return with him to his rooms.
We take the ferry across to Kingswear. It is only now that
I am fully aware of his poverty. I have seen him make a lunch
off a piece of bread and butter ; he has often refused to go to
cinemas with me or to have a drink ; but I have never realised

the cause—the need to husband his resources. Those of us who have never felt the lack of money so often do this—suggesting lavish meals, always assuming that the other person can afford to disregard expenses. And when we are met by a refusal or excuse—for people are often too proud to say ' I can't afford this '—then we accept what they say at its face value ; we really believe that ' It's more fun to eat sandwiches at a coffee stall ', or that ' The gallery is the only place to sit in at a theatre '.

His room is at the very top of an uncarpeted staircase, in a house whose façade is peeling, yellow and grimed and blotched. There is an unmade bed. Greyness of sheets. Papers littering a card table, pyjamas thrown over a chair, cigarette-ends on the floor. A pot full of stale urine under the bed.

" I'll make some cocoa," he says. But the gas won't come ; he fumbles in his pocket for a shilling.

" Here you are." I flick it across to him, placing myself gingerly on the bed.

" Thanks." He produces an aluminium saucepan with a ridge of sediment running round the inside and shakes the cocoa out of its packet. He is going to make it with water.

At that moment there is a deafening noise from next door. The room vibrates. Excruciating, epicene moans from a saxophone and crooner. Cauldwell pulls a face.

" Do you have to write through that ? "

" I don't really notice it when I'm writing. But when I'm reading—or trying to get to sleep . . . You see, I so often write all night and try to sleep during the day. It's hopeless."

He goes back to the cocoa, stirring it lethargically. A breath of wind detaches a sheet of manuscript and blows it against the door. It makes a dry, scraping sound.

Next door there is now a clatter of bones and an emasculated rhumba. If they could hear the real thing !

I notice a photograph on the table beside me. It is unframed, leaning against a tumbler of water—a woman of about thirty-five, tired, a little wan, the pores of her face unnaturally enlarged, her neck sagging as though with incipient goitre. She has a slight moustache, fair, because she must peroxide it. She is wearing one of those shiny black silk dresses which one sees on shop assistants, and a rope of pearls.

" My goodness. Who on earth is this ? "

Colour mounts to his forehead. " My girl."

" Your—girl ! " So this is a girl—the rubbed coarseness of the neck, the breasts that would sag were it not for the upward tilt of their brassière. I begin to chuckle, half in surprise, half in malice.

" What are you laughing at ? "

" It's—rather—funny. That's all." I look at the ageing face for a second time. " No, really. . . . She's old enough to be——"

" Give it to me ! " He darts forward and snatches at the photograph. The face is neatly severed from the goitrous neck. We each hold a fragment.

" Now look what you've done ! Now look ! " In a tearful rage he slaps me across the face with the flat of his hand.

This is too much. I punch him in the mouth. He begins to spit teeth and blood into a basin, muttering : " You swine. . . . You bastard. . . ."

" I'm sorry, old chap. I didn't mean to hit you so hard." Rage is a matter of seconds with me—a sudden paroxysm, and then nothing. " What's the matter ? Knocked out a tooth ? " I try to pat his shoulder.

But immediately he begins screaming : " Let me go ! Don't touch me ! Get out of here ! Leave me alone ! I don't want to see you again ! "

At that moment the cocoa boils over, sizzles, and finally puts out the gas. There is a hush in the radio programme. But, " Get out ! Clear out ! " he still yells at me, his face messy with blood and saliva.

The door slams behind me. Faces appear on the landing. I hurry away.

And that, I imagine, is the last of Frank Cauldwell.

June 6th, 1937

This morning he comes round to the house, says nothing of the night before. There is a gap in his teeth, through which saliva tends to trickle. He behaves as if the whole incident had never taken place. Should I offer to pay for a visit to the dentist ?

June 7th, 1937

He swims ten yards by himself and then collapses on to the sand, like a fish, white and panting and gleaming with moisture. In the afternoon he scribbles in a notebook.

June 8th, 1937

There is a fair on.

" I love fairs," he says rather surprisingly.

" So do I." (But I do not admit the reason. I do not tell him how much I enjoy being surrounded by a crowd while I win packet after packet of Woodbines in the shooting-gallery.)

" Let's go."

" All right."

We thrust ourselves through smells of sweat and scent, and acrid fumes from the merry-go-round. Sailors lurch against us with women on their arms. Strings of coloured lights sway gaudily. We are conscious of being rather aloof, of being spectators. A woman's hand rests on my sleeve in the crowd ; chapped, nails bitten and then varnished scarlet. Her thick, smiling lips reveal brittle teeth. Her legs gleam, bare and white and flaccid at the knees. Then a sailor picks her up.

At the shooting-gallery I say to Cauldwell : " Come on. I challenge you to a match. Do you shoot ? " My vanity is ludicrous.

" I'm sorry. I haven't any money." He turns out his pockets, ruefully smiling. " I paid my landlady this morning. And that's that."

" That's all right. I'll pay."

Of course I win. One round is enough for him. But I
continue, taking as prizes a teddy-bear that smells of sawdust,
a vase with flamingos on it, some raffia napkin rings, and four
packets of Woodbines. The Woodbines I distribute to some
sailors ; the vase and napkin rings are returned to the man in
charge ; and the teddy-bear is Cauldwell's. I have the admiration of the little crowd.

Swing boats. I have difficulty in persuading Cauldwell.
" They're horrible things," he complains, looking up at the
young men who pull muscularly at the ropes and at the girls
who accompany them, screeching, wind-blown, their skirts
billowing upwards to reveal pink thighs. " I hate them."

" Come on ! It's great fun. I don't believe you've ever
been up."

He looks uncomfortable : perhaps this diagnosis is correct.

I am in charge. A feeling of freedom, of being on the
high seas. The wind dishevels one ; one is so far above the
white, nondescript faces, peering up, appraising the exposure
of youthful thighs. If one thinks anything, it is how appalling
it will be to have to cease these aerobatics and come to earth.
I take a pleasure in swinging our boat higher than anyone else.
Again my vanity.

" Oh, do look out. We nearly went right over. Do be
careful." I am conscious of Cauldwell, strapped unhappily,
one hand to his mouth, his teeth unnaturally bared.

" This is fine," I say. " Don't you feel free ? Don't you
feel on top of the world ? "

He looks downwards and then looks away, out to the river,
coiling and gleaming like a noose about us. His hands grip the
sides, the knuckles white.

On our left a girl makes eyes at me. She is a farm-girl,
I imagine, with hands like bunches of bananas. Then her
skirt blows up, covering her rubicund face, while she cackles
with mirth.

" I'm feeling sick."

I had forgotten Cauldwell. He is crouched now, greenish, swallowing hard, a handkerchief to his mouth.

" Sick ? "

" Oh, do let's stop. Do let's go down. I've had enough. Please." He is like a child. I have visions of him being sick from up here on to those peering faces. I cease to tug at the rope. We swing lazily, hover, settle, the river ceases to hold us in its enormous snare. We clamber out into a circumscribed space—lights, faces, noise. Everything seems suddenly static and rather flat. Cauldwell belches and clutches my arm giddily.

" All right ? "

" I will be in a moment. I hate heights. And I'm a rotten sailor. Sorry."

A youth in a white artificial-silk scarf blows a squeaker into Cauldwell's face. He frowns. This makes me feel suddenly sorry for him : he seems to have lost all reserves, all self-possession.

" Come and have a drink," I suggest, and add hastily, " on me."

" Thanks."

When we are in the stuffy bar-parlour I turn to him : " I hope you won't mind my asking this. But when you said just now that you hadn't any money, did you mean that you hadn't any at all ? Did you mean that you were broke ? "

He looks into his glass, his greenish pallor changing to a blush. " Yes. I am broke. I've spent most of to-day looking for a job. No luck, I'm afraid. And I need three or four more weeks for the novel." In the parlour there are farmers discussing the year's prospects ; there are some rowdy youths, and two girls who laugh, throwing back their peroxided heads and clutching their sides ; there is an old man, half-drunk, breaking wind noisily ; the atmosphere is thick with smoke and din. But Cauldwell's voice is subdued, almost inaudible. He seems afraid of being overheard.

" Look. I've got an idea." I feel suddenly paternal towards

him. " Why don't you come and stay with me ? I could put you up quite easily."

His eyes flicker with the pleasure, and then go dull again. " That's very good of you. But I wouldn't make the ideal guest. As I told you once, I work most of the night and sleep during the day. And I hate being disturbed."

This sounds almost ungracious. But I persist. " I don't mind about that. I won't badger you. I have plenty of work to do myself. The spare room's at the top of the house. You can spent all your time there if you like."

He hesitates. " Well—thank you. If I could stay for—well —a week. . . ."

" Stay as long as you like."

" No. Only a week. A week will be enough. After that I want to leave Dartmouth. . . . I really don't know how to thank you."

" So you're going to leave Dartmouth after a week ? "

" Yes. I think I must. I've studied my subject from close quarters. Now I shall have to move away. I can't get it into focus otherwise."

I feel suddenly curious. " What *is* your novel about ? "

He smiles, watching the two women in the corner, stomachs stuck out, calves bulging, cascades of ash-blonde hair undulating round plump shoulders. " I never like to tell people about my work until it is finished. I don't know why. I feel that if the secret is shared it somehow evaporates."

" I see."

But the explanation does not satisfy me.

June 9th, 1937

Cauldwell moves over. A rucksack is the only luggage he brings. I think Clark disapproves of him. " Shall I unpack the gentleman's things, sir ? " He dislikes long hair, spectacles, untidiness. He can't imagine why Cauldwell should sit for three hours in his room on a beautiful June day.

June 10th, 1937

Cauldwell has not appeared all to-day. Clark tells me that
when he called him at eight he was up, dressed, and at work.
He asked not to be disturbed. At midday he went to the kitchen
and made himself a sandwich and a cup of tea. He hasn't been
seen since.

" I hope the gentleman's all right, sir," says Clark, when
giving me this information.

" That will do, Clark."

He limps out, disapproval on every line of his face.

June 11th, 1937

Cauldwell doesn't come down till lunch-time ; and immediately afterwards he goes to sleep in the study while he is talking
to me. I drop Brewer's *Dictionary of Phrase and Fable*—on
purpose—but nothing can wake him.

June 12th, 1937

Another swimming lesson : Cauldwell improves. But
when, in a moment of high spirits, I try to duck him he leaves
the water and sulks over a book. His back is peeling from the
sun : even to look at it is excruciating. But perhaps he will
tan afterwards.

June 13th, 1937

All last night Cauldwell was pacing his room or roaming
about the house. Eventually I put my head out of my door.
" For heaven's sake ! " I bawled.

Silence.

This morning, when I take *The Times* out to the summer-
house I find him asleep there. He has dribbled on to the cushion
of his chair, and waking up, he gives a sort of grunt. Then he
sees where he is, and apologises.

June 14th, 1937.

This evening I take out all the old family albums. Cauldwell
has asked to see them. He put them on the floor, then kneels
beside them, completely absorbed. There is a nostalgia in this,
which I try to combat. How the past tyrannises over one—
with photographs of Lucy on horseback, Lucy with her three
borzois, Lucy in a wheel-chair; myself self-possessed and
arrogant, leaning over a ship's rail, in bathing-trunks, in khaki,
in dusty field-boots, then lying on my stomach, a baby, pink,
cherubic, callipygous; Judith and Dennis snapped in Italy,
both naked, tanned, immodest, with a glaucous sea behind them.
I have tried to rid myself of this horla, the past. I have tried to
bundle it away with the lockets, rings, daguerreotypes, letters.
But the sight of these faces revivifies it. It is still potent.

Cauldwell always asks questions. " Who's that? . . .
And *she* was the sister of *him* ? And this is you, of course. . . .
No ? . . . Your brother, then. . . ."

Here is S. N. George, in the days when he was an Oxford
dandy, rather too conscious of looking like the picture of
Swinburne in his college hall; here is one of my A.D.C.'s, a
boy of eighteen, whose babyish face was blown off in the
trenches; Eckworth, diplomatic attaché, supercilious, erratic,
who cut his throat with a razor; Rolf, whom we thought a
genius, but who married a dull woman and begot dull children
on a small property in Cumberland; Andrée, smiling with
ingenuous voluptuousness as she poses on a veranda; youthful
faces, troubled faces, yellowing features corroded by time,
fashions and gestures of a lost era—these could once incite
anger or pity, contempt or lust, all dead, all forgotten, all
bundled away between the heavy covers.

" May I keep this ? " Cauldwell holds up a picture.

It is a photograph of me, a young man of eighteen in an open-
necked shirt, with a week's growth on my chin, staring arrogantly into the camera. I am frowning, eyes screwed together,
brows furrowed, deep lines running vertically on each side of

my mouth. In my hand I hold a riding-whip which I am flicking against a booted leg. My face is plumper, the lips fuller, more sensual.

" Why do you want it ? "

He shrugs his shoulders. " I feel it must be very like you at the time. . . . It is, isn't it ? "

" Yes. I suppose it is. You can have it."

Carefully he places it in his wallet, smiling.

June 15th, 1937

This evening Cauldwell has planned to leave. He is going to stay with some friends who run a boy's club in the East End—his services in return for board, lodging, and a little leisure. I see now that I shall miss him. All through breakfast I have tried to persuade him to stay : and the last swimming lesson is a melancholy affair. " If only I had another week," I say ruefully, " I think I could teach you to dive."

He, too, looks regretful. " I must go. Really I must. I can't finish the book without a change of scene. · I've got stuck."

His book puzzles me.

June 16th, 1937

A strange, rather disturbing, thing happened yesterday evening before Cauldwell left. I had gone up to his room to talk to him while he packed, but found him out. He was evidently in the garden. The room was littered with old news-papers, dirty collars, bus tickets, letters—and on the table three notebooks, small, soiled, at least one of which he always keeps with him.

In a moment of curiosity I opened the first of the notebooks and read at random : ' Ravaged face, superb physique. Some-thing curbed, controlled—I don't know what. Reticent, frigid, then suddenly voluble. Introspective ? In some ways, in others, not. There is power, certainly, but of a kind which frightens me. The way that face *vibrates* with personality even in a bad newspaper photograph—but vibrates is not quite the word. Burns perhaps. Strong, tranquil, steadfast. . . .'

At that moment there are footsteps and I close the book.

It is of me that he writes.

After this discovery I find that my hands are trembling, my mouth goes dry. When I talk to him I stumble over my words. It is as if I were drunk. Why? I cannot explain it.

" Write to me, sometime," I say when I see him off.

" Do you mean that ? "

" Certainly I do. I shall be interested to hear about the novel."

" Oh—the novel ! " He laughs. I do not think he has any suspicions of my discovery.

The train jerks and then slides forward. Hands wave. " Good-bye," he shouts. " Good-bye. Thank you so much. Thank you."

" Good-bye."

That horrible moment when one watches a train disappear. Everything flat, rather hostile. Things relaxing savagely.

So I am a figure in his novel. So that's it.

June 17th, 1937

All to-day I have thought about Cauldwell—in spite of a letter which I must write to *The Times*, and two articles.

Firstly : Will he ever be a good writer ? It seems to me that he is too obsessed with the novelist's rôle—with the outward manifestations. He loves to talk of how he creates : and this makes one feel that he is subtly imposing on one—and on himself. (As if to make up for some lack, some deficiency, he has to present himself as the typical artist—mildly eccentric, pacing his room at midnight, liable to sudden fits of inspiration. He is acting a part.)

Secondly : Those words of his, " When I am faced with my subject . . . I try to depersonalise myself ". Assuming from that entry in his notebook that I am a figure in the novel, does this explain that feeling I have of never being able to grasp the essential *him* ? Like water in sunlight there are sudden flashes : his confidences, the time I struck him—and then the whole thing goes blank.

Thirdly : How will I appear in the book ? Will it be as a caricature Blimp ? Or introduced for a few pages of comedy ?

These thoughts keep me awake to-night. I am sorry that he has gone.

June 22nd, 1937

I am in bed—in Croft's flat. Last night I came here to dinner, feeling headachy and rather shivery. Then, during dessert, I suddenly felt the table rise up towards me ; the light rocked ; there was the sound of a plate breaking. I had fainted.

An acute go of malaria. Croft insists on my staying here though I have suggested a nursing home. He is a wonderful nurse. I am too feverish to write more : my hand shakes.

Yes. I should like to go with him to the Amazon.

June 23rd, 1937

Much better to-day. I want to get up—in fact, have been on to the balcony when no one was looking—but the doctor is obstinate. Croft has been talking to me ; and then his fiancée comes in with some orange juice. I sense an antagonism, though she smiles and says " Good morning ". She does not sit down, she does not go away. She looks at me, her face overpowdered. A necklace of large wooden beads gives her an air of barbarousness : but otherwise she is dull, neat, solid.

Croft and I continue to talk about mountaineering, when suddenly she breaks in : " I can't understand it. I can't see the point. If one wants to risk one's life, why not do something worthwhile—medical research, anything. This desire to break records is so selfish—so senseless. There are so many other dangerous jobs to be done." Again she repeats : " I can't see the point."

" Exactly ! " I exclaim. " Exactly ! There *is* no point. That's the whole glory of it. That's why one does it."

She stares at me, bewildered.

June 24th, 1937

I suppose that *if* Croft is living with this woman my presence must be rather embarrassing for him. I can't see why he isn't more open about it. He always talks to me as if she went back to her room in Chelsea each evening. But I rather doubt it.

At any rate they are certainly in love. The trouble with these flats is that the walls are so thin. I hear them next door in the sitting-room.

" Darling."

" Darling."

" Do you love me, darling ? "

" Yes, darling."

" Say ' I love you '."

" I love you, darling."

" Darling."

" Darling."

As a commentary to their caresses lovers imagine this sort of thing to be inspired. But the feverish eavesdropper, propped in bed, finds it trite.

June 25th, 1937

This woman will make an ordinary, conventional figure out of Croft. Women do that. They hate a man to have anything inviolate—anything they cannot share. They want to drag everything out, like a trunk, ransack it, tidy it, label it, and then store it safely away.

It is she who has made a prude of him. When she brought me a hot-water bottle and I said something about " bed-pans " instead of " warming-pans "—a slip of the tongue—she blushed crossly and swept out.

I think she is afraid of me. At any rate she will not stay with
me if no one else is there. But perhaps she is one of those
people who hate being left *tête-à-tête*. This is not uncommon
among women. (An unconscious fear of seduction ?)

She is a pacifist. Yesterday, when we were discussing the
news, she said : " I suppose you would welcome a war ? "

" What makes you think that ? "

" Well—wouldn't you ? After all, you have everything
to gain—power, position, respect." (The aggressiveness of the
non-combatant !)

" I don't know that I have. War destroys, as well as makes,
military reputations. At the moment I am considered a good
soldier—on the strength of two minor campaigns in the Great
War and some buccaneering in South America. People admire
me for that. But if war broke out I might simply make a fool
of myself. Then where would my reputation be ? "

I don't think she believes this.

June 26th, 1937

If Dennis had lived I should like him to have been like Croft.
He cooks superbly, does housework, embroiders. It is only the
bowler-hatted multitudes, afraid of being thought effeminate,
who cry out : " That's not a *man's* job ". The true, the virile,
man usurps a woman's household function without shame.

S. N. G. comes to see me to-day. He is suffering from
prostatitis, ' old-man's complaint ', and is due for an operation.
He shows me his will. I see that bequests of five thousand
pounds have been left to his chauffeur and to me. I am not sure
that I like the conjunction !

June 27th, 1937

Illness makes one brood too much. Looking back upon
the person that I was I cannot see the connection between *then*
and *now*. I cannot believe that that young man has really
become this old one, that his body has turned into my body, in

this bed. It is as if my past self were a relative whom I no longer see—of whom I disapprove. Poor arrogant young relative !

June 28th, 1937

To-day I get up and sit on the balcony. Convalescence is even worse than illness—the weakness of the joints, the ache in one's back after the slightest exertion, the giddiness, lack of appetite, dryness of the mouth, the tendency to break out into sweat. These are, strangely, the symptoms of love as well as of sickness.

Croft and I begin a game of chess. One of his legs is crossed over the other : he massages the ankle with his hand. Tobacco smoke, silence, peace. Then Cynthia appears. " Darling, have you forgotten ? Have you ? " She runs her fingers through his hair, walks round the table, hums.

He looks up, his fingers still touching his queen. " What's that ? What ? Oh, yes. Just a minute, dear."

" But, darling, you *said* ten o'clock. It's now a quarter past."

He shifts uneasily. " Couldn't you wait—just until we've finished this game ? "

" But I *have* waited. My appointment's at eleven. . . . Shall I go without you ? "

" No, no. I'll come."

" But I don't want to spoil your game. Really—I can quite easily manage alone. No, really, darling. . . ."

But, of course, he goes. And I am left alone on the balcony. I watch them walk arm-in-arm, close, inseparably close, across the Heath. Her head is on his shoulder.

To-morrow I must leave.

June 29th, 1937

Dinner last night—my last dinner at Croft's flat—was a shocking affair. He opened a bottle of Hermitage in my honour : and Cynthia got tight on it. She did not have more than a couple of glasses, but soon she was giggling, caressing his hand, sitting on his lap. He seemed to be only amused by it all. "Darling—you're just the teeniest-weeniest bit tipsy." "I'm not!" "Yes, you are." "I'm not!" Her arms encircled his neck, plump, braceleted, her fingers rubbing his cheeks. He grinned at me. "She is drunk, isn't she?" He seemed to be proud of it, as though it were some accomplishment.

"Kiss me, darling. Give me a nice big kiss."

Again he grinned. "Not *here*, darling."

"Why not? Why won't you kiss me? Are you ashamed of me?"

"Of course not." A brief peck on the forehead.

"I don't call that a kiss."

"Don't you?"

"No. That wasn't a nice kiss." She snuggles up to him. "You're nice though, darling. You've a nice smell. You're nice and warm."

This embarrasses him; he draws away, passes me a cigar. "Now you be a good girl. Go back to your chair. There's a good girl."

She lurches to her seat, giggles, collapses. For a second she is quiet. Then she begins on surreptitiously smutty stories. ("Definition of a gentleman: Someone who takes the weight on his elbows. Definition of a cad: Someone who gives a woman two halfpennies when she asks for a penny.") I stare before me, bored, disgusted, pulling at my cigar.

But Croft is delighted. How amusing little Cynthia is! How clever! (She has done more than turn him into a prude; she has given him the prude's delight in anything that is furtively shocking.) "No, really, darling," he protests. "No, really." But he loves her for it.

This is what a woman can do to a man.

July 1st, 1937

The house seems lonely after my stay with Croft. I wonder what has become of Cauldwell and his novel.

There is a new paper-boy whom I catch stealing nectarines off the south wall. In a moment of rage I thrash him. But he doesn't seem to take any offence. I tell him to keep the fruit. . . .

July 4th, 1937

To-morrow, S. N. G. comes for a week-end before going into hospital for his operation. I am re-reading his last book ; and each time I am amazed at the note of frenzy. Is this S. N. G., dapper, shy, happy among tea-cups, writing *The Effigy* on the lawn of the Cheltenham house while his mother, the vast matriarch, played bézique with me over a fire in June ? How can one explain the brutality of these poems ? S. N. G. so cautiously amorous, inviting young writers to meet his mother or giving them dinner at his Club. It is difficult to reconcile the man and his work.

Yet once he said in a letter : ' The physically weak are obsessed with violence, the impotent with sex '. If S. N. G. had lived more adventurously, if he had been a libertine, would the poems have ever been written ?

July 5th, 1937

S. N. G. arrives. He seems harassed, preoccupied, a case left by mistake in the train, his clothes somehow ill-assorted, ill-fitting. His hand is clammy, chill, the fingers relaxed. He breaks into nervous sweats while one talks to him.

When I go up to his room it is already pervaded with a sweet exhalation—some sort of disinfectant. Medicine bottles, bound round with handkerchiefs in case they should break, now line the mantelpiece. A large roll of cotton-wool on the bed.

" Hullo," he says wanly as I come in. Out of his suit-case he takes the *Imitation* and some sleeping-tablets. " I have something to ask you, H. W."

" Yes ? "

He sits on the bed, slowly, carefully. " Will you be my

literary executor—if anything happens? You know what I want preserved. Only the three volumes. The rest is to be burnt."

" Certainly." I feel suddenly tender towards him—with the *Imitation* and the sleeping-tablets—religion and science— kept as analgesics against his fears of death, disease, discomfort. " But aren't you taking this operation rather seriously? After all, it's nothing very much, is it? "

His forehead again pimples with sweat. He shakes his head. " Honestly, H. W., I don't think I shall survive. I just feel it. My heart's none too good. . . . I—I may simply go under. So, naturally, I want to get my affairs in order——"

" Of course, of course. But I don't think you've much to worry about——"

" I have a sort of foreboding. It's not that I really *mind* dying. My work's finished—I can't add another word to it. And apart from my work—well, what is there? I have no one that I shall regret leaving very much—apart from you, of course—and I do believe in some sort of personal survival. I mean, there *must* be something—there *must* be : this can't be all, can it? "

I nod, not because I agree with him, but out of pity.

" No. It's not dying that terrifies me. It's all the frightful preliminaries—the indignities. After all, the operation itself. . . ." He stops short.

Yes : I can understand that. Poor S. N. G., being shaved, being wheeled about like one of the carcases at Simpsons, being bandaged and examined and fitted with a urinal ! It is easy enough to laugh at his dread of all this. But I myself remember how when I suspected infection in Aden I put off from week to week a visit to the doctor merely because I was ashamed of showing myself.

" It's been on my mind for weeks," he says. " I haven't been able to sleep because of it. I can't tell you how much I dread it all. I *hate* hospitals." His eyes fill with tears, as he speaks. " When I had my appendix out, there was an old blood-stain on the wall above my bed. It was horrible ! "

" Oh, nonsense. They don't leave blood-stains about."

" But there was," he reiterates. " There was."

We go down to dinner.

July 6th, 1937

After dinner yesterday I showed S. N. G. the Forsdike letters. I had not meant to show them to anyone—I don't know why : certainly not out of loyalty to her. Yet here I was handing them to him. Perhaps I accepted, subconsciously, his own belief that he would not survive the operation. Perhaps the thought crossed my mind : Dead men tell no tales. I do not know. All that is certain is that, suddenly, on an impulse, I had gone to the bureau, unlocked the box, and given them to him. There was still a faint scent on them as they passed through my hands. " What do you make of these ? " I asked.

He read them slowly, without comment, while I watched him, his gold signet ring flashing under the electric light, the shoulders of his dinner-jacket grey with scurf. Then, at the end, he folded them, and handed them back to me, still saying nothing, his gaze preoccupied.

" Well ? What do you think ? Crazy, aren't they ? "

" I shouldn't have said crazy. I can understand it."

" But, my dear man——"

" I can see an otherwise quite rational person writing to you in that fashion. After all, my dear H. W., you are a personality. I've learnt that myself."

" What do you mean ? "

" When I was a boy of eleven I went to private school— and you were a leader of a gang. Do you remember ? You were a horrid little savage—and your gang was horrid. But I joined it. Why ? Simply because of this personality of yours. I loathed all the things you did—roasting new boys on the hot pipes in the changing-rooms, stealing from the tuck cupboard, tracking Mr. Bowley and the under-matron. But there it was. You had this fiendish personality."

" Well ? "

" Now, as you know, H. W., I agree with very few of your opinions. We've hardly an opinion in common. But even now, to-day, if you wanted me to do something wholly disreputable— well, I think I should do it. I wish it wasn't so, but it is. I wish such personalities didn't exist : they're dangerous. But the power is there—the magnetism—and I, for one, feel it. And not only me. How do you think that you, a European, succeeded in turning a handful of South American insurgents into a formidable fighting force ? Your personality. One still hears of the love those men had for you. Well—is it such a step from that devotion to this ? Imagine someone whose life has been aimless, dull—and then your picture, the story of the South American campaign, your books. Is it so hard to see it happen ? "

" But she worshipped me before we had even met——"

" Why not ? Your story was romantic enough. Someone once said that your face was ideal for a recruiting poster. And then there was this thing over and above—something supernatural, uncontrollable—an aura ; if you like—your personality."

I began to laugh, without humour, profoundly disturbed, but afraid of showing it ; pretending that all that he said seemed ridiculous to me, when he continued : " Oh, yes ; you have a personality, H. W. It is unique. I only thank God that you have never tried to use it to the full. You could do anything with it—anything. . . . And that frightens me."

So he too is in the conspiracy.

July 7th, 1937

The best love letters are written by those no longer in love. When I said good-bye to S. N. G. this morning we were both inarticulate.

Before he went he showed me the new pyjamas he had
bought for the nursing-home. " Feel them. They've a most
lovely texture." His wan enthusiasm heartens me.

Will he die ? Will he recover ? I do not know. Presenti-
ments mean nothing. I often thought that I should be killed
in the last war. But I cannot help sharing his melancholy.

" Take care of yourself," I say, watching him settle himself
in a first-class carriage, with the *Spectator*, the *Criterion*, and the
London Mercury. " Take care of yourself. I shall ring up the
nursing-home to-morrow. I'm sure all will go well."

He smiles distantly, almost coldly, sinking down into his
seat and folding his blue-veined hands. " Don't bother to
wait."

" But I'd like to."

Silence. He looks out of the other window, his head turned
away from me, at some men on the line. The heat is oppressive.

Then : " Good-bye, good-bye." The train moving, coach
by coach, drawing him away, jerking beside the unimpeachably
blue river until it reaches a hazy distance and is lost.

I feel suddenly sick.

                                              July 8th, 1937

Last night there was thunder—on the right. What sort of
portent is this ?

I lay awake for hours, head aching, sweating, naked, without
bedclothes. Was it an attack of malaria ? Or only the heat ?
I thought all the time of what S. N. G. had said to me. I was
wrestling with devils.

                                              July 9th, 1937

Throughout this morning I have said : " I must ring up
the nursing-home." But something prevents me—a fear which
makes my heart thump, my scalp tingle. I keep on putting it off
—' after I have finished this article ', ' after my bathe ',
' after lunch '. This is cowardice.

It reminds me of when Dennis was killed : and I dared not go down from the balcony. . . .

From SHIRLEY FORSDIKE, Barbizon, France, *to*
Sir HUGH WEIGH, Dartmouth

July 15th, 1937

MY DEAREST,—It has happened ! A letter has come from you ! Oh, such a cold, disapproving letter—but a letter none the less. To-day I left my room where I have been brooding all these days and went for a drive in the Forest of Fontainebleau. This is the first time that I have been out of the garden since coming here. Your letter has done this. And now as I write, late, with Mother and all the guests asleep—all except the young Dutch couple on honeymoon who quarrel and do not turn out their light—I touch this one sheet of notepaper over and over again, I put my lips to it, because you, too, have touched it, your hands have rested there. Do not laugh at me for this : rather pity me. A letter is all that I have of you—a cold, disapproving letter.

If I could die ! If I had the courage ! But something prevents me—the certainty that some day, somehow, I shall be of service to you, that you will call me, that you will accept this love of mine. It is this that keeps me alive : it is only this that makes each day bearable—these days of summer, long, serene, but void, empty, like the smile on a dead face. (You see, I am being literary. ' Like the smile on a dead face.' But how else can I express this ache, this void ? I cannot write over and over again : ' I love you, I love you, I love you, I love you '.)

Plato was it who said that we all go through the world seeking a twin soul ? I think I believe that. I feel as if you had been torn from me—as if we had been sundered. And this one half must always cry out for the other ; must always hunger for it ; must always bleed : for nothing can heal it, nothing, till the halves be one. Why should I only be so certain of this—that we are halves, twin-souls ? Why should I only bear the ache ?

We belong to each other, inseparably. Claim what is yours :
return to me what is mine.

    . . . I came here to France because I was ill. Nothing could
be diagnosed, the doctors were puzzled. Should I have said
to them then : I am starving, I am bleeding to death ? Would
they have believed that ? But it is true, true.

Your letter : I have read it over and over again. When
I went for my drive this afternoon, alone, in a horse-carriage,
I kept on opening my bag, taking it out, looking at it, each
time as though I expected some miraculous change, so that what
was formal and cold might be tender, might be loving. And
each time my eyes filled with tears. You should not have written
to me like that. I had rather you had been angry : this coldness
freezes, kills.

You write : ' Be reasonable. No sane person could have
sent such a letter.' No sane person ! But are we ever sane
when we are in love ? And is it unreasonable, extraordinary,
for me to love you ? Is it strange that I should say to you :
' Take me, I am yours ', when you are a god. What else can
mortals do ? What else but this—to dedicate themselves ?
' I am yours ' : what else ?

A book has just appeared here in France, called *Pitié pour les
Femmes* ; it has caused a stir, my mother has lent it to me.
You must imagine a writer, Costals, a libertine, cynical, degenerate, a brute : yet to this man two women are willing to
concede *everything*—because they have read his books. Understand : they have not met him. Yet they love him, as I love
you. And they are starved—starved of all true companionship.
While I—I could have been married over and over if I had
wished it.

Does my love seem strange then ? Costals is amoral, a
cowardly degenerate : but you—you are noble, ascetic, good !
There is nothing strange here. There is nothing mad in my
wish to give myself to you. I am pouring my precious ointment
on your feet. Oh, do not spurn it ! Do not spurn it !

It is growing very late. Again I am weeping—as I always weep when I write to you. The young Dutch couple have turned out their light. If you knew how lonely I feel ! If you would answer this—tenderly, gently ! If I knew that you accepted my sacrifice ! That would be sufficient.

You must forgive the reproaches in this letter. They are unworthy of you. I must learn the complete resignation—to resign everything, even my grief—to make it all yours. I am not afraid of doing that. I put my soul into your hand. Do what you will with it, my dearest, for I am yours, yours only. Yours always. Even this intolerable anguish is yours, these tears.

I shall put out the light now. I shall try to sleep.

SHIRLEY.

PART II

PHANTOMS

WHEN Hugh Weigh first met Lucy Korrance at a dance at the Collector's bungalow (he ripped the train of her evening-dress and she was angry with him) it was said that she was 'wild'. For one thing, Mrs. Meakins, her aunt, had a story of how on their last visit to England she had spent a night on the river at Oxford with an undergraduate—and without a chaperone (Mrs. Meakins being the chaperone provided); and for another she had an irrepressible sense of humour. On one occasion at a dinner party, she offered a raw young sub-altern a concoction of vinegar and epsom salts with the words: "Do try this liqueur. It's supposed to be terribly, terribly old." "Hm, excellent," he murmured to the giggled derision of Lucy and her friends. But the more stuffy of her mother's guests thought that she might be going too far. . . .

Such were her idiosyncracies : and it was these, rather than certain more formidable traits—a tendency to lose her temper, be self-willed, strike the native servants—that really worried Mumsie. (Lady Korrance was always Mumsie to her girl : to her husband she was Memsie.) But everyone knew that she was young ; she would learn ; she would grow up.

Lucy had one other characteristic—one more endearing, conventional ; she was a snob. There was the occasion when her father had just been promoted and a dinner was given in his honour. After the ladies had gone into the drawing-room, Mrs. Meakins, who was pleased with her sister and wished to show it, said : "Tell me, dear. I suppose a *knighthood* goes with this new job ?" and the then Mrs. Korrance, being habitu-ally untruthful, replied : " Well, really, Beatrice, I haven't thought about it." Then her voice tinkled upwards in nervous laughter and she added : " In any case I don't care a ha'penny whether I'm Lady Korrance or not."

It was at this point that Lucy intervened. " I do," she said staunchly. " I shall be *proud* to be the daughter of Sir Basil Korrance." And she blushed in anticipation.

People agreed that this was the right spirit.

Not unnaturally, therefore, she decided to marry Hugh Weigh. He was, Mrs. Meakins had told her, heir to a baronetcy ; and when this advantage was coupled with good looks and the ability to ride, Lucy thought it sufficient. She had always wanted to be one of the aristocracy ; and, regardless of the fact that old Sir Humbert Weigh had been given his title by Queen Victoria and spoke with a Lancashire accent, this wish seemed at last attainable.

Mumsie repeatedly asked the young subaltern to bridge, tennis, and dinner ; Papa, when he carved, gave him the breast and wing ; and Mrs. Meakins contrived to ' leave the young people alone '—as far as propriety permitted.

It was in the garden that the first step was taken. " I just exist for my garden," Mumsie was in the habit of saying to enthusiastic visitors, as though she identified herself with the half-dozen coolies whose lives were devoted to its irrigation. It was certainly beautiful, flowering at the centre of parched roads, *maidans*, compounds. " It's like England," Mumsie would also say on occasions ; and this was the highest praise that anyone could bestow. There were lush lawns with sundials, bird-baths, and statuary ; there was a sunken garden ; there was even topiary, fantastic monsters, created out of the mind of one of the Indian gardeners. And all this was irrigated by a delightful stream which sloped artfully, made sudden water-falls, trickled into pools, and at intervals was spanned by bridges of wood. This stream—but the coolies knew where the water came from.

Hugh and Lucy strolled over the lawns, she twirling a parasol of vivid green. From her wrists dangled bracelets, lockets, charms, which tinkled as she walked. She was, as Mrs. Meakins put it, "a lovely girl". Hair piled on to her head in auburn turrets, swelling *embonpoint*, thighs moving firmly under rustling silk—these were the tastes of that era. Hugh approved.

"Do you ride?" she was asking. "I mean, do you find the time?"

"Oh, yes."

"Would you come riding with me? Susie's nearly sixteen —Papa's promised me another—would you?" This was the way she spoke, jumping from one thought to another, tripping here, slurring there. The parasol swung in an arc.

"That would be delightful."

"Oh, good! Couldn't we ride for miles and miles—I mean, right into the jungle—Papa won't let me—but if you said. . . ."

At that moment they came to one of the wooden bridges. How cool the water flowed! How clear! They both looked down, hands moving along the rail. Fingers met, momentarily. When they walked on, descending the little incline of the bridge, Hugh gallantly helped her. Slipping one arm round her waist, he pressed upwards that fine *embonpoint*.

"You brute! You utter beast!" She pulled away, tears of rage filling her eyes. The wide-brimmed hat quivered.

"But really——"

"Don't talk to me! Don't touch me!"

Over the smooth lawns she darted. The dress fluttered, the bracelets tinkled. She clutched her hat. Then she had disappeared.

Hugh stood on the bridge, gazing ruefully at his own reflection, dapper, dashing almost, buttons gleaming, teeth gleaming, hair gleaming with fixative. "Damn it," he thought. "Damn it. So she was frigid. So that was it. The little fool!" He felt enraged with her. He would like to smack her face. Any opposition annoyed him; with women he was used to having his way.

Then suddenly he decided : he would go and see Andrée. Andrée would understand. Dear Andrée !

But Lucy wept.

Hugh had 'had' his first woman when he was seventeen. He, S. N. George, and two other school friends had visited Paris for a week : in Paris he fell. Later, in retrospect, he never romanticised the incident as so many people do. It was a beginning ; and that was all. He was too truthful to romanticise his lust. His abnormal sexual energy was expended on women just as his abnormal physical energy was expended on hockey, polo, tennis ; and in either case without the expenditure he felt ill. But there was no romance there, no sentimentality.

For his school-friends, on that visit to Paris, it had been sufficient to drink absinthe in a Montmartre café where the sexes danced together—women mooning round in each others' arms, men swaying together. But to him this had merely seemed trivial : he had outgrown his adolescence. So that when, one evening, the others had set out, believing this to be Life and Sin and all the things that had been rigidly excluded from the tradition of Dr. Arnold, he complained of a headache and stayed at the hotel.

Later, after they had gone, he began to walk the streets with a perseverance which marked all his activities. He walked Les Gobelins quarter, because that was where the hotel was : had he known Paris better he might have seen the absurdity of this locale. It was raining as he explored those endless terraces and squares, to which clung, like a film of moisture, the gentility of a down-at-heel bourgeoisie. No one seemed to be out that night—only a cat that whisked through his legs, then stopped, returned, and pressed voluptuously against him. Far away, in the mist, there was asthmatic coughing. Lights blurred as though he were seeing them through tears.

For two hours he walked, hands deep in his pockets, the moisture gradually seeping through his clothes. Sometimes

3

he thought of the promised satisfaction—the warmth of it, the mastery. But more often he thought only of how best to succeed in his search, without any consideration of what would follow. The most important thing seemed not to release his energy but to find a woman. The means had superseded the end.

Footsteps clattering down an area, the sound of a woman singing, a church clock striking. The clammy touch of a lock of his own hair on his forehead. A desire to yawn. The ache of delayed realisation. This was all.

Then suddenly, as he strode along, head bowed, coat collar turned up, some syllables of French, murmured timidly from under a lamp-post. He shot round, smiling with relief, gesturing with one hand, oblivious that he was standing in a puddle.

Over her head she held a newspaper to keep her hair dry, a bony Jewess, pitiably thin, with a gold-stopped smile and a low forehead covered in a sort of rash. Her fur gleamed with pin-points of rain, her hands were large and clumsy. She smelt of wet clothes.

In her room her teeth chattered : and even when she was naked she grotesquely tried to warm herself after the fashion of cab-drivers—swinging her skeleton arms and slapping her flesh.

In their embrace she suddenly called out in impatience, because she was cold : " *Viens ! Viens, petit garçon !* " But he, because he was preoccupied and in any case did not know the idiom, did not hurry.

It was only later that he realised.

After that, few weeks passed without a repetition. But he was now becoming fastidious. Just as when he had first learnt tennis he was content to play with anyone, however bad, so at first he had pumped himself into drabs, syphilitics, inebriates. But later he was less easily satisfied.

It was when his regiment was sent to India that he met Andrée.

He had had an accident, riding into a heap of gravel on his motor bicycle and taking the skin off his face, when her father, a Eurasian jute merchant, had driven past in his carriage and seen him. He had almost hurried on, being naturally squeamish. But then his benevolence asserted itself. Grey, with the peculiar greyness of dark complexions, he drew up and got his Indian servant to drag Hugh on to the back seat. Once there, Hugh bled on to the dusty cushions, moaned, muttered, " This is very good of you, sir " ; quite failed to realise that Mr. Da Costa was ' not known ' at the Club, and fell asleep.

The next thing that happened was to wake up to an excited circle of women, Mr. Da Costa's family, some sending for the doctor, some cautiously attempting to remove his clothes in order to attend to his wounds, all of them talking. Andrée alone stood apart, watching him. He never forgot that gaze.

When the doctor arrived he was horrified to see Hugh sprawling on one of the many unmade beds that littered every room of the house, and hurried him off to the hospital. The Da Costas were not even thanked for their trouble. But the next morning, in spite of the doctor's warning, " They're awful people ", and the doctor's wife's, " The dirt they put up with ! " Hugh called on them. And Andrée was there.

She was fifteen, precocious as many children are who have spent their lives in the plains, plump as few are. She could not even be termed pretty : she bit her nails, her teeth were irregular, her face seemed to be all cheeks. But her body was young and strong, with breasts and buttocks that were far too large for their age, and feet that were far too small.

The first thing that Hugh noticed about her was the way her black hair was screwed into two little knots. " Pig-tails ", she called them ; and he had corrected, facetiously, " Piglet-tails ". But when they were in the garden together he got her to undo them and ran his fingers through the thick strands. Like a cat she at first rubbed herself against him ; then she pulled away, impatiently.

A few days later, a child now, in a white linen frock and sandals, she climbed a tree and dared him to follow her. At the top, scrambling from one branch to another, she ripped her skirt, disclosing a brown thigh. He touched her, and she did not move away. They stayed in the tree.

There was no opposition from her family. It never seemed to occur to them that Hugh might one day marry her. Obviously this was a thing which did not happen—an impossibility, given the society in which they lived. But they were honoured that he should pay her visits, send her flowers, buy her confectionery. Fortunately they were without sexual morality.

And just as they excluded, as a matter of course, all possibility of marriage, so Hugh did also. Apart from all incompatibilities, he was too realistic. He knew that for the moment Andrée was delightful : he loved her animal smell, the way in which she curled up in bed at his feet, her childish tears. But in five years, ten years—he could not bear to think of it. She would be like her mother and her twelve sisters—obese, clumsy, seismic, with a dry wheezing which one took to be laughter.

In any case, Andrée was already engaged to a young man, a Eurasian like herself, who had sung in the choir, been noticed by the padre, and was now a subordinate in the police. He never resented Hugh ; rather he was proud of the honour done to him. Hugh had made Andrée what is called a *demi-vierge*.

Then Lucy. But there had been that scene in the garden, and he was no longer asked to tennis, bridge, dinner by Lady Korrance. He had been dropped. True, Mumsie still talked to him in the Club or when they met in other people's houses, but Lucy ignored him, only staring, as if in reproach, when he entered a room in which she was already seated.

This change irritated him ; he was already in love with her—in spite of evenings on the veranda with Andrée, drives with Andrée, meals with Andrée. Thwarted, he took refuge in a ferocious antagonism. When passing her at the Club he looked the other way; he declined to partner her at tennis with an aversion which was obvious to everyone; and he took to staring at her critically, impertinently, on all other occasions when chance threw them together. Among his colleagues he spoke of her with a mixture of contempt and malice; and because they respected him, regarding him as their leader, they soon ceased to laugh *with* her and began, instead, to laugh *at* her. Lucy became the clown, instead of the wit, of the station.

But, suddenly, there was a change—an invitation to a picnic. At first Hugh thought it must be a practical joke: but in the evening Lady Korrance came up to him in the Club. "You got the invitation?" She sounded breathless, a shade too concerned.

"Thank you."

"You can come?"

"I shall be delighted."

Then, all at once, he was aware that Lucy was listening from an embrasure by the window.

Cameras, field-glasses, cold chicken in aspic—it was the usual paraphernalia; with Mrs. Meakins stopping the car at intervals to scurry behind a clump of bushes, the servants forgetting the soda-water, the guests forgetting to be polite. The truth was that it was too sultry. "I love picnics", exclaimed Lady Korrance. But she might equally well have said, "I love going to the dentist". No one expected her to be truthful. Then she scowled at the bearer because there were already blow-flies on the meat.

Sir Basil took photographs, Mrs. Meakins disappeared again ("Look out for snakes", was Lady Korrance's whispered advice), two subalterns threw a cricket ball at each other. They were all sprawling in the courtyard of a fifteenth-century palace. But they might, for all they cared, have been on Hampstead Heath. When Hugh examined some carving they

looked puzzled, even shocked ; and Lady Korrance, as though
to excuse her guest, exclaimed : " What funny beasts ! They
have two heads ! " and offered him another helping of trifle.

Then, having gorged—on cold chicken, hard-boiled eggs
(the salt forgotten), game-pie, trifle, chocolate mousse, liqueur
chocolates—the older of them yawned, went to sleep, or chatted
in small groups, while the youngsters discussed the feasibility
of playing rounders, squabbled over the rules, teased Mrs.
Meakins's dropsical terrier, and finally decided on a walk.
In twos and threes they wandered off into the jungle, led by a
young man who thought he knew a short-cut to the river.

Hugh was about to saunter after them, alone, when a hand
touched his wrist. It was Lucy, smiling, without a trace of
embarrassment. " May I come with you ? " The words were
the first she had spoken to him for four months, apart from
conventional greetings.

" If you like."

Again she smiled, magnificent in green silk ; then bending
her head slightly forward, as if in compliance to his wishes,
the plumes on her hat nodding, her eyelashes making delicate
shadows on rouged cheeks, she swung ahead. They did not
speak. Hers was a high-stepping progression, bird-like, her
skirt held high in a white-gloved hand.

" But aren't we going the wrong way ? " Hugh said at last.
" I'm sure the others——"

" Oh, no. I saw them. It's quite all right." Again that
smile, again the forward inclination of the head.

He shrugged his shoulders and they moved on through
punkahs of fern. The path had been beaten hard by the feet of
coolies, the air was shrill with birds. Then suddenly she turned.

" Oh, dear ! I do believe we've lost the way. I could have
sworn . . . but this is a dead-end." They had reached a
clearing, a few tree-trunks, some creeper, two lemonade bottles,
and a copy of the *Pioneer*—relics of some other picnic at some
other time. " Now what are we to do ? "

" We'd better go back."

She wrinkled up her nose. " I feel rather tired. Let's sit down for a bit." Raising her skirt she climbed on to a tree-trunk. " Come here. Sit down."

Obeying her he placed himself on the same perch. He wondered what would happen.

Then she was pressing herself against him, hands exploratory, mouth glued to his, body trembling.

" Dearest," she murmured. And her hat fell to the ground.

" Where have you been ? " Mrs. Meakins simpered when they returned too late for tea and a game of Consequences.

" We got lost," Hugh explained. " We thought we were following the others, but we came to a dead-end—a rather pleasant clearing."

" Good heavens ! Fancy Lucy losing her way ! That must be the clearing where we had our picnic last year." This from Sir Basil, who was only tactful with his superiors. " What's this, Lucy ? Lost your way ? You *have* got a memory." Then he began to chuckle indulgently.

But Lucy blushed.

" I couldn't be more delighted," said Lady Korrance when their engagement was announced ; and later : " Do call me Mother. After all—well—we've never had a son. And now we look upon you . . ." So she became Mumsie.

" Of course, I saw it months ago," Mrs. Meakins confided to a group of friends. " Months and months ago—even before they did." Then she sighed, thinking of the Rev. Pat Meakins—' padre '—who had been so slow that summer at Eastbourne, and was now buried in Gorakhpur under a marble inscription, ' Remember that the best of friends must part.'

" Congratulations, old boy," were Sir Basil's words, after a brief interview, during which the baronetcy, Hugh's grand-mother's probable fortune, and the likelihood of promotion

were all discussed. "I haven't a thing against the match."
Nor had he. Of course, there had been talk of a Eurasian girl;
the boy moved in a 'fast' set; old Phillips had seen a party of
them in the bazaar, and one guessed their errand.

But now all this could be dismissed as 'wild oats'. 'Wild
oats' meant anything that Sir Basil did not wish to find dis-
agreeable.

So it was all settled. His colleagues gave a party and they all
got drunk; the Collector gave a party and they all stayed sober.
Mumsie said she didn't believe in long engagements. Lucy
chose an emerald ring.

But Andrée had still to be told.

The Da Costas' house had been built in a swamp on a bend
of the river. For this reason the walls always sweated, the
verandas buzzed with mosquitoes, and they had been able to buy
it for almost nothing. Also, it was too near the bazaar; and it
was said to be haunted. But none of these things worried the
Da Costas. It was big; and that was sufficient.

In the bathroom there was a mausoleum: hence the stories
of ghosts. But as none of them used the bathroom, preferring
to wash, if they must wash, in the courtyard, on the verandas
or in their bedrooms, the ghosts left them alone. And so did
the English community.

That afternoon, when Hugh drove up in a tonga, a little
apprehensive, but fortifying himself with thoughts of Lucy, a
chuprassi sprawled on the steps, asleep, his mouth open, his
tunic undone, his turban over one eye. When he saw Hugh he
grunted, shifted, and went to sleep again. The steps were
blotchy where he had expectorated.

Hugh went in, smiling as he thought of Mumsie's orderlies,
saluting, standing to attention, opening doors needlessly—four
Sikhs who were old and pompous and scrupulously clean. But
he was not sure that he did not prefer this, entering unannounced
and letting in two dogs which might perhaps be pariahs or

might be Mrs. Da Costa's pets, then colliding with some naked children whose tummies were quaintly distended, and finally walking through a room where Mr. Da Costa reclined on a sofa, the springs broken, and discussed his affairs with a group of relatives. As Hugh passed he raised two fingers in greeting and smiled through discoloured teeth, while the relatives, men and women, lying in chairs or on the floor, nodded, fanned themselves to show how hot it was, and grinned. The air was wreathed in a sour exhalation of unwashed clothes, foot-rot, tainted meat.

Next door was Mrs. Da Costa, immense among cushions, doing nothing. She, too, smiled as she drew her kimono over gourd-like bubs. In a cage in one corner of the room was a canary, half-covered with a tattered yellow shawl : as Hugh passed it winked a rheumy eye. There were lizards on the ceiling, and on the walls the wings of squashed insects. The slats of the blinds gouged horizontal shadows on bangled arms, perspiring face, plump calves. A punkah swayed and then quivered to a standstill as the coolie took pan. But when Mrs. Da Costa screeched in Hindustani it jerked upwards once more, shifting the dull air in eddies.

On the veranda there was Andrée, reclining at full length in the torrid sun, she alone cool and undisfigured by sweat. She was reading a novel, the fingers of one hand resting lightly against her cheek, her breasts rising and falling as she breathed. Under her arms were blue shadows where she had shaved herself. The garden in front shimmered like a bead curtain.

" Hullo ! "

She turned round slowly, smiling at him, and the novel lay in her lap. " Hullo."

He drew up a chair, sat down, crossed his legs. " Christ, it's hot."

" Do you think so ? I like it."

For a while they said nothing more, both gazing out at the garden—if garden it could be called—where two dogs walked
    3*

in circles round each other, sniffing. Then Andrée burst into peals of laughter. "It's too absurd, those animals ! Even they find it too hot."

Silence.

Then : " Andrée."

" Yes."

" I came to tell you I'm going to get married. To Miss Korrance."

She said nothing. Only her eyelids flickered, as though at the dazzle. It was impossible to tell what she felt or thought. But at last : " Yes. I'm glad," she said. " And next winter I, too, shall be married. Vivian is to get his promotion then." She scratched lazily at her scalp.

He had always known that she would take it like this. Impossible to imagine her making a scene. Why had he been so nervous—the cut under his ear, where the razor slipped, that absurdly large tip to the tonga driver ? Why had he so mistrusted her ? Filled with a vast tenderness he stooped downwards, ostensibly to tie his shoe. Then, in that position, he rested his cheek against her thigh. How smooth it was, how soft through the white dress ! His hand stroked her knee, calf, ankle.

" Dearest." She ran grubby fingers through his hair. " Dearest. . . . You will come and see me sometimes—just sometimes ? "

" Of course."

Again the unresisting flesh, the ache that seemed to begin in his loins and forced its way upwards to his throat. " Of course."

The promise was kept.

Lucy and Hugh went to Kashmir for their honeymoon. It was Lucy's choice because she wanted winter sports. But on the day after their arrival she dared Hugh to race her to their house on skis, slipped, and fractured her pelvic girdle. This kept her in her bed—and Hugh out of it.

On recovery, she followed Hugh to the station in the plains where he had since been sent. "Such bad luck," said Mrs. Meakins, referring to the accident. It seemed as if all the facetious references to the honeymoon that guests had made during the wedding breakfast had somehow been wasted.

Of the months that followed, in the sweltering heat of the small station, Hugh later remembered very little. In his mind there was only an eternal afternoon, walls sweating, bodies sweating, moist fingers resting on his side. Always there was promise of storms—the boom of thunder, sudden lightning, intimations of celestial pique. But no rain fell. Lucy lay beside him, and again and again, as one scratches an intolerable itch, arms met, lips closed on each other. Impossible to break away from that high bed and the weight of the ceiling. They were bound in a common doom—both anguished, resentful, humid.

This was the memory he bore with him, indefinite for the most part, without incident, a sense of heat and dazzle, the smell of damp flesh, incessant giving and incessant demand. Only a few details remained apart from this. Going on a parade, his lip bleeding where she had bitten him. (That morning he was particularly savage to defaulters.) Or coming from polo, grimed, sweating. "I'll have a bath," he said. But : "No," she pleaded. "Stay as you are. Stay as you are." And dirty as he was, his nails black, his shirt sticking to him, she drew him downwards.

This seemed to him almost perverse. And the way in which she delighted to run fingers over his muscles, making him harden them. And hair, not of his head, in her mouth. . . .

But of that time there was little else. Only the words of Lady Korrance when she came for a visit. "I can see that you are both madly in love."

The next winter he got leave and together they sailed for England. But first he went to see Andrée to say good-bye, making an excuse that he wished to meet colleagues he had left

behind at the old station, with Mumsie and Papa and Mrs.
Meakins. By an odd coincidence he arrived at the station on
the night before Andrée was to be married : they had never
written to each other, probably because she was almost illiterate.

Their meeting was intended to be ' platonic '. Together
they sat on the veranda, while in the house Mrs. Da Costa, Mr.
Da Costa, and a host of screeching relatives made arrangements
for the next day. Neither of them spoke, because they had
never had much to say to each other ; and now it seemed too
late to begin. Bats scissored down the sky with a dry creaking
of wings ; for once the garden ceased to look brown and cracked
like the ground of a badly preserved oil-painting, and wore a
downy bloom ; a fresh breeze blew from the river, bringing
not unpleasant smells. But Hugh was bored. Somehow he
felt it would be dishonourable to caress Andrée now, on the eve
of her wedding. But what else was there to do ? What else
did she expect ?

Soda-water sneezed into his tumbler as she pressed the siphon.
Then, handing him his drink, she said with a wry smile : " To-
morrow I shall be Mrs. Green. It seems strange." Was it the
moonlight that dilated her pupils and made her eyes seem
luminous ? Why did her lips tremble ?

" Let's drink to that," he said. " To Mrs. Green." Raising
his glass he sipped at the bitter concoction she had shaken out
of a row of bottles. Again he repeated the words : " To
Mrs. Green."

" Don't ! " Suddenly, and for no reason, she threw herself
on his shoulder, tears streaming from her eyes. Her breasts
shook convulsively as they lay against him. " I can't bear it !
I'm so frightened ! "

" Frightened ? But, my dear, why ? Don't you want
to—— ? Don't you love him ? "

" Oh, yes, yes ! Of course, I love him ! I'm really very
happy. It's silly of me to cry like this. It's just that I feel—
afraid."

" But why—why ? " he repeated, tender yet amused. It baffled him that after all she had experienced at his hands she should still have room for fear. Was she afraid of Green's clumsiness ? Or did she expect something more, some special miracle ? Almost without thinking he began to caress her.

So it ended in this—what he had been determined to avoid.

On the voyage home Hugh suddenly made a discovery— with Lucy's help. It was not a very original discovery, but for these two it was certainly a momentous one : for from that moment began the little quarrels, the raising of voices in public rooms, the scenes in the halls of hotels. The discovery was this : it is often those people who are most concerned to appear ' unconventional ' who are truly convention's slaves. At the station Lucy had appeared such a free spirit, even ' wild ' : Mrs. Meakins, Mumsie, all of them would have agreed that she was independent and went her own way. And yet, and yet . . . Why, for example, when Hugh suggested that they should spend their leave in Greece, did she reject the idea, not because she did not like it (he would have understood that) but because " Everyone goes to England when they have leave ". Why did she say, " You have failed me ", on that evening when he somehow forgot that the Captain had invited them to play bridge and instead gossiped with some third-class passengers in their cabin ? Why did she burst into tears when he said that he did not wish to accompany her to Simon Artz, but preferred to take a car into the desert ? Why, why ? Could it be that Lucy who had always pretended to despise social functions—Lucy who had given herself to him on that picnic, resolutely, defiantly —could it be that she, too, was like the rest of them ? It certainly looked like it.

So they didn't go to Greece. So they bought turkish delight in the company of one governor-general and consumed it in the company of another. So they became ' good sorts ' and ' dears ' and ' nice people '. So they spent their leave at Bournemouth.

" Restful ", said one of the passengers who advised this place to them. But Lucy did not find it so. Now that they lived in a small and dank and economical pension, artfully concealed from the sea by three bigger and more expensive hotels (but ' only three minutes from the front ', said the tinted brochure), now that there were no servants, no dogs, no horses to beat or tame, she became suddenly fretful, ill-at-ease, petulant. She changed. Perhaps, after all, she wished that they had ignored what people said and gone to Greece.

" But I feel so shut-in here. I know no one."

" Oh, come, darling. . . ."

" No—no one ! No one that is worth knowing. I hate it."

" There's nothing to prevent our going away."

" Where on earth could we go ? "

" Anywhere."

" But it would only be the same."

Suddenly she began to ask questions about his grandmother, his father, the baronetcy. Once she said : " Of course, as I am the only child . . ." and then stopped, blushing.

She made him take her each evening to the grandest hotel in the town. How it bored him ! For hours she prepared for this, lacing her figure, tinting her face, piling her hair into monumental turrets. And then, after it was all done, they sat together, glum, unspeaking, sipping sherry in the lounge while her sulky eyes roamed among the other guests. Then home— to bed.

She resented the money he spent on books, excursions to the country, the hire of a yacht. All these things she regarded as hostile to her. They drained his time and his energies when she should have them exclusively. They were almost as hateful as those other enemies—his friends.

Once, coming home from a day in the New Forest, he thought she greeted him with undue effusiveness. Yet some-how she seemed constrained, triumphant. " Let's have some wine," she said at dinner : and later, in their room, she began to whirl round and round in a waltz, her skirt swinging out-wards, the colour mounting to her cheeks. Then she collapsed on to the bed, dizzy, laughing, coughing.

Suddenly and for no reason he felt angry with her. He had to repress the desire to strike her face. " I'm going to bed now," he said, and went into the dressing-room.

Then he saw what had happened.

" Where is that book ? " he demanded.

" What book, dear ? "

" The book that was by my bed."

" I don't know what you are talking about."

" You know perfectly well. The one that arrived this morning. S. N. George's new book."

" No, really, dearest——"

" Don't lie to me ! " In a sudden rage he caught one of her wrists and twisted it. " Where is that book ? What have you done to it ? "

She moaned, struggled ; tears ran down her cheeks. " Let go ! You're hurting ! Let go ! "

" Where is that book ? " he repeated, suddenly seeing the whole scene in the mirror above the mantelpiece and feeling ashamed of himself. But he still gripped her wrist, still shook her.

" I burned it."

" Burned it ! "

" Oh, darling, it was horrible. I couldn't bear to have it lying in our rooms. I didn't want you to read it. I picked it up quite by chance, you see. And then . . . You do under-stand, don't you ? You're not cross with me ? "

He looked at her in incredulity. " Horrible ? What do you mean ? What's wrong with the book ? "

" That first poem . . . It was all that I read. It was—' On the Statue of a Greek Boy '—or something like that. I—I didn't know that men thought such things. It frightened me." She rested her head in his lap, where he had sunk on to the bed, the warm tears splashing his hands.

He could not help being tender towards her : " There's nothing to be frightened of—nothing to upset you. You see, S. N. G. was trying to recapture the spirit of a Greek sculptor— and he must have felt rather like that. The Greeks thought differently from us, that's all. It's not a matter of right or wrong. . . . Theocritus, Virgil——" How could he go on ? He knew he could never explain to her. Gently, but resolutely, he freed himself from her grasp.

But : " Yes. Yes, I see," she said, seeing nothing, seeing only his anger. " You must forgive me then. I—I know so very little, I suppose. I mean, Mumsie—I never realised that people could feel that sort of thing. It still seems queer to me. I can't help it. . . . If it had been anyone but S. N. George——" She broke off, her eyes fell to the carpet. With one finger she began to trace the acanthus pattern on the eiderdown.

" What do you mean ? " Again fury made him breathless.

" Well, dear—it's only—to be frank with you—I've never liked him. He's very kind, of course," she added hastily, " and he must be frightfully clever. But sometimes I'm afraid—of his influence—on you. . . ."

" On me ! Are you mad, Lucy ? What sort of influence can poor S. N. G.——"

" Oh, not him only ! " Suddenly eloquent, she rose to her feet and began pacing the room, clasping and unclasping her hands, the tears streaming down her cheeks. " It's all your artistic friends. They frighten me. I don't understand them, I suppose. But they seem evil, somehow—somehow unhealthy. And when you're with them, dear, you change, you know. Oh, yes, you're different, dear—quite different. It's your whole attitude. As if you were two people—*my* Hugh, and *their* Hugh. . . . I don't think you really belong to them. They're unlike us. They don't believe in the same things as we do. It's silly to try and imitate them, merely because they are clever——"

" Be quiet ! " he shouted at her. " Your insane drivel will drive me out of my head. Be quiet—do you hear ! "

She clutched the mantelpiece, her lips white. " Darling ! You've never spoken like that before. We've quarrelled, yes. . . . But you've never——"

" So you resent my friends. So that's it, is it ? So you want to condemn me to the imbecilities of Mrs. Meakins and Colonel Hale, and the rest of them—for life. So you want to have me to yourself, away from whatever is real and valuable——"

" No, no, dear ! No, no ! You've misunderstood me ! How can you be so cruel ! I like so many of your friends—so many of them." Piteously, she sobbed on the bed, choking, face downwards, nails scratching on the pillow. He could not help feeling compassionate towards her. " Be kind to me, dearest. Try to understand. I know I'm not very clever. . . ." Then through paroxysms of weeping again came the words : " It's—just—your—artistic friends. . . ."

Faced with such anguished stupidity what could he do but go out ?

There was a reconciliation, of course, with them both clasped in each other's arms, naked, before the gas-fire in their hotel bedroom. Not very romantic. Not even comfortable. Or so Hugh thought, one side scorched, one frozen. But Lucy said : " I've never been so divinely happy, dear—unless we count that time in the jungle—the first time." And Hugh meditated, wondering why the thing they had attained in the discomfort of noonday, with the heat and the flies and the danger of being seen, should no longer be attainable in Miss Acre's pension, Bournemouth, before a gas-fire. It was, he decided, not solely a matter of place.

The next day they were quarrelling once more—over something so trivial—so unimportant. Perhaps this is the way to quarrel. Perhaps this is the art of quarrelling. To quarrel over nothing.

When they came in from a ' stroll ' along the front—they called it a stroll though Hugh was always inclined to turn it into a scamper—Lucy, as usual, went up to the reception desk, where Miss Acre presided behind a telephone, an inkstand, and a carafe of water, and asked if there were any letters.

" Oh, three for me ! " she said proudly, triumphantly, as Miss Acre handed them to her. " Three ! How lovely ! "

Hugh was looking over her shoulder. " But, dearest—two are addressed to *me*. That only leaves one."

He said this laughingly. But Lucy flushed, threw down the letters, and ran upstairs, as though he had offended her for ever. Miss Acre and such of the residents as were in the lounge exchanged delighted and scandalised glances.

Hugh followed Lucy slowly, determined that there should be no scenes, above all no tears. But she was already weeping on the couch where they had staged their reconciliation three nights ago.

" What is the matter ? " he asked coldly.

" You know p-p-p-perfectly well ! "

" No, really, I don't."

She sat up, suddenly, abruptly, her face red and ugly with grief. " Was it necessary to humiliate me in front of Miss Acre and all those people ? " she snapped.

" But, Lucy, dear——" He tried to lodge himself beside her on the sofa, failed, and instead stroked her hair.

" Don't touch me ! " she screamed piercingly. " Leave me alone ! Don't touch me ! "

" Lucy, dearest—do pull yourself together. You're behaving like a child."

" Beast, beast ! I hate you, I hate you ! " Out into the passage she rushed, down the stairs, into the street. " I'll never come back ! Never, never, never ! "

More glances, eyebrows raised, Miss Acre, overcome, sipping water from the carafe—Hugh perceived all this as he ran after her.

" Come home, Lucy ! " he shouted breathlessly as they dodged between the traffic. " Don't make such a fool of yourself."

" Never ! I'll never come home ! I don't want to see you again." At that moment she almost tripped against the pavement : if she had, the whole scene would have ended in farce. But somehow she regained her balance and scurried on. " Go away ! " she yelled.

" Certainly not. When you're in this state—it would be unsafe——"

" Go away ! I'll call a policeman ! I warn you ! Go away ! "

How people stared ! The excitement ! Later, it was said that one old woman had thrown a fit in her bath-chair. But as she had been throwing fits for an odd sixty years there was nothing remarkable in that. What was remarkable was the stir, the bustle, the end to lethargy. Livers ceased to be sluggish, attendants trundled their bath-chairs as though they were wheel-barrows.

" Lucy—what are you going to do ? "

" That's my business. Go away ! "

" Where are you going ? "

" Go away ! "

" If you don't answer, I shall have to follow you. Can't you see what a fool—— ? "

" That's right ! That's all you think of—your precious dignity ! "

" But, Lucy, what are you going to do ? "

" If you must know—if it'll get rid of you—I—I—I'm going to kill myself." Again she began weeping, a handkerchief pressed to her mouth.

" No, Lucy. Don't do that. . . . Lucy, listen to me ! I love you, dearest. I love you ! Why should you want to kill yourself ? " But already they were nearing the cliffs and Lucy was walking resolutely towards them.

Then, in sudden exasperation, he caught her by the shoulders, turned her round, and slapped her face, hard, three or four times. "You little fool," he said. "For heaven's sake pull yourself together. Everyone's staring at you."

At first she went rigid with rage. Then : " Darling ! Oh, darling ! " She was in his arms, kissing him, stroking his hair. " I thought I'd lost you. But that was you—the old you. So you do care. You do care ! . . . Hit me again, darling."

But he only gaped at her in amazement.

Soon after this Tiger, Lucy's Tiggs or Tiggo, joined them on their strolls, their excursions, their meals. Apart from two dark stripes on an otherwise weak-whisky coat he was not in the least like a tiger. Lucy was nearer the mark when she called him a lamb. He was woolly, and skittish, and silly.

Impossible to forget the day when they bought him. For on that day Hugh had experienced something, a vision one might have called it ; but a vision must be decisive, and this decided nothing ; it only made conflicts, posed questions, showed a diversity of ways.

He and Lucy had driven into Southampton, bickering aimlessly, without passion ; and as they drove he had suddenly felt the complete emptiness, the triviality of all they did. It was as if a light had been blown out by the wind, leaving everything dark. And he found, most terrible of all, that he no longer cared if the light *was* out. He simply did not care.

That was the beginning.

Then, driving past the docks, he had suddenly seen the big ships, smelled salt and tar and the less pleasant smells ; and for no reason, he had drawn up, there, in the middle of it all, with Lucy protesting and threatening to get out and walk.

Climbing out of the car and leaving her he walked to the edge, his hat in his hand. It was then that the thing happened. It began with a ship's siren which reverberated, plangently, like a gong, across and across and across the bay. And for no reason a great longing filled him, a great ache, which seemed to drain him of all strength and strike upwards as if it would smash through the bones of his chest. What he saw then could never be described : perhaps he saw nothing. Perhaps all that he experienced was a special miracle of light, a special absence of all sound. But afterwards he knew that he associated with that moment islands, tropical birds, women singing, the touch and scent of enormous blooms. Happiness would be too commonplace a word for it : and besides, this was an anguish.

And somehow Andrée was a part of all these visionary splendours, no longer a child, naïvely voluptuous in a white cotton dress, but a figurehead, carved by the wind, a figurehead on a ship with sails. And the crooked was made straight, and rough places were made plain. . . . For that second only. Afterwards everything tumbled into chaos again ; and two drunken sailors lurched against him ; and Lucy called out from the car petulantly : " Oh, do hurry, dear. Do hurry. I'm getting so hungry."

And that was that.

Lucy appeased her hunger on scones and cakes and ice-cream at a café in the New Forest. It was then that Tiger, Tiggs, Tiggo was found.

As they ate, this dog, half puppy, ceased to scratch itself and came and watched them. Saliva trickled from its mouth. Then, all at once, it had jumped on to the flowered silk of Lucy's frock and was reaching for the scone that she held in one hand. Its eyes were small and avaricious, its tongue was red.

" Darling ! " Lucy exclaimed, suddenly forgetting to look peeved, and twisting her finger in its woolly coat. " Oh, look ! He's like a tiger. And he loves me. . . . Don't you, darling ? You love little Lucy." (The inference being that Hugh did not.) Turning, she said : " I must have him, Hugh."

" Have him ? What on earth do you mean ? "

She touched his sleeve decisively. " Buy him for me."
" But, my dear Lucy—he's not for sale. I really can't——"
" Buy him for me."
So Tiger, the mongrel, was bought for a five-pound note.

He became Lucy's ally, brushed, overfed, the fleas evicted.
When she and Hugh quarrelled she had a way of talking to the
dog which infuriated him : " I'm sorry, Mr. Tiggs. No walk
along the front this morning, 'cos Master's very, very cross—
very, very cross. No walk for poor little Tiggsie-Wiggsie. No
walk for poor little Lucy. No walk. Master's cross, that's
why." And Tiggs would wag his tail.

When she wept on the couch she would embrace the animal,
murmuring : " No one loves little Lucy. No one loves her
any, any more. But Tiggsie does. You *do* love me, don't you,
Tiggsie ? You'll never leave me ? You'll never leave poor
little Lucy ? "

" Oh, for God's sake shut up ! " Hugh would bawl at her,
exasperated, losing his temper as she hoped he would. " I can't
bear this sentimental drivel."

But : " Oh—oh—oh ! Tiggsie, did you hear that ? Did
you hear Master shouting ? " was the only response.

She certainly loved the dog, with the animal-love of those
who have failed in human relationships. But given this love
how could one explain the scene that he witnessed one afternoon, by accident ? Lucy was sitting on the tennis lawn of
the hotel with Tiggs, while he was upstairs writing letters.
Suddenly bored he looked out of the window. Someone had
taken down the tennis net, and Lucy knelt by it, where it lay
in a heap, and played with Tiggs. Over and over she rolled
him, patting his distended stomach, pulling his ears. Hugh
thought it rather a delightful picture, with Lucy in a green
cotton dress, her hair piled on to her head. Then, still play-
fully, she pulled a bit of the net over Tiggs : Tiggs struggled,
collapsed. More of the net. And again more. Tiggs was

being wrapped round and round like a cocoon, entangled, fighting, catching his ears and nose and tail in the meshes. Then, when he began to squeal, she watched him for a while, smiling. Finally she left him, going into the house.

Hugh met her on the stairs. " Tiggs is squealing," he said.

" Is he ? I wonder why. I've only just left him."

She followed Hugh out on to the lawn. Then, with a sudden cry, as though it was only now that she saw it, she ran forward : " Oh, poor Mr. Tiggs ! He must have been having a roll—and now look ! Help me, dear. . . . Oh, the poor darling ! His paw's caught. He might have been suffocated." Tears glistened in her eyes.

Kneeling down together, side by side, they began to undo the net. Hugh did not tell her what he had seen.

A week later old Sir Humbert died while playing croquet in the grounds of his Hampshire house. His death was said to be caused by excitement at the possibility of beating his neighbour, the colonel. At any rate, Hugh and Lucy arrived to a hushed house, the blinds drawn, the housekeeper in tears. The croquet mallets and balls still lay out on the lawn, unheeded.

After they had seen the body Lucy and Hugh went into the drawing-room and sat down, beneath sabres, tusks, skins. They shivered ; there was no fire.

" Darling—I'm terribly sorry," Lucy said. " Were you awfully fond of him ? "

He nodded mutely.

" I know how I should feel if Mumsie, or Papa . . . Oh, I do hate death. It terrifies me." She came across to him and caressed his face. " Poor darling ! Poor, poor darling ! "

At that moment the family solicitor was announced. He stumbled into the room, blindly, peering from the back of gold-rimmed spectacles, his face greenish. He had known the family for years, for years and years. " Oh, dear," he began in a voice that was pitched oddly high. " Oh dear, oh dear ! I can't believe it. . . . So sudden. No warning. . . . Only the other day—the Hunt Ball. . . . Oh, Mr. Hugh ! "

" *Sir* Hugh," interjected Lucy emphatically.

And a few days later, back in Bournemouth, she suddenly said : " I suppose we could go abroad now."

" Abroad ? . . . Oh—yes. I suppose we could."

" Oh, let's ! Oh, do let's ! " She clapped her hands with excitement.

So before moving into the house they went to Switzerland—on the legacy.

Then the war. Strange that what was for others disruptive, explosive, unsettling, should be the means by which these two resolved conflicts, found satisfaction, found peace. On his leaves they no longer quarrelled. They were passionate once more—in taxis, on walks, even in a box at the theatre. And Hugh begot a son, Dennis, who was strong, and tough, and quick tempered. And at the age of two the boy threw a brick at Lucy and cut her cheek. And Hugh thrashed him.

Lucy had turned the house in Hampshire into a convalescent home : while Hugh won distinction in the Balkans and later in France. For both of them these were full, satisfying years. It was as if a tree that had seemed withered had suddenly showered fruit into their laps.

Mrs. Meakins said that Lucy was wonderful, quite wonderful with the patients. She often attended operations ; she bandaged and washed them ; she wrote their letters home. Some deep-seated craving had at last been satisfied. Power, perhaps. Pity, perhaps. Perhaps something far more subtle and dangerous.

Hugh, too, was satisfied, leading impossible expeditions, heroically showing young boys how to die, winning medals and mentions and articles in the daily press. Of course, there was the danger ; comradeship ; ambition surfeited. But something more, something added. A craving as formidable as Lucy's. (What was it ? Was it this that made people say that they were ' wonderful people ' ? Was it this that won the war ? Impossible to tell. But it was there, urging them, thrusting them forward, mastering them.)

When Hugh was to be decorated and given a new command some friends gave a dinner for him. He arrived for it from the Front, dusty, tired, grimy. There were too many speeches, too many courses, too much to drink. And always, at the other end of the table, he saw Lucy, sitting next to a Cabinet minister, superb in emeralds. His head ached.

Then afterwards, as he put on his coat, an acquaintance came up to him, talked for a while, and said, in the course of their conversation : " Sad about poor Eckworth, wasn't it ? "

" Eckworth ? What do you mean ? "

" Didn't you hear ? You must have heard."

" No."

" Cut his throat with a razor. It was in all the papers. Horrible business. . . ."

" But why ? "

Shoulders were shrugged, eyes raised. They talked of other things.

But in the car Hugh thought again of Eckworth, who had been at school with him. One of his letters, the last, was still in his wallet now. He had written this :

" . . . So Maurice and Tony and John were all killed in that last offensive. This eternal Tchekov play is driving me mad. Am I to be left like the old servant in *The Cherry Orchard* ? I can't tell you how horrible it is to see one's contemporaries go off, one by one, to be killed—and still I toddle along to the Foreign Office, see the latest Shaw play, read S. N. G.'s new book. If the others resented it, it wouldn't be so bad. Or if I was in discomfort—on a minesweeper, on the land, anywhere. I can quite see why so many of us pacifists volunteer for dangerous jobs. You see, no amount of principles can remove that feeling of guilt—the utter humility of the thing, the abjectness. Often

I feel like throwing the whole business up and putting on a
uniform. But would that be an answer ? I mean, if I believe
that war is wrong—if I would rather die than kill a fellow
human being. . . . And so it goes on, the interminable conflict,
with oneself, within oneself. I'm boring you, I expect. Forgive this letter. . . ."

And now he had killed himself. The taxi drew up, Lucy
got out. How cold it was ! How his head ached ! Slowly he
walked up to his room and stretched himself out on his bed, in
soundless, intolerable anguish, one hand twisting the sheet.
For the first time, he cursed the war. . . .

Then Lucy came in. " Tired, dearest ? I bet you are. But
you were wonderful—wonderful. Your speech . . . Oh, you
can do anything—anything ! It's all yours—the whole world."

And she lay down on the bed beside him, her cheek touching
his.

The war over, he came home, no longer a subaltern but a
general, and went to Hampshire and wrote his first book. It
was a time when ' revelations ' and ' exposures ' were becoming
popular ; and though he had never written with this in mind,
only telling the truth, the brutality of it all, the picture of men
who were no longer men but beasts, the incisive presentation
of his own personality, all this made for success. The press
published angry letters from ' Cui Bono ', ' Ex-officer ', ' Mother
of Six '. A liberal M.P. misquoted a paragraph. Someone
tried to throw a stone through the London flat, but mistook the
number. Begging letters, angry letters, laudatory letters
arrived by post. A critic wrote in a Sunday paper : ' A book
for the discriminating few '. And it sold twenty-five thousand
copies.

General Sir Hugh Weigh was becoming a cult.

It was soon after this that the first of Lucy's many disorders
began. She had always tended to hypochondria, seeing doctors,

taking medicines, submitting to diets. But with the war this had suddenly ended. Perhaps she had been too busy looking after the bodies of others to interest herself in her own.

One night, long ago, out in India, when Hugh was working on the veranda alone, late at night, she had suddenly appeared to him in a flowered wrap, her face white, her lips trembling. He had thought she was asleep.

"What is it?" he asked, thinking she had had some night-mare.

But mutely she drew aside the folds of the wrap to show her naked body underneath. "Feel," she said. "Feel here. There's a lump. It hurts." Her fingers rested on one breast.

He touched it, experiencing, even at the moment, an ashamed thrill of pleasure. Beneath it the acetylene lamp inked great shadows. "But there's nothing," he said. "Nothing at all." Again he touched that softness.

"Oh, don't lie!" she exclaimed, drawing away. "I'm not a child. It's cancer."

"Of course, it's not cancer. I promise you, Lucy. Don't worry, dearest. . . . But to-morrow you can see the doctor—to reassure you——"

"There you are!" she cried. "The doctor! So you know! So you're hiding it from me! You want to pretend——"

"Lucy, what is the matter——?"

"Oh, it's horrible, horrible! This'll mean an operation. I can't bear it! I can't bear it!" Convulsed, shaking with tears, she clung to him.

"There, there, my dearest! It's nothing. Really, it's nothing. There's nothing the matter with you."

He carried her back to bed, quieted her, gave her a sleeping-draught.

The next morning she said nothing about it all.

In Switzerland something similar happened. She was brushing her teeth at night while he waited for her in bed, when

suddenly she gave a short scream. " Look, Hugh, look ! " she
cried, when he appeared in the doorway of the bathroom.
With a horrified forefinger she pointed to the wash-basin.

" What is it ? "

" I've just spat some blood. I've only just seen it." In the
basin was a trickle of saliva threaded with scarlet.

" But that's only your gum bleeding," he reassured her ;
thinking : " She's so suggestible. It's because she saw that
consumptive."

" No, no ! It's not my gum. It's from my chest. All
to-day I've felt blood in my throat. But it wouldn't come
out." Touching her flushed cheek she said : " I think I've got a
temperature. You know what that means, darling ? "

" What nonsense ! " he exclaimed. " It's your imagination.
Here—let me get the thermometer——"

" No, no ! Forget about it. Let's pretend it hasn't happened.
Let's pretend there's nothing the matter—right to the end. I
don't want to be an invalid—a tie to you. . . ."

This decided him. " You're going to see the Hofrat to-
morrow morning," he said with great firmness. (They had
made friends with the German principal of the sanatorium.)
" If you've got this thing——"

" Oh, no, no ! " She backed against the wall in terror.
" Don't say it ! Please don't say it ! I—I'm so frightened,
dearest. It's such a horrible illness. . . ."

This time nothing, no sleeping-draught, no soothing words,
could put her to sleep. But the next morning the Hofrat
laughed jovially : " A few scars—nothing else. Perfectly
sound. Your wife has too much imagination." And as though
to insult her he even refused a fee.

Perhaps her hypochondria had been a sort of prescience :
perhaps she had known all along that she was doomed, so that
she took each symptom, each trivial malady, as the beginning
of that final disintegration. Or perhaps there had been in her

PHANTOMS **93**

some morbid craving so that, without knowing it, she had desired to suffer. In that case one can understand why, with the coming of the war, her hypochondria abruptly ceased ; for the war would have satisfied that morbid craving with wounds, amputations, sickness ; she would no longer have desired some cataclysm within herself, for the cataclysm was there, in others.

She behaved very differently when it was the real thing, when death was really upon her. There were none of the tears, the hysteria. Hugh came home one day from Aldershot, tired and knowing nothing ; and as usual she dined with him, asked him about his day's work, talked of the garden, accompanied him to the children's nursery. But when, late that night, he climbed into bed and touched her body she drew away with a sigh, a light sigh, inexpressibly mournful.

" What is it, dearest ? "

" Hugh—I haven't really had a chance to talk to you seriously. I've got to have an operation, soon, in a week or two."

He knew, even at that moment, that there was no reason to argue with her as he had always done on those other occasions. The bed suddenly felt cold and immense, a curtain bellied outwards in the wind. " But I never realised——" he stammered. " Why didn't you tell me ? I didn't even know you were ill."

" I didn't want to frighten you. But to-day I saw the doctor. He says it's serious. I haven't really been well since Judith was born." She spoke in a flat, conversational voice, resting on her elbow in bed, her hair coiled in two plaits.

In this same tranquil way they continued to talk for a long time, Hugh shivering with the cold or the fear he felt. He could not bring himself to caress her, though at that moment, in the glitter of winter moonlight, she seemed more beautiful than she had ever been, her breasts and arms gleaming like mountains of snow, her body giving off a subtle perfume.

Then, after many minutes, she slowly sank on to the pillow, turned away from him, and fell asleep. She breathed evenly.

That was the beginning. Much followed afterwards, as each faculty, each member, rebelled. Finally, her brain was attacked ; it, too, would have to be probed and lopped and scraped by the knife. And then she, who had been dying with such infinite resourcefulness, suddenly broke down. " No, no, dear," she pleaded when he went to see her in the nursing-home before her operation. " I can't bear it—not my brain. There's something—I mean, do you really think that one has a right to do that sort of thing ? Amputation's bad enough : a balance is upset—one ceases to be wholly oneself ; one becomes spiritually lopsided. But this——! This is far, far worse. I may not be the same when I wake up. I may not think or feel the same things. I may be someone quite different. There are things that are sacred ; there are things that are better left alone. . . . Oh, I do believe this ! It's not that I'm simply a coward. Having suffered so much . . ." Clutching at his coat, sobbing, trying to raise herself from the bed, she screamed : " Take me away from here ! Don't let them do it ! I'd rather die ! Take me away ! "

But the doctor came in and gave her an injection. And she fell asleep, smiling. And for six hours they explored what lay within her skull.

It is impossible to say how close is the link between the corporeal and the spiritual. In some bodies, devoured, eaten away, corroded, the flame of the spirit blazes brighter. In others it gutters, goes out, relinquishes the shell that is cracking about it. With Lucy body and spirit disintegrated together. Almost, but not entirely. There was still her terrible stoicism. But stoicism is not enough, as anyone who has lived with an invalid knows. There must be something more : and this something Lucy simply did not possess. She was incapable of letting go, of relinquishing things : and the art of letting go is the art of being an invalid. She still had desires, she grew more, instead of less, possessive. As the things which were truly hers and hers alone—her faculties—deserted her, she craved what belonged to other people, to her husband, her children, her servants. She wished to live on their sensations, vicariously, through them.

And because they would not have this her voice grew plaintive, she read letters left in empty rooms, listened at doors, probed for secrets, made scenes. It was impossible not to pity her. If only she had given up, if only she had relaxed her devouring grip on life.

Often, when Hugh came back from town, she was waiting for him, her face ravaged, propped on a couch, waiting, doing nothing.

" Where did you go, darling ? "

" To the Club."

" What did you do there ? "

" Oh—I don't know. The usual things. You know what one does at the Club."

" No—I don't."

" Dined, drank a little, talked a little. That was all."

He was marvellously patient with her. Picking up a paper from the table he began to flick over the pages. But she would not let it rest.

" Darling ? "

" Yes."

" You don't think I'm very suspicious, do you ? You're not offended ? "

" Of course, I'm not offended."

" You do see that I ask these questions because I love you so much ? Now that I'm ill I'm so terrified of losing you. You do see ? "

" Yes. I see."

" It's so horrible not being able to go out with you any

more. . . . But you do still love me ? Darling, you do still love me ? "

" Of course, I still love you."

" Don't say it like that, darling. Say it nicely. Say ' I love you '."

" I love you."

" Promise ? "

" I promise."

" I don't disgust you ? "

" Lucy, my dear, what a thing——"

" I don't disgust you—the bandages, smell, everything ? "

" Of course not, my dear."

" You're speaking the truth ? "

" Of course I'm speaking the truth."

Like a formal incantation the conversation was prolonged infinitely.

But he was lying. That evening he had spent in a small restaurant in Greek Street with a girl he had met in the tube. Later, he had gone to her flat. There had been other evenings, in other restaurants, in other flats, for months and months, long, long before Lucy's illness.

When a habitually truthful person lies, without shame, without scruple, then the person to whom the lie is told must stand condemned.

But Lucy was, in a sense, already condemned. And he continued to lie to her.

Tiggs had been Lucy's ally in the days before the war ; he continued to be her ally till the end. He had grown immensely stout, he had eczema, he soiled the chairs, he suffered, poor dear, from empyrema. (So Lucy said, who was never at a loss for a medical term.) All day he sat with her, on the same couch, in her bed, curled up against her body, his dry nose resting against her breast : and all day she fed him off her plate, on grapes, on chocolates that friends had brought : and all day she talked to him. "Doesn't Tiggsie want to go out and chase rabbits?" (Tiggsie had never caught a rabbit in his life.) "Doesn't Tiggsie-Wiggsie want to play in the garden? Does Tiggsie love his mummy so very, very much? Does he? Won't Tiggsie leave his little Lucy?"

To Hugh this seemed like a criticism of his own visits to London, his games of golf, his walks with the children. And soon Lucy had another ally—Miss Thompson, her new companion, who spoke ever so 'naicely', and cut out pictures from the *Tatler*, and powdered her face a dead white. She was about thirty-five, with a chin which suddenly collapsed into landslides of goose-flesh. And unlike Tiggsie she had a voice.

Mutely, maternally, she adored Lucy: and perhaps from jealousy hated Hugh and the children. When they came in from a walk together and were met by her in the hall their enquiries after Lucy were always answered: "She's as well as can be expected—poor dear!" Then there was a shake of the shoulders, a toss of the head. "She's such a plucky person—no complaints, no grumbling. Goodness knows, she's got enough to worry her." Saying this, Miss Thompson would leave them, creaking upstairs in patent-leather shoes over which bulged fatty ankles.

When Hugh went to see Lucy in her room, Miss Thompson, 'Tommie', was always there, listening under the pretence of filling hot-water bottles or emptying bed-pans. Her face was set in a cynical smile. So that he found it impossible to be tender or even affectionate because this woman seemed to see all his actions as a pretence.

She always said "Sh!" when she passed the children, whether they were making a noise or not. She complained that the servants stole groceries, cheeked her, spied on her. And when, finally, Lucy had to have two nurses she insisted on staying in the room with them, all day, all night, sleeping in a chair by the bedside, because she refused to believe that they would care for her poor darling as she had. In the end, because the nurses

4

complained so much, she had to be ordered to leave and go to her own room.

Goodness knows what she insinuated to Lucy. Goodness knows how she troubled those last few months of consciousness. She brooded over the house, an obese Fury, against whose corseted waist clanked a bunch of keys.

When the end came and nothing more could be done, when all that could be cut away had been cut away, when the body had been purged and stimulated, injected and drugged, then the doctors shrugged their shoulders, took their hats from the hall, and gave up. But first they told Hugh.

He decided to leave Lucy in ignorance of her doom: she was convalescing after her last operation, still in great pain. But whether Miss Thompson told her, or whether she had the supposed clairvoyance of those who are going to die, she knew as soon as he entered the room.

" It's the end, isn't it ? "

" My dear, what do you mean ? Dr. Swan is most hopeful——"

" Oh, Hugh, don't lie to me ! " She laughed as she lay back among pillows, Tiggsie nestling against her. " It *is* the end, isn't it ? "

There was no use in prolonging the deception. " Yes," he said with a queer, abrupt gesture of anguish. " Yes. They can do nothing more now." Then kneeling beside her bed he took one of her hands, ringless now, because the fingers had grown too thin, and bent over it. " Oh, Lucy ! Lucy dearest ! My poor Lucy ! "

She watched him for a while, in surprise, in amusement, while with the hand that he was not holding she stroked Tiggsie. Then suddenly she pulled away : " Oh, stop it, Hugh ! What's the use ? I'm so sick of it all. I'm sick of pity, and medicines, and the smell of formalin. I'm going to get up."

" But my dear Lucy—— ! You can't——"

"Oh yes I can. If I'm going to die, I'm not going to sit in bed and wait for it. At the moment I feel perfectly well—perfectly well. I'm going out into the garden."

And after much argument she had her way. She put on a flowered silk dress and a large yellow straw hat and went out on Miss Thompson's arm. She looked old, and she was rouged like a harlot. When the children came up to her she smiled distantly : and when, not having been told, they said : "We're so glad you're feeling better now," she only inclined her head with strange condescension.

For two days she moved about the garden, cutting the heads off roses, reclining in a deck-chair, trailing over wet lawns in a rustling frock. Already she seemed to have become a ghost, a legend.

Then on the third day at lunch, even while she was sipping beef-extract and breaking toast in weak fingers, she suddenly groaned, clutched her side, tipped forwards, bruising her forehead and splashing water out of the vase.

They carried her upstairs.

But even that wasn't the end. There were another three weeks.

Of that last period, lulled in bandages and morphia and febrifuges, Hugh remembered only one incident. He had gone up to the sick-room to see Lucy, on tip-toe, wrinkling his nose at the smell of disinfectant. But she was asleep, her hands carefully placed outside the blankets, like a child's. He noticed for the first time the decalcification of the nails.

A new nurse sat beside her, reading a book, a buxom girl with undisciplined hair under the starched cap, an unpowdered face, large feet. She smiled at him as he came in, blushing a little : and because he could not talk to Lucy and wished to be friendly he asked her : " What are you reading ?"

" *The Conquest of Mexico.*"

He looked surprised. "Where did you get hold of that?"

"You brought it up for Lady Weigh. I hope you don't mind, sir. I had nothing else——"

"Oh no, of course not." He waved a hand in dismissal. "Do you like it?"

"Oh yes. Oh yes. It's a wonderful book." She was too inarticulate to say more. But he could see it had impressed her.

"Would you like to go to South America?"

"Oh, yes. I should. I should." Again the struggle to fit her emotions to words. "If only I could save up enough money—fifty pounds even. . . . I've always wanted to travel."

"Yes. It's a great thing," he said, sinking down on the end of the bed. "And Mexico's a great place. I hope you get there."

"You've travelled a lot, haven't you, sir?"

"Yes, I suppose I have."

"I read that book of yours. I did so like it."

At that moment Lucy turned over, groaned, cried out. The nurse hurriedly took a china basin and held it under her chin. Then, tears rolling down her cheeks, Lucy began to vomit a greyish-green fluid. . . .

All that remained of that devoured body, the shell, the husk, was burnt at Golders' Green. "My poor girlie," sobbed Lady Korrance, who had come up from Henley-on-Thames in a Daimler and was staying at Bailey's Hotel. "Still—it was a beautiful sight. A beautiful sight. I wish she could have seen it herself." A widow now, she wore mourning from Bradley's.

Afterwards, a will was found, made two or three days before the end. Half of Lucy's little fortune was left to the R.S.P.C.A.; Tiggsie and the other half was left to Miss Thompson. But the nurse was to have fifty pounds—' for a ticket to South America '.

" So kind," said Mrs. Meakins of this last legacy.

He was handed the ashes. But before that final symbolical action, before Lucy became three lines in the newspaper and a handful of photographs, some decisive change had already occurred in Hugh. Looking back, he saw the beginning of it in two incidents which had happened within a week of each other : out of these two incidents had come a transmutation, they had been decisive.

The first incident was when his car broke down, in London, just by Shepherd's Market. He had been in the Club when a telephone message had come through : Lucy had had a relapse ; she might die in the night. It was very cold and bright that evening, there was frost in the air. His hands were trembling as he drove, his mouth dry. He felt many things. Relief, that this should at last be the end, not only for poor tormented Lucy but for himself and the children. Exasperation, that he should have to leave a glass of whisky and a circle of friends to drive for two hours through darkness and cold. Fear, that the sight of her death might suddenly unnerve him. But no grief. He was an entirely honest person ; and he could not grieve for her.

The Lucy he grieved for had died long ago, an Edwardian beauty, high-stepping, in green silk, whose parasol had swung in diminished arcs as she ran away from him. He could not grieve for this twisted woman who whimpered and retched in sleep, clutched at him with claw-like hands, asked questions. She was only pitiable, like an animal which cannot get well.

He cursed when the car broke down, tried to mend it himself, failed, and eventually wandered down an alley in search of a garage. His teeth chattered, the cold seemed to make a heavy aching lump in his chest. Over and over again he clapped gloved hands together, distended his cheeks, stamped. Far away a church clock sprinkled the hours on the crisp air—two o'clock. And Lucy was probably dead. Voices cajoled him from doorways, someone brushed against him and giggled, a dog barked ; and for no reason he found himself thinking of that distant night in Paris, with the " *Viens, petit garçon ! Viens, viens !* " He smiled.

" Could you please tell me where I can find a garage ? "

The policeman peered at him, tall, stupid, a droplet glistening on the end of a long nose. Then he gave some directions. But the premises were locked, there was no one there. The mews seemed deserted. But no. Above, in the room above, uncurtained, a fire threw roseate handfuls of light and warmth. Numbed fingers felt for the bell, pressed it. Click of a light, footsteps. Someone humming " The Man who broke the Bank at Monte Carlo ".

" Yes ? Who is it ? Is it you, Mr. Warrington ? " The voice was soft, sleepy, with a trace of a West Country accent. One hand touched her coiled hair, the other drew her wrap together against the cold. She seemed very tall, possibly because she spoke from a step above him, and she brought with her smells of cigarette, spirits, perfume.

" Is the garage open ? My car's broken down. It's rather urgent."

She stared at him for a moment, without speaking, her eyes gleaming as though with tears in the moonlight. But she was smiling, her teeth white, large, gleaming like her eyes, and her black hair gleamed in great coils, and her arms gleamed. " He's gone," she said laconically. " There's no night service. He doesn't live here. He's nothing to do with me."

" Oh—I see. I'm sorry." He hesitated for a moment, swaying before her, undecided, at a loss what to do. His teeth began chattering again. " Then perhaps——"

" Why don't you come up ? " she put in, slowly, distinctly, as though she were speaking to a foreigner. " You seem cold. Why not ? " Again he smelled those female smells—Coty,

'*Soir de Paris*'; again the arms gleamed, visionary, lulling. The cold struck up at him from the pavement.

"Thank you," he said. "Just for a moment. This frost . . ."

"Just for a moment," she echoed, leading the way up uncarpeted stairs in a pair of feathered mules. One hand hitched up the long wrap so that she shouldn't slip; and he saw bare legs, downed with hair, and ankles grey and soiled. She spoke over her shoulder: "I was expecting someone else, an American. He should have been here three hours ago. But as he hasn't come . . ." She laughed, a deep-throated laugh, and shrugged her shoulders.

The room was lit only by an immense fire piled with logs: but this gave light enough for him to see stockings, a rubber corset, a dress thrown over one chair, copies of *Esquire*, the *New Yorker*, *Bystander* lying in another; a crucifix over an unmade bed; some tea-cups in the hearth, with cigarette ends, corks, a handkerchief; and on a table, a cactus, spiky, stiff, painted white.

"Well?" she said, turning to him. She was about thirty-five, with a scar on her throat, not beautiful but voluptuous.

"Well?" he responded.

"Do you want to undress?"

Slowly he slipped off his overcoat, his scarf, his dinner-jacket. She watched him all the time, her eyes bright, enormous as though with belladonna. He said nothing, perhaps felt nothing. Lucy was certainly forgotten, the car, the children. The fire was hot; a dry wind came off it, like a sirocco, making his skin tingle, his eyelids prick. He sighed, deeply, for no reason that he could think of.

Then she, too, undressed, slipping off her wrap, and crouched in a chair, waiting. The fire pelted her body with red blooms; her body glowed as though the fire were lambent beneath its flesh. She rubbed one foot against the other, crossed her hands over her lap, a gesture of modesty.

He touched her, first her breasts, then her thighs, then her belly. She put out a hand and touched him. The fire threw up great ruby chunks of light.

When she saw him down the stairs and out at the door they were clinking milk-pails in the near-by street and it was already morning. Rain fell, horizontally, into her face. She shivered, heavy with sleep, yawned, rubbed the back of one hand against her cheek. "Tom'll be there now," she said, pointing to the garage doors where a mechanic showed a greasy rump from under a Morris.

"Thank you." He, too, was sleepy, tousled.

Then, suddenly, she put both her arms round his neck. "Come again," she whispered. "Come again, my dear."

"Yes," he said, "I will. I will."

It was only later, driving through the desolate countryside, hungry, haggard, his eyelids dropping incessantly, that he realised that he had paid her nothing : and she, strangely, had made no demands. This omission irritated him. And yet, and yet. . . . Did it not give him an excuse to go back ?

Lucy had not died that night. She had survived miraculously, and was to survive for another week. But she seemed to know that he had failed her : for when he went up to her room she said nothing, did nothing, but stared at him fixedly, the tears rolling down her cheeks ; and when he took her hand (remembering that other hand on his shoulder) she drew it away with an exclamation of anger or surprise.

Miss Thompson, too, showed her disfavour in numberless ways. When he made the excuse that his car had broken down she shrugged her shoulders and smiled ; and even as he spoke to Lucy, she came and elbowed him away with a thermometer in a small glass. He noticed then, for the first time, that her plump hands had dimples in place of knuckles.

He went back to the room near Shepherd's Market on the night of Lucy's death.

After it was all over he felt that he must get away from servants who had once hated her and now wept; from Miss Thompson who drew blinds; from the heavy weight of silence and mourning which lay upon the scene. So he took out the car, and drove through the night, and went to the room, and found her there.

"You've come back," she said, meeting him as she had done on that other night. "I knew you would." And with a gesture of tenderness she slipped an arm over his shoulder.

Again it was the fire, the untidy room, the removal of the wrap. But something had slipped, had gone astray; so that even as he caressed her, upon the unmade bed, he was suddenly absorbed, abstracted. He suddenly got up and, still without saying anything, began to put on his clothes.

"What is it?" she asked. "Aren't you well? Aren't you well, dear? Are you going already?"

He did not answer her. But as he went to the door he took some notes from his wallet. "For you," he said.

She looked at him, her eyes filling with tears, still naked, her shoulders heaved miserably so that the breasts sagged. She shook her head. "No," she said. "That's too much. I don't want anything. You took nothing."

"For you," he repeated.

Mutely she put out a hand, crumpled the notes into a ball and tossed them on to the bed.

Then, as though she knew she were seeing him for the last time, she caressed him, momentarily, a brush of the fingers, with great intimacy.

"Good-bye," she said.

"Good-bye."

And she began to hack at the fire with a poker.

4*

These two events, these two visits to a woman whose name he did not know, were decisive. Perhaps not as decisive as they would have been in a novel or film. He did not immediately change, overnight, as they say. She was not the last person that he slept with. But from that time began the asceticism which became his most characteristic trait. His ferocious sexual appetite was curbed; blunted ; he lived simply, with the rigour of a monk ; he slowly became a misogynist.

Why ? Was it a sudden remorse ? Or was it the feeling, ' Never again ', ' Once bitten . . . ' ? He was not sure himself. Only the cynic or sentimentalist can really be sure. But the change was there.

While Lucy had lived he had taken little notice of the children. They were there, like the dogs, to be petted or taken on walks or told to be quiet. But now they were his responsibility. And he set about the task with great thoroughness.

For the children the change was impossible at first. Life with Lucy had been so different. Not that they had ever really loved her. Coming back that morning from Shepherd's Market, with Lucy lying dead upstairs, he had found them quarrelling in the hall. " What is the matter ? " he asked. At first they would not answer. Then Judith said : " Dennis says he can have Mummy's walking-stick now. But it's a lady's stick. Shouldn't I have it ? "

How easily they had accepted her death—with relief almost ! And he could not scold them, could not say : " You are being heartless " : for he, too, accepted it in the same mood.

No : the difficulties of the change lay elsewhere—in the need for adaptation. They had got used to one kind of life, and now Father was forcing another on to them. And children are creatures of habit. When so much is unstable within they like stability without.

With Lucy they had been left alone for long periods to do as they liked under the supervision of Miss Kahn, a benevolent

German governess. Then suddenly, without warning, there would be a visit to the nursery : Judith's nails were dirty, Dennis had ink on his collar, she would like a word with Miss Kahn. And afterwards everything went on as it had always done.

Or she would have them up to her sick-room. They hated that. There was always Miss Thompson in one corner saying, " Sh, children ! Don't talk so loud ", or, " You'll have those bottles over " ; and there were smells, strange, terrifying ; and there was Lucy herself, panting, breathless, one hand pressed to her side, while with the other she forced chocolates or grapes upon them. " Come nearer, my pets," she would say. And an arm, skinny, blue-veined, encircled their waists. It reminded Judith of the witch in *Hansel and Gretel*.

But now it was all different. Miss Kahn left, in tears, with a good testimonial, and Captain Allbright, who was over forty and had lost an arm in the last war, took her place. Not that he was any more formidable. He was short-sighted, and his face twitched nervously when he spoke to them. It was easy to squirt ink behind his back or throw bread-pellets. " Oh, do stop it ! " he would say plaintively, still a boy, who became excited over bird-nesting or tree-climbing.

No : he didn't make much difference. It was Father himself. A few days after Mother died a time-table appeared in the nursery. This was the outward symbol of the change. The old easy-going ways disappeared : the clock became their master, ticking, always ticking, on the nursery wall. Time for work. Time for lunch. Time for games. Time for bed. Time, time, time. They had not been aware of it before. Miss Kahn would say, " Now for some fresh air," and they would troop into the garden. Miss Kahn would say, " You look sleepy, Judith," and they would be hurried up to bed. But now even Captain Allbright watched the clock : he, too, was its slave.

They became typical of all motherless children—Dennis

tough, independent, insensitive ; Judith old, too old for her
years, maternal yet tomboy, a useful fielder when Hugh joined
them in cricket. But it was Dennis, rather than Judith, who
felt the greatest change. Hugh didn't care about Judith then :
she sniffed, she tended to howl, she wet her knickers, she was
a woman. But Dennis, his son . . .

So he planned for him. ' Issues from the hand of God the
simple soul. . . .' Issued from the hand of God the complex
soul with all its separate aims and claims ; and Hugh set about
simplifying it. What was fluid, unstable, uncertain became
suddenly petrified. Do this, do that, Hugh said. He was
like a dentist freezing a nerve. And the whole essential glory
of childhood was sheared off like a crop of hair.

Discipline : he believed in that. Every morning, all the
year round, Dennis had a cold bath. No very great hardship
there. He did the same thing himself. And the morning-room,
what Lucy used to call her ' Watteau Room ' because the
furnishings had faded from bright blue to grey, this was now
a gymnasium with boxing-gloves, a punch-ball, parallel-bars.

Round the grounds of the house they made a track for
running, ' The Cresta ' Hugh called it. This was for winter
use when the ground was too hard. In a white polo sweater
Dennis circled six times, his hands clenched. If only he could
do it in under ten minutes ! But he never could. And each
day there was the shame of saying to Father's question at
lunch : " No, sir. It took eleven minutes." So that in the
end, before that winter was over, his eyes used to fill with tears
of exasperation even while he ran.

For the great thing was to succeed. And yet . . . When
Cousin Paul had come to stay with him and Dennis had lost
to him at ping-pong, because he looked miserable at his defeat
Father had thrashed him for ' not being a sport '. It seemed as
if one should care, but not show it.

Cousin Paul was pink and plump, about Dennis's age, the
son of a stockbroker and Hugh's sister. Sometimes Dennis

envied him. When he was staying at the house Hugh constantly matched the boys against each other—at boxing, tug-o'-
war, tennis. But as soon as Paul had had enough he would say,
" Oh, Mummy, I *do* feel tired " ; and she would answer,
" Well, of course, dear. Come and sit down."

Dennis never said things like this. He never dared to. So he
went on, doing everything that Father told him to do, though
his arms ached and his back ached and his head became dizzy.

But he loved Father. And by suffering in this way he
thought he could prove his love. And, of course, *if* Paul beat
him at ping-pong, well, didn't that mean that he had let Father
down ?

He wanted to be like Father, to have to shave and to smoke
a pipe and wear a uniform. He loved Father's smell, and his
strength when they wrestled, and the touch of his hairy
forearm.

But, of course, he never said so. That would be unmanly.
It was terrible to be unmanly. Father said that Paul was an
effeminate prig ; and that was because he kissed his mother
in public and once said, " Oh, Mummy, you oughtn't to have
worn that hat ! The other's much, much nicer." And Paul
called his father ' Pop ', and said ' O.K. ', and played an April
Fool on him by giving him an inverted egg-shell instead of an
egg at breakfast.

But Dennis called his father ' Sir ', and saluted him when he
saw him. And the most Father ever did to show that he was
pleased was to flick one of his ears or slap him on the bottom.

But he loved Father, oh yes, he loved him. And in the
innocently erotic dreams of childhood he and Father no longer
wrestled, but lay silent and motionless together, all conflict
gone ; and Dennis's face rested on his chest ; and his arms
encircled him in a snare of love.

It was inevitable that Hugh's ambition should consume the
boy. He was too frail a vessel for that heady spirit. He was

too young. One way or another he would be destroyed. Either he would become an automaton or he would die. These were the only solutions.

This is myself, Hugh thought, as he wrestled with the boy or taught him to dive or hurled a cricket ball at him. Bone of my bone, flesh of my flesh. . . . And all that he could do this boy would also be taught to do. To be a light unto the Gentiles. . . .

So when, after a day out among the mountains in Wales, with only some raisins to eat, Dennis ran into the dining-room and said, "Gosh, I'm hungry," and began to gnaw at some bread, his father reproved him. One must not be a slave to the body. One must always be master. A lack of self-restraint. . . . But the boy was only seven.

One winter they went to Switzerland to ski. Then Dennis was to be seen every morning on the mountain-side in nothing but a pair of shorts, wiry, dark-skinned, his muscular legs scarred where he had fallen doing impossible things for love of Father.

They had two rooms, one in the hotel itself and the other in the annexe. And these two buildings were separated from each other by a glass conservatory four or five feet in width.

One afternoon Judith and Dennis played dominoes in the bay of the window of their room while Hugh wrote letters on the balcony of his. He had thrashed Dennis a short time before because he had shirked his cold bath by going into the bathroom, letting the water run, and then coming out—dry. This was Deception, and not Playing the Game. So Dennis was beaten, as he had been beaten so often before, and as Hugh imagined he would be beaten so often again. "Take down your trousers. . . ." And Dennis never so much as whimpered.

But now Hugh felt it was time to forgive. So he shouted across : " What are you both up to ? "

" Playing dominoes, sir."

"Dominoes!" Hugh put aside the pad on which he had just been writing. "That's a pretty poor sort of a game, eh?" And Dennis blushed as though at a reproof. "What about another game of chess?"

"Oh, yes, sir. Please, sir. Now, sir?" So he was forgiven. So Father still loved him. So he was not entirely worthless.

"All right. You come across here. Get the board and come across here." Judith had already disappeared, shrugging her shoulders irritably. She was always left out of it. "Hurry, though. Double quick!"

"Yes, sir."

Dennis ran towards the door; but before he could open it Hugh called: "Here! Come here! Come back!"

"Yes, sir?" He stood once more in the embrasure, with closely cropped hair that curled in spite of his efforts to straighten it. A snake-belt encircled his waist. His tie was held neatly with a tie-pin, his shoes gleamed. "Yes, sir?"

"Why don't you jump?"

"Jump, sir?"

"Yes. Jump, sir," High mimicked back. "Get on to that ledge—and jump. It's only four or five feet. You've jumped that often before."

But it was such a drop. Supposing he fell? Supposing he missed his footing? He stared downwards, white-faced, ashamed, his fingers fiddling with the snake of the belt.

"Well? Come on! Aren't you going to do it?"

He shook his head, miserably, his eyes filling with tears against his will.

"Funked it, eh?... Oh, in that case, I'm not sure that I want a game of chess." Hugh took up the pad again. But out of the corner of his eye he was watching Dennis.

Slowly, biting his lip, the boy climbed on to the window-ledge, clutching the frame to steady himself. His hand trembled, the knuckles went white. Far, far away, in a field, he could

see the three Dutch children they had played with that morning.
They moved in red fur over a white expanse.

"Changed your mind, eh ? That's right. It's nothing very
much. You can do it. You can do it easily."

He tensed the muscles in his legs. "You can do it easily...."
And he would be forgiven ; and this would be the proof—
the proof that he had dreamed of. That's right. ... It's
easy now. You've only got to jump. Father's eyes and
father's voice, and the ache of the muscles in his legs. And
the game of chess. And the dream he had had of saving Father
from some extraordinary doom—cannibals, was it ? It's
nothing very much. ... Oh, it's nothing very much. And
far away, in one corner of his vision, were the Dutch children
rolling in snow. And behind him Judith sang to herself in
the dressing-room where she slept. And this was the proof :
and afterwards there would be no conflict, but his face on
Father's chest, and his arms holding him, and. ...

A dry sob broke from his mouth as he hurled himself forwards.
Hugh held out arms, held them outstretched long, long after
there was any chance of catching anything. Far away, below,
there was a crash of glass, a tinkle, a silence. And still he held
out his arms, as though petrified.

Someone ran out and screamed ; the Dutch children stopped
playing and raced across the field ; two consumptives who
were doing a 'horizontal' on another balcony threw aside
rugs, hot-water bottles, magazines, and hung over the side.

He could not go down. And then suddenly he glanced
across to the embrasure ; and there was Judith. And she was
looking at him, without reproach, in acceptance, in love.

In the English church they sang, "Time, like a never-ending
stream", and Hugh, who stood mute and held a prayer-book
in cold fingers, thought then of the flux of time, time flowing
constantly, bitterly like Judith's tears, time bearing its sons
away, time bearing his son away, in a black box, as it would

bear away those flowers, sweet and fresh from a mountain-side ;
and to-morrow they, too, would disappear on the cruel wave,
they, too, would be slack and faded. And as he thought all this
Judith clutched the pew and her eyes closed and tears splashed
on to the prayer-book ; and Miss Poulton, the consumptive
from the hotel, pulled out the ' vox humana ' and made the
organ wheeze as if it, too, had only one lung ; and the choir-
boys showed sleek hair, and quavered, quavered shrilly at the
descant ; and the padre looked round at the congregation, and
his nostrils trembled as he stifled a yawn.

So Judith became Father's girl, a familiar sight on golf-courses,
in tweeds and brogue shoes that flapped : and she called him
' Fibsy ' and he called her ' Pynx ' ; and she learnt to whistle,
and did exercises with him before breakfast, and cut the finger-
nails of his right hand.

And she was spoiled.

" For some reason it was rather moving," the General
tended to say when recounting one particular incident in his
South American campaign. Quite simply what had happened
was this : a half-caste boy had let himself be killed instead of
Hugh.

They were walking through a ravine when a volley of
shots rang out : and when Hugh looked down there was the
boy with a wound in his groin. He did not survive. And Hugh,
in exasperation, had cried to him : " You fool ! You little
fool ! " as he used to do when the boy upset something or
forgot something or committed some blunder. And the boy
grinned at him sheepishly, this too reminiscent of other, less
honourable occasions ; and then he turned over and died.

Afterwards, anyone else would have romanticised the incident.
But not Hugh. He never forgot that he hadn't liked the boy ;
for one thing, he had been inefficient, he wouldn't learn ; and
on his thighs were small ulcers, the mild form of syphilis that is

common in those parts; and the others had laughed at him because he was unclean, and soiled his bed, and grunted in his sleep.

So all Hugh would say in retrospect was this: "It was strangely moving." Strangely: because it puzzled him that he should be moved by an act of idiocy; and he still could not see why the boy had done it.

He did not yet know his powers.

PART III

LABYRINTH

FOR as long as she could remember there had hung above that bed a photograph of Father and an oleograph of the Sacred Heart.

When she was a small child she had thought that if only she were patient enough, if she waited enough and lay awake enough, her father would one night speak to her. But the miracle never happened. The lips never trembled into speech. For hours she listened, tense against her pillow, while an owl shrieked in the forest, and Mother and Cousin Maurice laughed and tinkled glasses downstairs, and the moon moved from the wardrobe to the wash-basin and then across her eiderdown. Sometimes she thought : " Yes. That's him. He hasn't forgotten." But it was only a voice in the road or the wind shaking the door.

Her father was dead. He had been killed when she was four years old and she could remember him hardly at all. There had been walks with him in the Forest of Fontainebleau ; yes, she could picture that. Whenever they came upon litter left by some party of tourists he would stoop down, make it into a little bonfire, and then set it alight : so that it seemed as if their whole walk had been somehow rare and exciting because of these beacons. Yes, she could smell the smoke now, as it curled in ringlets from soiled copies of *Paris Soir*, the Continental *Daily Mail*, the *Frankfürter Zeitung* : and she could feel his hand, moist, strangely salt when she kissed it. But his face—that she could never recall. The photograph told her that he had a moustache under which hid a weak mouth and chin ; and that his eyes were prominent, like her own. But nothing more.

The face in the photograph never really seemed to exist; it was a conglomeration of features of a kind which she never could fix in her mind. Had his face been like that in life? And was that why it had faded, when other, more trivial, things remained—his smell, so English, the product of soap and tobacco; the way that he spoke, swallowing the end of the sentence, so that one said: "What's that? I didn't quite catch"; the touch of his hands, and a salt taste on the lips?

On those walks he would often stop to sketch: and the results still cluttered the attic. A stranger would have had difficulty in telling his work from hers—fastidious, careful, and, oh, so dull. He painted trees in water-colours, and did some etching, and sometimes tried to draw the rocks that fill those parts. Not for the first time a young man of talent had considered himself a genius. But in this case failure had unmistakably claimed him for her own: so that even when he was a student at the Slade one could say with complete confidence: That man will never succeed at anything.

But what was so clear to others never seemed to have occurred to him. Not even Mother's doubts could cloud the glittering vistas through which he moved. To the end he believed that somehow, some day, a critic would go to the Royal Academy and proclaim him for what he was. (For like many people of his kind he was 'hung'—rather ingloriously perhaps, 'skied' even; but he felt it to be an honour.)

Mother was never taken in. She had known immediately, instinctively, although she had never looked at a picture in her life. It was she who persuaded him to take pupils, usually American girls; and this was the beginning of the hotel.

Not only his features but his personality eluded Shirley. What had he been like? What sort of man had he been? She could not tell. She only knew that he had spoken softly—and had pretended to blow smoke-rings through his ears, and that she had loved him. But she guessed other things—his

kindness, his shyness, his self-consciousness—from the few
incidents that she had hoarded up in her memory.

When she had to go behind a tree or a bush on their walks
it was he, not she (reversing the usual rôles), who called out :
" Are you sure no one can see you ? Oh, do be careful ! Do
hurry ! I heard voices."

Once, he took her to Fontainebleau in a pony carriage and
began to trail her round the Palace : but at the second state-
room she sat down on the floor and howled with boredom
and fatigue. He had not been angry at this, though he had
planned the excursion weeks ago. Instead, he took her to a
café where they could sit in the open, and ordered for himself
a glass of beer, for her a *café glacé*. But when she had dipped
her spoon into the concoction and sucked it she again began
howling, because it was ' cold ' and made her teeth ache.

" Very well," he said, smiling. " I prefer *café glacé*. Would
you like to change ? "

" Oh, please."

So they changed over. And half-way through she had to
be taken into the street to be sick. But she never regretted
this incident. It was something memorable, like the first time
she could blow her own nose.

And now he was just a photograph. Often, although she
had ceased to expect that miracle of speech, she paused to look
at him as she moved about the room ; and each time she was
inflicted with an intolerable ache, an emptiness ; and sometimes she stretched out on the bed, and sometimes she prayed,
but most often she opened the large scrapbook and read and
stared and thought of the General.

Her father had come to Barbizon almost by accident. He
had begun by migrating to Paris from a two-storied house in
Edgware because he had heard someone say at the Slade :
" It's the only place to paint in." This was typical of him. He
believed that if one learnt the requisite rules and did the requisite

things then somehow the elements coalesced and the result was a masterpiece. Paris was quite ' the thing ' at the time : so one went to Paris.

His father who travelled up to the City each morning from the house in Edgware, and his mother, who sang prettily and had once been spoken to by King Edward, were a little anxious at his departure. But his mother gave him a medicine-chest and his father gave him advice ; and he took a room in Neuilly ; and there he began to paint, conscientiously, in great boredom and without meeting anyone.

Paris was dull he decided. He could paint as well in Edgware. And this ' special quality of light ' that the students talked about—well, had he found it ? Regretfully he shook his head as he took a solitary stroll, and a solitary bock, and a solitary meal.

If only he had some friends ! But the men he met at classes filled him with disgust. He began to think nostalgically of musical evenings at home, with Mamma and Aunt Hester singing duets. Mamma had a charming voice, but Aunt Hester, who had ' trained ', played the oddest tricks with her vowels. When Mamma started off on the old ballad :

> The ploughboy kisses,
> Those golden tresses.

Aunt Hester joined in with :

> The play-boy cusses,
> Those go-olden trusses.

Oh, but he could forgive even that ! He was so lonely.

Then one day he had been to the Louvre to admire the " Mona Lisa " and the rest (but he walked hurriedly past things like Reuben's " Fertility led Captive ") ; and as he strolled he was drawn into a little knot of people who were listening to a professor lecture on Millet ; and Millet had painted " The Angelus " at Barbizon.

And Ralph Forsdike thought : " Well, if Millet can do it, I can ! " And, of course, when he discovered that Barbizon was less than forty miles from Paris that settled it. If it had been ten miles farther he might not have gone.

So he came to Barbizon and found it delightful (as indeed it is) ; and each morning he painted, and each evening he went for a stroll. He was still bored, certainly. But there is something rather less shameful in being friendless in the country. Besides, this was a period of waiting ; he could afford to wait ; he was only twenty-one. At any moment he would be ' discovered ' and then there would be commissions, and society, and perhaps a knighthood. Oh, yes, he could afford to wait. (But fortunately death spared him that. He never had to wait for an appointment which would not be kept, year in, year out, until he grew old. He died believing, *Qualis artifex pereo*. And that was something, even though Mother immediately carried all his paintings into the attic.)

Mother had been ill up at the farm : she was a young girl then, Denise Polnay, daughter of a farmer. One day she had attempted to ' bring off ' a baby : and, as in most things, succeeded. But the injury crippled her for several months.

Ralph had heard this story from his landlady at breakfast : and though shocked profoundly (he simply couldn't look at his kidney and bacon) he found himself pitying the girl. Then later, by a coincidence, he went to sketch in one of their fields. They were finishing the harvest, on an expanse now bare and dry except for the sheaves ; it was very hot, with a haze tingling and distorting the atmosphere. When Ralph began sketching the scene he suddenly noticed a girl, in a low-waisted frock of blue linen, who limped slackly, a sheaf under either arm. Her face was white, she had large thighs and arms and a single violet-dark plait of hair circled her head three times. After that, he ceased to sketch the corn-field and watched her instead. For a while she moved slowly, even resentfully, at her task, until, with a shrug of her shoulders, she dropped the two sheaves that she was carrying, without even placing them in a stook, and wandered off to pick blackberries from the hedge.

Still he watched her, absorbed, distracted ; until, looking down, he discovered that his hand was sketching her in on the cartridge paper, in a few bold strokes which obliterated the feathery outlines of trees and reapers and sheaves. This was strange, for he had never attempted figure-drawing before. And stranger still, he was drawing her nude.

At this discovery he blushed, hurriedly threw his things into a rucksack, and made for home. His cheeks burned, so that when he came in his landlady exclaimed : " You do look hot, monsieur." In sudden shame he went to the wash-basin, wreathed in china roses, and sluiced water on to the back of his neck with a sponge. Someone had once told him of this remedy at the Slade.

But he was to see her again. One evening he went down to the river, as he often did, to swim. Cows pulled at willow-herb along the banks or plashed in mud ; bats circled ; the sun was sinking, a mass of scarlet viscera, in the west. Suddenly he had glimpsed her, appearing from trees with a poodle at her heels—a comical dog, clipped like a lion ; in panic, he had thought of racing to the bank and slipping on his clothes ; but already she was inexorably upon him. With a wide swing of bare arms she flung a rubber ball into the water for the dog. It plopped quite near Ralph, he started, and she laughed.

At first, in embarrassment, he stood with the water up to his neck : he was as modest as if he had no clothes on, though in fact he was wearing a serge bathing-costume of the period which was far less revelatory than the tight cotton trousers of the reapers he sketched.

She sat down on the bank, and again and again, like a shuttle, the ball shot outwards and the dog shot after it. There was no

shyness about her : nor did she behave as if he were not there.
She accepted him tranquilly.

Then, when his teeth began to chatter and his arms were
going blue, she suddenly said : " Is it nice in there ? Is it
warm ? "

At first he thought she was mocking at him. " Y-yes,"
he said through chattering jaws. " Y-yes. It's beautifully
warm, really."   And as though to demonstrate how pleasant it
was he began to kick out and eventually to swim discreetly on
his stomach.

" I think I'll come in," she said, and disappeared behind
some bushes. A moment later she was back in only a chemise.

With extraordinary grace she climbed on to a tree trunk and
dived in.

Later she ducked him.

Later the sun burned out, and the cows wandered away,
and everything was tranquil.

Later, at one o'clock, he was again sluicing cold water on to
the back of his neck.

When the war broke out Denise said : " Don't go. We're so
happy. Why should you go ? " But for once he did what he
himself wanted instead of what she told him to do.

In the train, going to the Front, he suddenly began thinking
of how on the eve of his first departure for Paris he had said to
Mamma : " Sing for me " ; and she, because she was sentimental, began on " Danny Boy " ; and at the words, "But
come ye back", her cheeks had started to trickle with tears.
But she had continued singing, without shame.

And now, at the recollection, his own eyes filled and his own
throat ached with grief.

Although it was growing dark, and it was nine o'clock,
Shirley still played in the courtyard of the hotel. She buried
an old spoon under the rowan as treasure, and clapped two pieces

of wood together to scare birds, as she had seen them do in the fields, and sometimes she sang to herself in a tuneless alto. Miss Cory and Miss Witherby, the two English ladies who wore their grey hair in plaits over their ears, so that they looked like telephonists, and always walked close, arm-in-arm, passed her and murmured to each other : " Disgraceful ! She ought to be in bed. Only four. . . ." And they moved on in black silk and Queen Alexandra collars.

Shirley pulled a face at them, their behinds so close that they seemed to have only one behind between them ; shiny and rolling and hard. Then she picked up handfuls of dust and threw them into the air, shouting : " Bang ! Bang ! Bang ! " These were the shells of which she had heard much recently.

" Shirley ! Shir—ley ! " A window was thrown up and Mother shouted to her. " Come here, dear ! Come here ! "

" What is it ? " she asked sulkily. " What do you want ? "

" Come here ! "

" Oh, all right."

Was it bed ? Was it an errand to the baker ? Was it cigarettes for Cousin Maurice ? Or did Mother want help with her curlers ?

Slowly she mounted the stairs, lingeringly, sometimes pausing to listen to conversations in other rooms. She wore a faded blue pinafore with a butterfly embroidered on it in yellow wool : but the wool was unravelling, a piece hung loose for her to fiddle with. Her hair was in plaits ; she hated plaits ; Cousin Maurice pulled them.

Mother sat before her kidney dressing-table, half of her hair twisted into papers the other half falling over bare shoulders. She looked comical like this. Her fingers massaged the lobes of her ears from which she had just taken off ear-rings. One breast poked out of her wrap, her eyes gazed at her own reflection. On her upper lip was a faint moustache, her legs gleamed with hair.

" Yes, Mummy ? "

Without saying anything she handed Shirley a piece of paper and continued massaging her ears. Shirley stared at it.

" But I can't read," she said at last.

" Maurice ! Maurice ! " Mother swung round, another breast popped out. " Maurice ! "

Cousin Maurice appeared in black-and-white silk pyjamas from the dressing-room. He had obviously been listening at the door. " Yes, my dear ? " he said. " Yes ? " Manicured hands slipped into the folds of his sleeves, after the fashion of the Chinese.

" Read it to her."

" But Denise. . . . You yourself——"

" Read it to her."

He turned to Shirley, came close to her, so that she smelled lavender-water and bay rum and Russian cigarettes. His feet, in slippers, were red and swollen, as though after a hot bath. " It's like this, my dear," he said. Then, articulating each word with undue precision, he told her : " Your—father's—dead."

" Dead ? Dead ? Daddy dead ? " She stared at him under her matted fringe. Then she ran across to her mother : " Mummy, what does he mean ? What is he talking about ? "

Denise repeated : " Your father's been killed."

" Killed ? Then—then—he'll never come back—— ? "

" Oh, Maurice, take the child away ! I can't stand it ! I can't stand it ! "

For once Cousin Maurice was kind. " Come along, Shirley," he said. " You must go to bed." His slippers flopped loudly at the heels as he took her to her room. " You must be a brave girl," he added. " Your mother needs your help."

When she was in bed he felt in the pocket of his dressing-gown and took out some cough pastilles. " Here's a sweet for you," he said.

She took it gratefully. " Good-night," he said. The light clicked out.

The hot and bitter taste of menthol filled her throat.

Cousin Maurice wore a *toupet*. It was an old story. When they were children—he, and Denise, and the rest of them—they had a maid called Sophie who was deaf and dumb and almost a lunatic. They all teased her, for years and years and years. Until one day, in a sudden fit of rage, she picked up a copper of boiling water and threw it at them. Most of the water fell on Cousin Maurice's head.

Hence the white scars on his neck and forehead : hence the wig.

Cousin Maurice was a furrier in Paris. But soon after Father's death, and indeed before it, he took to spending weekends at the hotel in Barbizon ; and Shirley noticed that when she took round the bills to the other residents there was never one for him.

She hated him, with the vindictiveness of children. Once he asked for the salt and she passed him sugar. Absentmindedly he ladled it into his soup, and then pulled a horrible face, wrinkling up his lips till the gums showed, white and flabby. Another time, she saw his tennis trousers in Mother's room beside her work-box ; Mother had just been sewing buttons on to them. Hurriedly, Shirley pulled out a pair of scissors and slit them up the back.

Next day, when Cousin Maurice went up to change, he came down again looking rueful and puzzled.

Once, at a Christmas dinner, among a crowd of Mother's relatives, he crept up behind her and pulled a cracker on her bare neck.

" Maurice, you are a tease," said Mother, laughing.

But Shirley, white with anger, screamed : " How dare you ! You beast ! You brute ! " She rushed at him waving her arms round her head.

" Steady ! " he said, catching her. " Steady ! You must learn to take a joke."

" You wait ! " she said, breathless and kicking in his grip.
" You wait ! You wait till my Daddy comes home."

There was a hush : everyone stared ; the relatives ceased
blowing tin-whistles and giggling at mottoes.

Then Mother said, tranquilly, in a loud, clear voice : " I've
told you, dear. Daddy will never come home."

Father's belongings were kept in two trunks in the attic.
Shirley often crept up there to touch old shoes, suits that
smelled of moth-balls, collars that were now out of date. And
the pictures. " They're lovely," she thought ; and it was this
that started her off with his black paint-box.

Smelling the clothes, holding them to her cheek, running
fingers over them, she felt the same things as when she looked
at the photograph. Father was near, oh, so near. If she were
still enough, if she sank deep enough into these emanations
from the past, if she held her breath and concentrated on the
touch of the flannel that he had once worn, on the aroma,
then he could materialise. He was there, in the whole atmosphere of the attic. If only he would appear !

One day Cousin Maurice came down to lunch in a morning-
coat with the wide lapels and facings of another era.

Shirley stared at him, her fork half-raised to her mouth.
" Where did you get that suit ? " she asked.

" Shirley ! " her mother protested, her face reddening.
" It's very rude to ask those sort of questions."

" Where did you get that suit ? "

Cousin Maurice speared himself some hare out of the casserole,
tucked his napkin into his collar, and began to eat.

" It's Father's, isn't it ? You've taken Father's clothes !
That's it, isn't it ? " She rose from the table, her face crumpled,
her body trembling.

" Sit down ! " Mother commanded : in those days she was
too indolent ever to be really angry. " What *are* you making

this fuss about ? What do you expect to be done with the clothes ? They might as well be used."

Cousin Maurice masticated with large white teeth ; he grinned ; hair grew out of his ears. " Exactly," he said. " The clothes were just rotting up there. Don't be such a silly little fool." With one finger he flicked at his nostril ; then he took out a scented handkerchief and blew. Turning to Mother he said : " Really, the child——"

He got no further. Shirley had tried to stab at him with her knife. He leapt to his feet : " My God ! The little demon ! " Down the hairy back of one of his hands trickled scarlet gouts of blood. He put it to his mouth, but clumsily, so that it smeared across the sagging fold of his cheek.

Mother ran out into the courtyard after Shirley ; the child was screaming, while Miss Corry and Miss Witherby hung out of a window together, cheek pressed to cheek. " I'll teach you ! " said Mother. " I'll give you a lesson." She suddenly felt light and happy with power—' drunk ' with it as they say. She experienced what one feels when squashing a cockroach or smacking a dog for a misdemeanour.

" No, Mummy ! No ! " Shirley screamed, rushing round the rowan tree under which was buried the spoon. " No ! " She tripped, fell, grazed her knee. She sat up, dusty, groaning.

Mummy thrashed her and put her to bed. Then Cousin Maurice went up and thrashed her. Then she was sick all over the floor. So that meant another thrashing.

Her father's photograph remained mute.

After a while she ceased to expect the miracle. He was dead, he would never speak to her. After she had stabbed at Cousin Maurice, then, if at any time, he should have comforted her, he should have said : " You have done right ". But the lips were still shut beneath the moustache, the hand still rested on a chair. It was useless.

She realised then that our ancestors are more subtle than

this. They do not make an obvious intervention, they have no language. They speak, but not with words ; they tyrannise over us, but not with their presences. They are powerful because they do not materialise ; that is their strength.

So she gave up waiting at night. She no longer watched the photograph. For the dead were dead.

But the oleograph would bleed. She had read of such things. If she had faith enough the Sacred Heart would bleed, as a sign. It was for this that she now watched. Often, in a white cotton nightdress, she would rise from her bed and reach out an arm and touch the oleograph. Always she expected to find something sticky and warm. But the material was cold, shiny, sleek as celluloid.

She had begun to go to church. Her mother was a Catholic, so she went to the Catholic church. But later, surreptitiously, she would also go to Sunday school in the English church. Often she went there when there was no service, and prayed and lit candles and gazed at the waxen Christ who hung there with gaping stigmata.

" The Lamb of God. . . ." The phrase lingered in her mind, like a benediction. It made God suddenly lovable, not frightening. A woolly lamb. . . . She could nestle against it ; its fleece was warm. She could run fingers through its fleece.

Then, at a service, she heard the words " . . . washed in the Blood of the Lamb ". At first, the idea seemed terrible to her. But later it gave her an odd shock of pleasure. Sticky and warm. . . . She looked upon it as a barbarous but somehow delightful ritual. " This is love, I suppose ", she thought, as though she could already see a time when school-fellows of hers would mix their blood and swear eternal fidelity. Christ, divided and eaten : that too was a shocking and yet delicious thought. . . .

At Sunday school she always tried to sing louder than any-one else, as though in this way she could prove an abundance of love. But since she was incapable of keeping a tune in her head, and in any case chanted through her nose, the result was hardly pleasing.

Once, only once, she experienced what she believed to be religious ecstasy—at the age of nine. She was wandering through the empty church, the heels of her shoes ringing with an unnatural loudness. Incense filled her nostrils ; the air seemed thick and heavy. She ran fingers along a brass rail, making a smear where there had once been the brightness of polish ; she knelt on a hassock, praying and fingering her dark plaits at one and the same time ; she looked up at the ceiling, intricate with carving, and down at the floor where whole families lay buried. Through stained windows pressed a ruby light. " The blood of the Lamb. . . ." Her fingers as she held them in an attitude of prayer were warm with it ; the whole church was drowning in its viscid fountains.

Then she stood before the waxen figure of Christ. It was not a beautiful image, as so many are : this Christ was the work of a nineteenth-century artist, a realist, who gave Him a grey-green skin, creased sides, distended ribs, pink nipples. The wounds yawned like chasms of a violet colour. But as she looked at it, her gaze fixed on the bearded yet effeminate face and then on the pitiable slope of the shoulders and then on the fragment of clothing, a mere rag, that covered the loins, tears began to trickle down her cheeks and she was sobbing. She found pathos here.

But then, a moment later, she was tingling inside, her tongue seemed enormous, it felt as if her eyes would burst through their sockets. And she felt such joy. Both hands moved up in a gesture of love ; she clasped the feet of the Christ ; she kissed the wounds, bearing on her lips an accumulation of dust.

A wind seemed to be blowing against her breasts, and then against her throat. It was dry and hot : the pain was almost intolerable. Moving upwards, it fanned her cheeks and then

her forehead. Yet in spite of the agony of it she welcomed it ;
again she stretched hands towards the Christ ; a scream tore
from her, as though from her entrails.

Afterwards, she lay for a long time on the chill floor, scraping
her nails against marble and mosaic. She was tired ; she was
at peace ; she murmured explanations to someone who was
not there.

The sagging Christ looked down ; the red light glowed on
etiolated flesh.

But one sign was not enough. She was a person who sought
many signs. She needed continual reassurance.

After her first communion the relatives gathered at the
house, and gossiped, and ate, and made jokes. Cousin Maurice
proposed a toast to Mother : and Mother blushed. Later, he
pulled away Uncle Raymond's chair so that the old thing
landed on the floor. This was considered very funny.

But through all the noise and the congratulation Shirley
moved aloof. She felt a curious exaltation, akin to that moment
before the Crucifix, but this time it was suppressed, an ache,
which must somehow be released. It was as if there were
something hard and stubborn within her ; and by a great
exertion she must thrust it forth. All that day it remained,
this sensation of something within her ; all day she smiled
distantly at remarks made by humorous relatives, all day
she fasted, all day she sat with her hands folded over her
stomach.

That night she prayed. She wept as she shaped the words ;
she trembled with a power too huge for her ; she clutched
the sheets of her bed, choked, dug her nails into the flesh of her
arms in nervous spasms. " Our Father," she prayed. " I
believe in God . . . the Father almighty." " Gentle Jesus . . .
look upon Thy little child."

Then she climbed into bed and drew the coverings up to
her neck. She was still shivering. But the great weight was

5

expelled. She felt light, elated, dizzy as one does after a haemorrhage. "It will happen to-night," she said. "The Heart will bleed. . . ."

Turning towards the wall she closed her eyes, she sighed in acquiescence.

Many hours later she woke up as she knew she would. The house was silent ; the guests were gone. Slowly she clambered into a kneeling position on the bed. Her joints cracked noisily, her breath came in gasps. The white nightdress fluttered in a wind, as her communion dress had fluttered. The soles of her feet gleamed white, her arms gleamed white. Gently, caressingly, she raised one hand and then the other ; they moved towards the oleograph ; she murmured to herself fragments of prayers : "Lord, I am unworthy . . . Who, like a raging lion . . . Our ghostly adversary . . ."

Then a sob broke from her, she threw herself back on to her pillow. Still on her palms was the chill touch of paper. There had been no blood. . . .

Her teeth bit deep into the stuff against them. In a gesture of mutilation she struck her breasts, again and again, with her fists. Tears poured from her eyes.

On trains she was always sick.

After a few minutes in her seat she began to walk up and down the corridors, as though in this way she could persuade herself that she was not boxed in, irrevocably, and moving at forty miles an hour. Sometimes she hung her head out of a window and took deep draughts of air until cinders blew into her eyes or her hair became dishevelled : sometimes she talked to other passengers, or counted up to a hundred, or tried to read. But always there was a growing sense of confinement, a growing nausea.

She began to pray, her lips moving restlessly : "Oh, God, don't let it happen. . . . Please don't let it happen. . . .

Please don't let it happen." The words fitted themselves to
the clatter of rails. She thought of what she had eaten—
potato soup, roast pigeon and spinach, ice-cream and pistachio
nuts. She thought of Uncle Maurice using a toothpick to
remove slivers of white meat. She thought of him crossing
plump hands over his stomach and belching, and saying :
" That was good, Denise. That was very, *very* good." She
thought of the glass of milk she had drunk, and freckled hands
squeezing at leathery dugs. She thought of the acids that
Cousin Maurice said were in everybody's stomachs, and the
advertisements in the paper, and the time she had vomited
in the corridor of a train and how angry everyone had
been.

She clutched at the rail in front of her. " Please, God. . . .
Oh, please, God." Her eyes pricked with tears of shame and
impotence. The sight of someone swaying with every jolt
of the train made her turn away, her gorge rising hot and
sour with vomit. Then someone else crashed against her.
" Sorry. I'm so sorry. These corners . . ."

With a gulp she rushed for the toilet.

But she was not sick. On the floor was the fragment of a
paper. Only a fragment. The rest had presumably been used.
She stared at it for a while and then picked it up.

The photograph was of a man whose eyes were screwed up
against a dazzling light : he was wearing a uniform of white
drill ; his face was oddly lined.

She began to read as best she could, her back wedged between
the basin and the door. It was a short paragraph, describing
an obscure campaign in an obscure state in South America.
It said little of how one man, a foreigner, had turned a handful
of men into a well-disciplined force : rather, after the fashion
of the press, it recounted how his life had been saved by a
half-caste boy ; how he had performed an amputation without
anæsthetic ; how he had a horror of publicity.

This cutting became the first of the scrapbook.

For one term she went to a boarding-school in England. Her English relatives paid for this. For many years they had made a figure of romance out of Shirley—having never met her. So they badgered her mother, and plotted, and talked of "giving the poor mite a start in life"; and finally Shirley was shipped off to them.

Of course, they were disappointed. She was not a friendly person; she said none of the amusing things that can be repeated to visitors; she was plain, and dull, and tended to cry for no reason.

Six months was sufficient. After that, they felt that they had done enough for poor Ralph's child. Shirley was shipped back.

The school was by the sea : the pines were so healthy, and the headmistress was the niece of a baronet, and there were a number of rules, one of which ran, "No girl may faint in chapel." The school was called a 'Ladies College'; and the fees were sufficiently high to make it so.

At the school was a girl called Barbara Maul. Her parents were said to be 'artistic'; she had red hair in a plait, a gold brace over her teeth, and eyes that filled with tears when it was cold; in her locker was pinned a photograph of Pavlova, dying swan on the stage of a provincial theatre. Her mother had seen Pavlova when she was *enceinte*; Barbara was to be a ballet dancer she had decided. So every Saturday afternoon Barbara joined Miss Moore's classes in the town; and once she danced Hiawatha in the end of term show.

But she did other things than dance. She wrote poetry; she painted; she played the piano.

It was the piano-playing that began it all.

She and Anna-Marie Blech were to play a duet arrangement of the finale of the Beethoven Fifth Symphony at the school concert. Anna-Marie was a Polish Jewess, plump, unattractive,

but a competent musician. Barbara played with 'expression'
—and all that that usually implies.

In the drawing-room Miss Mixton watched her pupils with
anxiety, as one by one they walked up to the piano and
treated the parents to "Hark, hark, the lark," "On Wings
of Songs", Beethoven Sonatinas, and 'bits' of Mozart (the
easy bits).

Then came the turn of Barbara and Anna-Marie. Miss
Mixton patted Barbara's hand as she rose from her seat and
made for the piano : it was a gesture of faith, of reassurance.
Barbara was fiddling with her plait, rubbing her fingers
together as though they were cold, and biting her nails. She
was nervous. Anna-Marie needed no such encouragements.
Decisively, she elbowed the last performer out of her way
and put the music on the rest. Then she drew a deep breath,
nodded to Barbara, murmured "One, two three" and
thundered out the opening chords. The muscles swelled in her
calves as she thrust at the loud-pedal.

But poor Barbara couldn't come in. Twice she missed her
beat ; twice Anna-Marie stopped and went back to the beginning ; the "One, two, three" became sibilant, viperish.

But no. "Try again," said Miss Mixton, wondering in
exasperation why Barbara made such a fuss. One beat or
another, it made no difference to the parents. "Try again,"
she repeated. "Third time lucky, you know." She smiled,
first at the two girls and then at the audience. "Come along,
Barbara."

But third time was no longer luckier than second or first.
In dismay Barbara rushed from the room, her cheeks pouring
with tears. Anna-Marie, unmoved, began a Brahms Berceuse.
But Miss Mixton had already gone, in uncrushable silk, after
the child.

Barbara was crying in the lavatories.

"What is the matter, dear ?"

"I'm so unhappy ! I'm so mis-er-able ! "

" But why, dear ? " Miss Mixton turned Barbara's face from a wall which was decorated with glaucous tiles. " But why ? Why on earth ? "

" Oh-oh-oh ! "

" But Barbara, darling—— "

" I've let you down ! And I did so want it to be a success —for your sake. I practised all yesterday afternoon—and it went p-p-perfectly. . . ."

" But what does it matter, dear ? It doesn't matter a jot. Who cares what they think ? " She stroked Barbara's hair and wondered how many parents had noticed her absence. " Now buck up, old thing ! Parents don't matter."

" It's not the parents ! It's—you. . . . Oh, I did so want to show you—— "

" But I *know* that you can play it. I've heard you often. I know that you can play it beautifully. So if, just once— because of nerves, and parents, and everything else—well, if just once it goes wrong—well, what does it matter ? "

" Oh, Miss Mixton ! "

" Barbara ! My dear ! "

She, too, was crying now. They clutched each other, damp cheek pressed to damp cheek, while the electric light gleamed at them from each rectangular tile on the wall.

" My poor dear—you mustn't worry so ! "

" Miss Mixton ! Oh, Miss Mixton."

At that moment Shirley appeared from one of the lavatories and grinned sheepishly.

Such things cannot be forgiven.

" Oh, do look ! Oh, look, girls ! "

Bare feet pattered over the expensive parquet floor, plaits swung.

" My goodness ! What's this ? How priceless ! " They jostled each other, giggled ; someone climbed on to a bed. Barbara stood in the centre of them all, holding a large book

that had been bound in newspaper. Her toe-nails were varnished
daringly.

"Give it back! Oh, please, give it back! It's private!
Oh, don't you see? . . . It's private. Oh, please. . . . Oh,
please give it back." Shirley, in flannel pyjamas, ran round the
circle of girls, trying to clutch at the book, until someone
pushed her and sent her sprawling across a bed. She began to
whimper, but her eyes remained dry.

Barbara asked: "What *is* all this? Who is this General,
anyway?"

"It's nothing. . . . Oh, please. . . ."

Her face was suddenly slapped. "Oh, stop that row!
Nothing's going to happen to your precious book."

Shirley began to bawl. A tall girl with a worried expression
said: "Go easy, Barbara. We don't want the hag in."

Barbara lowered her voice to an inquisitorial whisper.
"Who is this, anyway? Who is this General? Have you
got a crush on him?"

"I don't know what you mean."

"*I don't know what you mean!*" The words were mimicked
back at her. "Of course you know. Don't pretend. . . ."

Only a lie could save her. Inspired, she retorted: "He's—
he's—he was a friend of my father's. His best friend. They
fought in the war together. My father saved his life. And—
and when my father died he said to him: 'Hugh, look after
my child.' Those were his last words—his dying words."
The danger past, she was lying for the sheer pleasure of the thing.
All the fantasies with which she had consoled herself in secret
suddenly became real. Of course they were real. If the girls
believed them, then she did. And if they all believed them,
then this somehow made them true.

Barbara stood alone, the book still in her hands. Everyone
had clustered round Shirley's bed.

"Then you really know him?"

"What's he like?"

" Oh, do tell us about him ? "

For hours she talked, while the late June sunlight dimmed and deepened, and the shadows under the yews spread outwards, out and out, and Miss Mixton and the Maths mistress ceased to play clock-golf on the lawn and went in to a cup of cocoa, and Matron fell asleep over a book of Michael Arlen. She told them all the details that she had scraped together from newspaper articles, conversations in trains, *Who's Who*. " Yes, he shot a lion . . . He swims wonderfully . . . In South America . . . He told my father . . . They were together right through the war . . . Oh, yes, in Bulgaria—*and* Russia . . . Oh, yes, all the time. . . ."

It was dark now ; faces gleamed, arms gleamed under coils of hair ; the flat voice continued, evenly, but with a suppressed throb of excitement. The sheets seemed hot and twisted about her ; her heart pounded ; her eyes ached. She stared into the night outside, where Orion stretched, and the yew trees made furred patches against the smoothness of the sky's cheek, and the late birds twittered drowsily.

But Barbara slept, or appeared to sleep, one arm hanging out of her bed and pointing to the floor.

On Sundays, most of the girls walked in pairs ; but Shirley always walked alone.

This time, however, as they all began to congregate outside the changing-room a twittering throng of girls surrounded her. " Oh, *do* walk with me ! Oh, please walk with me ! Shirley, please ! " For the moment Sir Hugh Weigh had taken the place of Mr. Ivor Novello.

Shirley looked round her in embarrassment, small and squat, with the school hat pulled unbecomingly over her ears. It was as if she were afraid that her leg was being pulled. How could she choose ? And having chosen, what would she say ?

Then she noticed Barbara, who stood on the outskirts of the

little circle, waving a hand from which dangled a gold bracelet (all personal ornaments were forbidden) and crying : " Shirley ! Oh, please, Shirley ! " By turning up her school hat in front and pinning a brooch on to it she made herself seem oddly adult.

Shirley pushed her way towards her, blushing. No words would come.

Over the South Downs seventy girls moved off, for a moment petrified into a crocodile. Strangely, Miss Mixton was ' taking ' the walk ; and Shirley knew that on such occasions Barbara was one of the vociferous crowd who clamoured and fought for a ' side '. She realised then how greatly she was being honoured.

As they turned up a slope where lovers sprawled in ungainly beatitudes ("Don't stare, girls ! ") Barbara spoke for the first time :

" Shirley ? "

" Yes."

" I'm sorry I was so horrid about your scrapbook. I was a pig to take it from your locker."

" That's all right." She longed to be gracious, but could not find the requisite words. " I didn't really mind."

" Shirley ? " This was more tentative : the gold bracelet gleamed as she fiddled with it.

" Yes."

" Can we be friends now ? I mean, real friends."

" Oh, yes. Oh, please."

Fingers pressed her arm through the dark-blue macintosh.

" It must be marvellous to have a man like that as your guardian."

" Well—he's—he's not exactly my guardian. Of course— well—it comes to that——"

" Like a father, really."

The words filled her with an extraordinary pleasure. " Yes," she said. " Yes. That's it. Like a father." For no reason

5*

there was an ache in her throat, her eyes misted. But she
was elated, she was content.

" Your father's dead ? "

" Yes."

" You don't mind my asking ? My father nearly died when
he had his appendix out. It burst. But he got all right again.
He's in the Foreign Office. . . . Did you love your father
very much ? "

Shirley nodded. " I can't remember him very well. But
he was awfully nice."

" Were you very young then ? "

" Oh, yes. Only four." For the first time she was telling
somebody. In a moment she would mention the photograph,
and Cousin Maurice, and the box of old clothes. " He was
killed in the first week of the war."

Barbara's head jerked suddenly towards her. " In the first
week ? "

" Yes. He just went away—and never came back."

The snare snapped shut. " But you said—that night—you
said that he had saved the General's life—that they were comrades—comrades, you said—oh, right through the war. You
said they went to South America together——"

" I never said——"

" Oh yes you did ! If you like we'll ask Felicity—and
Beatrice——"

" No, please don't do that ! "

" Then you *were* lying ? "

" But you—you were asleep——"

" Of course I wasn't asleep. I heard every word. So you
thought you could take us all in, and——"

" No, honestly Barbara. What else *could* I do ? "

" Have you ever met this creature—this General Weigh ? "

" Well——"

" Have you ever met him ? Answer me ! "

" Well—no."

" I see."

She shook her wrist so that the bracelet jingled. She smiled.

The crocodile moved on, threading the fanatical lovers. Tears poured down Shirley's cheeks, but she made no sound. This was the end, she decided. This was the end.

No one likes to be deceived. " The little bitch," said Felicity, as she pulled down from her cubicle wall a picture which she had torn out of the *Sketch* while waiting to have her teeth filled.

This was the opinion of all of them.

Mr. Ivor Novello in Tyrolean shorts was restored to locker-doors, albums, picture-frames. Shirley, after a few days of ' baiting ' was sent to Coventry. At meals no one passed her anything.

The incident had its ironic sequel.

As they were filing out of a lecture on " Early English Brasses " Barbara beckoned her into a darkened music-room.

" But it's time to go to bed," Shirley protested, fearing some unseen torture. " Matron will——"

" Matron won't be round for another ten minutes. Don't be frightened. I'm not going to hurt you."

" But, Barbara——"

" Oh, come on."

In the twilight, in a room which smelled of peppermints and eau-de-Cologne, Barbara faced her. She put out a hand : " I've made you so unhappy. I'm an awful beast. Oh, do forgive me, Shirley. Say you forgive me."

" But I—I——" It was impossible to say anything. When one most wanted words they eluded one.

" I betrayed you. I see that. Oh, I do see that." She put an arm round her. " I trapped you. It was horrible of me.

But you see—you see. . . ." She broke off. " Shirley, may I tell you a secret ? "

" Oh, yes ! "

" Promise not to tell anyone ? Promise ? It's between you and me—no one else ? Promise ? "

" I promise."

" Cross-my-heart ? "

" Cross-my-heart."

Barbara drew Shirley towards her so that her hair brushed the other's wan cheek. " I've never told anyone here before. You're the first person I've told. You see—there's something queer about me." Her hand tightened on Shirley's wrist ; her voice thrilled.

" Queer ? "

" Yes. It's in the family, really. Mother—she was an actress, you know—a famous actress—before she married Father, that is. Well—I get it from her. She calls it her ' temperament '. But it's not really that."

" What is it then ? "

" Shirley. You're not frightened are you ? "

Mutely she shook her head. Then she started as the school cat whisked past the window after a rabbit. Her heart began to pound.

" It's a sort of—madness." Barbara went to the window, rested her elbows on the sill, and stared outwards into the gathering darkness. " No—not madness. That's too strong a word. But something—something queer. It makes me do things which I don't really want to do. I didn't want to betray you, Shirley : honest, I didn't. But then one of these fits came over me, and it—it happened. . . . Oh, I felt so miserable about it afterwards. I cried all that night in bed."

" Did you ? Did you really ? " No one had cried because of her since the day when her mother had thrust her, head first, into the world. " Did you really cry ? "

" Oh, yes, Shirley. I was so unhappy, you see. I'm very

fond of you, really. I want to be your friend. You do see that, don't you?"

"Yes."

Shirley stood by her at the open window. The wind blew strands of Barbara's hair across her mouth. It was sweet and fragrant on the lips.

Barbara put an arm round her shoulder. "Say you understand," she whispered intensely. "Say you understand. Say you forgive me."

Someone, a school servant, was turning out lights in the corridors and the schoolroom; they could hear the clicks of the switches, the ring of her shoes on vacant concrete. A mournful sound. Then there was silence.

Huddled together, they both wept luxuriously for a full five minutes. Afterwards, they scurried up to bed, hand-in-hand, just evading Matron by a passage and two steps.

But the next day, strangely, Barbara said nothing to Shirley. The whole incident might never have occurred.

Soon after that first and only term she spent at boarding-school Cousin Maurice died.

He was to have come down for his customary week-end by his customary train. But the day wore on and the dinner Mother had cooked for him grew cold, and she, who was usually so indolent and placid, rang up the station and walked down to the end of the drive, and said repeatedly: "I can't think what can have happened to him."

"Couldn't you ring him up?" Shirley ventured at last.

"Ring him up? How can I? He closes the shop on Saturday afternoon."

"But couldn't you ring him up at his home?"

Mother flushed. "No, I can't do that," she snapped.

"Why not? Hasn't he got a phone there?"

"Oh, do stop these absurd questions!" Mother shouted in exasperation. "You don't understand. Do go away!"

"But *why* not?" Shirley reiterated as she scurried for the door.

She was to learn why, later.

Eventually, Mother did ring up Cousin Maurice at his home : and a wife, whom Shirley had never known to exist, told her that he was ill, dangerously ill.

Mother said : "Oh, I must see him ! I must see him !" Tears ran down her cheeks. She went into the garden and cut all the roses, with a dry snip-snip of scissors. Then she wrapped them in tissue-paper and said to Shirley : "Do I look all right, dear ? Do use your wits for once. Do I look all right ?"

"You look lovely, Mummy."

"Good. I want to show that woman."

Her cheeks were still blotched with tears.

The next morning she returned, her eyes red with grief and sleeplessness. Shirley was eating breakfast. Removing the fur which Cousin Maurice himself had given to her, removing the cloche hat and the black net gloves, she sank into a chair.

"He's dead," she said.

"Dead ?" Shirley looked at her blankly. She felt an extraordinary elation, her head sang. "Dead ?"

Then with a sudden choking groan, as though she were trying to retch, Mother collapsed across the table. "Dead, dead, dead !" she screamed, her rings knocking on the smooth mahogany. "He was dead before I got there. I never saw him alive." She writhed in the chair as though in physical anguish, her eyes poured, saliva ran from her open mouth.

She was thinking of the death's head, strangely bald, shrunken and topped with white scars, that had lain propped in a darkened room. She had put her lips to his forehead, while his wife looked on, silent, tearless, in a stiff black dress, and the children whimpered next door.

But Shirley was thinking of Mother on a late summer evening

in a silk wrap, massaging the lobes of her ears ; and in her hand was a telegram ; and Father was dead.

At the funeral Mother and Cousin Maurice's wife, both in widow's weeds, sat close together, their hands clasped. Mother was enormous, magnificent, her plump throat clasped in three folds by a triple necklace of pearls. But Cousin Maurice's wife was thin, and sallow, and the only jewellery she wore was a worn circle of gold on her wedding finger.

Afterwards, they wept together ; and Mother said : " We are friends now, aren't we ? "

And Cousin Maurice's wife blew her nose, nodding.

He had his successors : and as Shirley was then growing up, while Mother herself was growing old, a certain jealousy was felt for the daughter. Not that these middle-aged shop-keepers and travellers were ever interested in the child. They always preferred Mother, who dyed her hair red, and wore rubber corsets, and joked coarsely and raucously. But Mother never ceased to humiliate Shirley. " My dear child," she would say in front of one of her ' friends ', " you're as flat as a rolling-board. But don't stoop so. It doesn't help." It was always assumed that Shirley was to be an old maid : " My poor girlie ! I doubt if we shall ever marry her, with a figure like that. What do you think, Paul ? Perhaps we can find some gentle-man whose tastes are not quite—orthodox. Really, she might be a boy." And she screamed shrilly in laughter, while Shirley got up and left the room.

Worst of all, Shirley was treated as Mother's *femme de chambre*. Mother had a certain sense of propriety which made it im-possible for one of the servants to bring up her breakfast when she was ' entertaining '. So this task devolved on Shirley. She grew used to knocking on the door, not once but repeatedly, so that she might be heard above the spurts of laughter and the raised voices.

"Come in!" yelled Mother. And then: "Ah! It's my little Shirley. My innocent little Shirley. The child knows nothing, you know. Put the tray down here, dear. . . . No— not on Uncle Henri's knees! Whatever next!"

In nausea she would leave them as soon as possible, bearing with her an image of some tousled ' gentleman ', the hair thick on his chest where his pyjama jacket divided, and Mother smoking a cigarette as often as not between stained fingers, her face creased, and greased with Crême Pomeroy, and surrounded by a wig-like mat of red hair.

The nicest of them was Théo, who had a short fringe, and was plump, and spoke in an oddly soprano voice. His pleasures so often coincided with Shirley's : he liked to go to the shooting gallery up the road, and helped her with the house she was building out of bamboos, and bought ice-creams for her and himself. Once he took her to the cinema in Fontainebleau and wept throughout.

Afterwards, they walked back through the Forest, and he climbed a tree, and waved his arms, and began to sing, " *Auprès de ma blonde* ". Then he climbed down, rather sheepishly, and said : " We'd better hurry. Your mother will wonder what has happened to us."

They walked on, in silence, until suddenly he turned to her : " Your nose shines dreadfully, you know."

" Does it ? "

" Why don't you powder it ? " he suggested kindly.

" Mother won't let me use make-up—yet."

" But that's not make-up. Why, even I use powder—after a shave."

" Do you ? . . . Do you think it would make me look better ? "

" Of course it would. You take no trouble with yourself. You don't care how you look." As though to modify the harshness of these criticisms he slipped his arm through hers :

" One simply must take trouble, you know. Appearances do
count. Look at this waistcoat of mine—double-breasted—
latest style. It's damnably uncomfortable, one can hardly
breathe. But it gives a man an air. People stare at him. You
take my advice. Just think a little more about how you *look*."

" Yes, I will, Théo. If you really think it will make any
difference."

" I'm certain it will."

He began to whistle, pleased with himself, full of self-
importance, while his dainty little feet moved forwards under
white spats.

That evening, after dinner, Shirley crept up to Mother's
room. She had seldom been in there when it was empty. She
fumbled for the light on the dressing-table and clicked it on.
Smells, unnoticed before, now filled her nostrils—stale perfume,
perspiration from the soiled jacket and trousers over the chair,
smells of the medicine Mother took and the marigolds, drooping
in a vase, and Théo's hair-oil. On the bed was a koala bear
with a zip-fastener down its back : it had been stuffed with
Mother's nightdress and Théo's pyjamas. Their slippers lay
side by side. On the bedside table was a glass for Théo's teeth,
and a Bible which he sometimes read.

Shirley looked at herself in the mirror, turning her face this
way and then that. She moved the light, she pulled her hair
up on to her head. But whatever she did she looked drab,
dull, untidy. About her lay bottles with great globular stoppers,
curling-tongs, bits of newspaper which had been scorched
where the tongs had been tried on them, some false hair. She
took this last, fixed it as a fringe on her forehead, and then
began to giggle. But a moment later she was crying. Why
did she always look so ridiculous. Why did the false hair
make Mother seem so chic while she looked absurd in it ?

She lay for a while on the enormous bed, which had in its
centre a hollow, a cradle. She imagined Théo and Mother

lying on either side, and then slowly, slowly, tumbling downwards into the centre. Oh, it was useless. She put out a hand,
took Mother's medicine bottle, and removed the cork. Her
tongue ran round the rim, she pulled a face. It was bitter,
crusted.

Then she got up and returned to the dressing-table. She
looked for powder. Ah, here it was. A large and bedraggled
puff was stuck in what looked like an ornamental soup-tureen.
She did not realise that this was for toilet use only. Tentatively,
she touched nose, one cheek, the other cheek. Then, bolder,
she took up a pair of tweezers and began to pull at her eyebrows.
She winced at the pain, made a gap in the centre, and then left
off in fright. With two combs she scraped her hair upwards.

At that moment there were footsteps. In panic she pulled
out the combs, tried to tidy the table, upset a perfume bottle.
The nauseating liquid trickled on to her bare legs. It felt as
if she had wet her knickers.

"What *are* you doing in here?" Mother came in. Then
seeing the damage she shouted in one of her sudden paroxysms
of rage: "You slut! You bitch! Get out of my room!
Get out! At once!" She rushed towards Shirley. "Making
yourself up! Using my things! How dare you!" She looked
around for something to hurl at her, picked up the enormous
puff, and threw it in her face. Shirley burst into tears.

But no sooner had she done this than Mother, with one of
her sudden changes of temper, began to laugh shrilly. "You
idiot! You little idiot! You don't know how funny you
look!"

Shirley gazed at herself in the glass. Her face was caked
in a uniform white, except where the tears had made runnels.

Mother still rocked with merriment; already she had
collapsed on to the bed. "Oh, it's priceless!" she sobbed.
"You—look—so—crazy!"

Shirley rushed for the door. But there she collided with
Théo who had come up at the sound of their voices. First he

gaped at her ; then he said, " My God ! What have you been doing ? " ; then he, too, was laughing hysterically.

Weeping, caring nothing for the pain, she scrubbed her face with a nail-brush over the kitchen-sink.

For as long as she could Mother made her wear the clothes of a schoolgirl—black woollen stockings, blue tunic, strap-shoes. At eight o'clock she was packed off to bed : so that it became difficult to remember a time when she was allowed to play in the garden for as long as she liked. If anything exciting was to happen—a dance at the hotel, a visit to Paris—Mother always said : " You're too young, Shirley. You're far too young." She wanted her to remain perpetually adolescent, clumsy, gauche. She could not bear to think of her coming to womanhood just at the moment when her own powers were waning. She thought that by holding Shirley in this bondage she could hold time in bondage also.

It was not surprising that the child did not reach puberty until she was eighteen.

In that year one of the English aunts, whom Shirley had never met, left her a few hundred pounds in her will. She would go to the Slade she decided, where Father himself had studied. In this way she would become an Artist. How magical that sounded ! She would escape Mother, and her ' gentle-men ', and the yearly visits of Miss Corry and Miss Witherby. She would be free.

Somehow, she never got to the Slade. But the next year saw her at an art school in South Kensington, where she won most of the prizes. She found that she could, with the greatest of ease, reproduce the style of the principal, Mr. Blain. It was an ' academic ' style, not dissimilar to her Father's. Outside an art school or an academy it would not have had much success. But for the moment she was the best pupil. Both she and Mr. Blain were thrilled.

He was a kindly widower who might have passed for a civil servant. He was interested in birds and plants and had a 'flatlet' off Baker Street. He played the recorder.

At the end of her last term he asked her to tea, and she helped him press some wild-flowers in a room with jars full of tadpoles in it, and acorns growing shoots in old medicine bottles, and a model yacht which Mr. Blain sailed on the Serpentine.

When they were eating their tea before a gas-fire Mr. Blain said : " And what are you g-going to do when you l-leave the school ? " He always stammered when he talked of anything other than his hobbies.

Shirley thought of her father and said : " Well—I really wanted to continue studying in Paris."

" Paris ! " His light-blue eyes widened, he ceased for a moment to masticate buttered scone. " D-do you think that would be a g-good idea ? "

" Don't you ? "

" Well — w-wouldn't it be serving both G-God and M-Mammon ? "

She was not sure what he meant by this. But she knew it was a form of disapproval.

" What else can I do ? " she asked.

" Of course, there's advertising," he began brightly, in a manner which he usually kept for prospective parents. " Plenty of possibilities there. Plenty of money."

She wrinkled her nose, and he broke off. " But you've too much talent for that. Leave the commercial side alone."

" Yes," she said. " Leave the commercial side." It was pleasant, sitting like this, drinking out of a cup without a handle, while they discussed her whole future.

" I'll tell you what ! " he said suddenly. He sat up with a start, so that the plate on his knees tilted at an angle and spilled melted butter on to his trousers. But he did not seem to notice it : and she did not dare to point it out to him. " I've got a f-friend," he began. " She has a shop in Chelsea. They make all their own stuff—trays, all that sort of thing. Why don't you join her? It's interesting work. And with my recommendation . . ."

"Oh, yes. It sounds lovely."

"There's a studio there. So in your f-free time, you could paint—seriously, I mean. And then, in no time—why, you'll be hung, you mark my words. You'll be famous."

"Oh, no . . ." she protested. But she felt that his words were somehow prophetic. Like Laura Knight, she thought. The picture of the year, reproduced in *The Times*.

"Shall I speak to my friend—Miss Mincer?"

"Oh, do. Oh, please."

It was all settled. In the silence, the warmth, she ate cup-cakes from the Lyons' round the corner. Life seemed suddenly full, rounded off, complete.

It was only when they said good-bye that she felt something missing. Their handshake seemed a sketch, a suggestion. But of what? She did not know. And he was too shy, too frightened, to enlighten her.

She never went to his flat again. Except for occasional visits that he paid to Miss Mincer the last she saw of him was when, one by one, the leavers went to his study to say good-bye. She was the last on the list.

It was difficult, when she was summoned into the small, untidy room, crowded with paintings by 'promising' pupils, to realise that if she ever came here again it would be as a stranger. She saw then the pathos of it all—the pathos of all departures, from however uncongenial an environment.

He began: "I haven't really much to say to you. J-just good-bye—and good luck. It's been a real pleasure to have you as a pupil—and—and as a f-friend. . . ." Then he blushed, for this last addition was not part of the speech as he had already delivered it sixteen times. "Just one thing before you go," he continued. "I—I have here a—a little gift—a token. Only a token. Nothing more." He pushed aside papers nervously, with both hands, as though he were doing a breast-stroke through them. "Ah, yes," he said at last. "Here it is."

"But this is very kind of you," she began.

"Oh, it's nothing, it's nothing at all, really."

She took the brown paper parcel with a murmured "Thank you."

"Good-bye," he said.

"Good-bye."

Their hands met. Then she went out.

It was a book called *Eyes and No Eyes*, by Claud Blain, F.R., brought out nearly twenty years ago by a firm of educational publishers. On the fly-leaf was the dedication : "To Edith, beloved wife", opposite a colour reproduction, "Flea-bane by river-bank".

Other students brushed past her, carrying canvases, paint-boxes, rucksacks. Their voices were shrill with plans, excitement, talk of the future. As they went out they left the door open behind them, and a wind, sharp with the promise of snow, blew down the corridor. She shivered and moved away.

For no reason her eyes were filling with tears.

At Miss Mincer's she learnt how to put lacquer on to trays and paint on to boxes. On a handloom she made scarves with ravelled ends. Lampshades were decorated with an acanthus pattern. She made the things, Miss Mincer sold them.

It was a shop in a side street in Chelsea, "Lucky Finds", with a doormat which said "Welcome" and a scrofulous Sealyham whose growl implied the reverse. In the shop sat Miss Mincer, polishing her nails on a buff, knitting, or reading a book from Mudie's Library (Subscription C). She wore a flowered smock and ankle-socks above court-shoes. It was impossible to tell where she had come from, or how she had found herself among reproductions of Van Gogh's "Sunflowers", framed copies of "Trees" in William Morris calligraphy, a couple of Paisley shawls, one of which had a cigarette burn through it, and of course the scarves, the lampshades, the boxes, the trays.

Next door was her great friend Miss Plumpton. "Oh, yes, we're *bosom* friends," she told Shirley. Miss Plumpton kept a tea-room where she also served two-course luncheons at one-and-six a head. The cakes were craggy, but tended to suddenly crumble if one persevered hard enough. From Miss Plumpton's ears dangled gold ear-rings, her hair was wrenched back in a tight little knot. " Spanish ", she would have called it, forgetting that the effect is not so easily achieved when the tint has changed from black to grey. Once upon a time she had been on the fringe of Chelsea's artistic sets, but at the present her only cultural pretensions were back numbers of *Time and Tide* and a badge from the League of Nations. " I was a model for Augustus John, dear," she confided to Shirley. " That was more years ago than I'd really like to confess." She giggled, as though at some rare audacity : but whether the artist or the passing of years was the cause, one could not tell. " Oh, yes ! " she sighed. " I've had a full life. I've known them all." She shook a meagre handful of currants into what was going to be a castle pudding and then continued : " But that's all over now. It's all right for a bit. But it doesn't really do, you know."

" No. I suppose not." Shirley was not very certain to what she referred.

" Yes. It's all over now," she continued. " Funny to think how crazy I was about art, and poetry, and that sort of thing. The time I first heard Scriabin's " Poème d'Exstase " ! There was an air-raid on : but I walked home, blithe as a lark. And Stephen Phillips—and Rhoda Broughton. . . . I don't suppose you read Rhoda Broughton now. And the time I saw George Moore in Ebury Street . . . I'd never touched one of his books. But the girl who was with me said, ' That's George Moore ', and really the way . . . Oh, how I do love to hark back to it all ! It makes poor Mincie laugh until the tears come into her eyes. But it's all over now. It's all over."

And as though to bear witness to this sad declension, this rejection of *la vie bohème*, around the four walls of the chintzy little room flapped marine birds by Peter Scott.

One day, when Miss Plumpton's help, the adenoidal Clara, had to go to the hospital to have her " dubes seed do ", Shirley was lent for the afternoon. It was a slack time at the " House of Martha " (as the tea-room was called, both Mincie and Miss Plumpton being converts to Anglo-Catholicism) ; and Shirley heard much more of old Chelsea.

"You know, dear," said Miss Plumpton suddenly, "I do think it's nice the way you don't use any make-up. I like a girl to be *natural*." She sighed : "I only wish the men did." Then seeing Shirley blush she said : "I do hope you didn't mind my saying that. But I've thought for so long that you'd make such a *nice* wife for some lucky man. You mustn't worry about having to wait, you know. I'm sure the Prince Charming will come along in the end."

Shirley turned away in embarrassment to serve two regulars with rock-buns and Indian tea. But when she returned Miss Plumpton said : "I've got a nephew whom I very much want you to meet. He's a medical student at the hospital up the road. I'm sure you'd get on famously."

"I should like to meet him."

"Would you ? That's the spirit !" Miss Plumpton swung her gold earrings in pleasure. "He's coming over this evening. Why don't you get Mincie to bring you along. After supper," she added hastily in case of misunderstanding.

"May I ?"

"Of course ! I'll have some tea for you. He's a dear boy. My god-son."

"Waitress ! I say, waitress !" Someone in sealskin and a wooden necklace was calling for her. She scurried off.

Mincie brought her knitting in a bag which she had made out of samples from Derry & Toms, and Jo-Jo, the Sealyham, and some soda-mints in case of trouble. Miss Plumpton had changed for the occasion into a black velvet garment which was tied with an embroidered girdle a foot or more below her waist : over it she wore a ' coatee ' with half-length sleeves, edged with greyish-green fur. Shirley, in her desire to satisfy Miss Plumpton's preference for ' natural ' girls, had washed her face in soap and water and then left it. It, like her hands, had a rubbed appearance.

They were all introduced, they all sat down, and Jo-Jo jumped into Mincie's lap. Shirley looked at the young man. He was large, and seemed to have been poured into his clothes hot : his shirt gaped open, his trousers were pulled dangerously tight across his buttocks, his collar was creased. His face was pink and benign, until one encountered the glasses, which enlarged his eyes until one seemed to be seeing them in an aquarium. His hair was brushed straight off his forehead : but suddenly it rebelled, just after passing the ears and stuck out in tufts. He was fiddling with a crystal set.

Miss Plumpton said to Mincie : " Mincie dear, shall I get the tea now ? What do you think ? "

And Miss Mincer said : " Just as you like, dear. I really don't mind."

So Miss Plumpton went out and rattled Poole pottery next door, and eventually appeared with the tray and the tea. " I *think* the kettle was boiling," she warned them, optimistically. " I wonder if you'll like this sort of tea. It's Yerba Maté. They drink it in Uruguay—or is it Paraguay ? At any rate the Culpeper place said it was excellent—and very good for the digestion." She addressed these last words to poor Mincie who had difficulties in that quarter.

After this, they all sat in silence for a long time, while Miss Plumpton lapped tea noisily, and poor Mincie was noisy in quite another way, and Jo-Jo was fed on brittle flakes off the

Chelsea buns, and Shirley stared into the fire, her face becoming
more and more red, and the young man inserted a piece of
wire into the crystal set and made it twitter, and then said
" Damn ! "

Then Miss Plumpton began : " Really, the other day, such
a funny thing——"

But immediately she was silenced by the young man who
said : " Sh ! Oh, for heaven's sake ! I'd almost got it to
work. That was the Midland Regional, that was."

So again they were silent, while the young man squeezed
out for them, as though from a tube, a thin trickle of sound,
a ghost, which Miss Plumpton triumphantly pronounced to be
" Yes, we have no Bananas ". Other similar melodies followed.
Still none of them talked.

Eventually, Mincie yawned and said, " Jo-Jo wants to go
walkie ", and they all, except the young man, got up and
kissed each other. Miss Plumpton kissed Jo-Jo, and Miss
Plumpton kissed Shirley, encouragingly, on the forehead, and
Miss Mincer kissed Miss Plumpton, once on either raddled
cheek. But the young man never moved.

" Good-night," they called to each other. " Good-night,
dear. So kind of you. . . . Mind the step."

" Good-night," the young man muttered, pulling ferociously
at a knob.

The next time Shirley saw him was when Miss Plumpton
had gone to see her Harley Street specialist. She was always
referring to her ' trouble ' ; and occasionally, in her less
boisterous moments, one would hear her exclaim : " Oh,
what it is to be a woman ! " Shirley for some reason associated
these pronouncements with her visits to the doctor. She never
had positive proof.

When the visits were made Shirley ' took over ' at " The
House of Martha ", serving stewed breast, mashed swedes,
and apple and junket to a dozen or more customers. After

the apple course, the plates were always lined with what looked like toe-nails : Miss Plumpton was too haphazard to core an apple with any success.

Shirley saw him sitting by himself, by the window, his elbows resting on the glass top of the wicker table. On the mat, which she herself had stencilled, was placed a copy of *Pearson's Weekly*. Sometimes he shuddered with what she took to be laughter.

It was very important to make the right impression. She went into the kitchen and examined her face in the glass. How pale she looked ! If only she had some rouge. . . . But hadn't Miss Plumpton said . . . ? With both hands she began to pinch her cheeks until they were filled with colour. Then she licked her lips and patted her hair.

" Hello," she said. " Have you been served ? "

" Oh—hullo," he murmured, without looking up. " Is Miss Plumpton away ? "

" I'm afraid so. She's seeing her—— " She broke off. Was it quite the thing to mention the specialist ?

" Oh, never mind. I'll have the lunch. It's on the house, you know. She doesn't mind."

" Swedes or spinach ? "

He pulled a face. " Either—both. If they're hot."

She scurried off. In the kitchen she piled his plate with the choicest morsels of meat. In two heaps she placed swedes and spinach.

" Oh—I say ! " he remonstrated when she set it before him. " I didn't really mean both. I couldn't."

" Shall I take it away ? "

" No, no. Doesn't matter now. I'll leave it to one side." He still read *Pearson's Weekly*, jabbing his fork towards his mouth, snatching the raised meat in sudden gulps, then loading once more, in careful tiers. He was a methodical eater, demolishing his plate according to plan. One imagined that he would make a competent surgeon.

Meantime, in the kitchen, Shirley was picking pips, 'toe-nails', and peel out of his helping of apple. She found a half-empty carton of 'coffee cream' and poured that over it. Then she watched him from behind the bead curtain until he was ready.

Muscles rippled up and down his pink cheeks as he ate. One of his knees was perpetually agitated. A woman tried to sit down in the place opposite him, but he grunted, "That's taken", and she wandered out. Sweat glistened on his upper lip.

Shirley took him his pudding, and saw, with satisfaction, that he was able to eat it without surreptitiously having to pick his teeth as the other guests did. *Pearson's* was now propped against Miss Plumpton's 'daffs', crushing their heads sideways.

At last he got up to go. Shirley ran forward, smiling.

"I hope you liked your lunch."

"Oh—yes." Crossly he fumbled in his pocket. Something clicked down on the glass-topped table. Then he wound one of those lengthy school scarves round his neck, an affair of three colours of a particularly dazzling kind, braced his shoulders, and went out.

Shirley crossed to the table. On it were three half-pennies.

"I know it will be hung," said Miss Plumpton, as they clambered into a taxi and the canvas was placed across their knees. "I know it will be hung. I feel it." Later, she had the satisfaction of going to the private view ("The last time I came to a private view it was to see a portrait of myself, *au naturel*, so to speak"): and she was able to stand for a long time before 'No. 406', so that everyone would know that she knew the clever girl who had painted it.

The picture was entitled "Miss Adelaide Mincer", and showed Mincie watering the geraniums in the window-box on the second floor. It was never sold, but returned to "Lucky

Finds" and was hung beside a gold-illuminated text: "If
you don't succeed at first . . ."

But, unlike her father, Shirley knew already.

It wouldn't do, she decided, just as she was dipping her
paint-brush into a tumbler of murky water. She left it there
and stared into space, her chin cupped in the palms of both
hands. A robin leapt on to the window, chirruped and then
disappeared; the girl opposite practised her double-stopping
with tense shrills of cat-gut; the room shook convulsively
as a remover's van thundered past. But she noticed none of
these things. Abstracted, she was thinking.

I'm only partly living, she thought. That's the whole
trouble. I'm not really alive at all. That morning she had
begun by getting their breakfast of thin slices of toast, tea,
Cooper's marmalade; Mincie read the *Daily Sketch*, and
murmured, "Oh, these poor Chinese! Another earth-
quake!"; then she said, a little crossly: "I do believe you've
used yesterday's milk for the tea. It tastes rancid." After
breakfast Jo-Jo had to be taken for a walk. "See what sort of
duty he does," were Mincie's instructions. "His tum-tum
is rather upset. And *don't* let him eat garbage at number
sixteen." George Arliss was on at the Gaumont: Mincie and
Miss Plumpton liked him: perhaps they could all go to the
matinée. Outside the town hall a beggar pulled her sleeve;
he had no nose, and was selling bootlaces; really it was most
offensive. Then someone, a young man in Oxford bags and
a pork-pie hat, poked Jo-Jo with his walking-stick because he
was making a mess on the edge of the pavement. Shirley
blushed hotly. On the counter at "Lucky Finds" was a box
for the R.S.P.C.A. and another for the Anti-Vivisection
League.

When she returned home she set to work on some lampshades. Mincie had a new 'line', as she called it. She sent
Shirley up to Charing Cross Road to buy second-hand stacks

of music ; then one threaded them in pleats with pieces of
ribbon, and sold them for twelve-and-six each. She did this
all morning and part of the afternoon, until Miss Plumpton
came round and asked if she would kindly go to Mudie's for
her. Mudie's had none of the things that she wanted : no,
there was such a run on Lady Eleanor Smith's *Red Wagon*,
but would *The Virgin and the Gipsy* do instead ? Shirley said
" Yes ", until she discovered that it was by D. H. Lawrence.
So she took back Marjorie Bowen, whom Miss Plumpton
called ' reliable '.

And now she was alone in the studio, painting the single
rose that flopped in an old scent bottle. " But I'm only partly
living," she repeated. " I'm only partly living." It was not
like this in the novels that she read or the films that she saw.
There, each incident had its own significance ; each incident
led on like the rungs of a ladder ; there was always a promise
of something more exciting ; until, at the end, George Arliss
was made *Duke* of Wellington, and Chaplin walked into the
sunset, and Marlene said, " Yes. Oh, yes ", and was embraced
by a sheikh.

Lacking all wisdom, she thought : Life should be like that
too, little realising that so much is greyness, a void, in which
we work that we may eat and eat that we may work. The
philosopher said, " I feel, therefore I am ". It would be a
mistake to assume, " I am, therefore I feel ", if feeling means
more than the ache of hunger, the wish for sleep, the everyday
experience of everyday things.

She began to pace the room in a sudden anguish, clasping
and unclasping her hands. I must get away, she thought.
Oh, I must begin living. Soon it will be too late. Time
passes, and nothing is done. Time passes.

She walked resolutely down the stairs and gave notice.

But how was she to begin ? If she had had money she would
have gone on a cruise, or taken a trip to America, or done

something equally adventurous. But all that was now left
of the legacy was twenty pounds. Someone else might have
' blown ' it all in a few weeks of excitement. But Shirley had
ancestors who had been peasant proprietors. She must hoard
this meagre amount—' in case '.

A job. But what ? She could go on painting trays for one
of the big stores, but would that really be much different ?
Then she thought of other, more eccentric, possibilities—a
shop-girl perhaps. But shop-girls were only paid thirty-
shillings a week. She *couldn't* live on thirty shillings. So what
was left ? There seemed to be nothing.

Suddenly she remembered Mr. Blain. He would probably
have ideas. She rang him up, and after much hesitation he
arranged that they should meet at the Strand Corner House.
Over a marble-topped table she told him about her wish to
' Live '. " Yes, I see," he interjected slowly. " Yes, I see.
Quite so. Quite so."

" What about a school ? " he asked at last.

" Teaching ? "

" Why not ? "

She clasped his hand as though at some wonderful discovery
they had made together, quite oblivious of the shocked way
in which he drew back and winked his hairless eyelids. " That's
it ! " she exclaimed. " That's it ! Of course ! "

Her enthusiasm should perhaps be explained. She had only
spent a term at boarding-school : so that now it seemed a
world full of possibilities. To be a school-girl had been one
thing : but to be a mistress. . . . Phrases came into her mind
—' intellectual companionship ', ' good talk ', ' the cameraderie
of the common-room'. But of course. Why hadn't she
thought of it before ?

In her memory were stored imagies, magical symbols. On
late summer evenings Miss Mixton and the Maths mistress
played clock-golf on the lawn beneath the dormitories. The

mistresses had their private jokes and illusions, passed on over
the heads of their charges at meals or on the playing-field.
The common-room was a place where no girl might go without
permission. And after eight o'clock, when for them the day
was over, a second lease, a strange life from which they were
excluded opened out like a blossom within a blossom. In
those days it had always seemed as if the girls were in an ante-
room, while next door, in the main chamber, other secret
and exciting things went on. The mistresses could join the
girls, but no girl could ever cross the threshold into that alien
world.

But now it would be possible. The journey would be made.

It was not quite as she had expected.

Her best friend became Miss Tree, who was forty-five and
had dry, brittle hair and a dry, brittle voice. Miss Tree taught
French and Shirley helped her. She had a little money, which
meant that she could wear tailored tweeds and run a two-
seater and have a radiogram in her room. She was the only
one of them who seemed to have a life wide enough to swallow
the school and still leave room for other interests. She lectured
to the W.E.A., and sometimes motored in France, and had
for the last twenty years been making desultory notes for a
book on the Peninsular War. At the school she was feared,
disliked, and despised in turn. She was harshly candid, could
afford to be independent, and had the reputation of being a
highbrow.

At meals, instead of the witty conversation that Shirley
had expected, she had to listen to what funny little Muriel
said when asked to decline *mensa*, and how Miss Cox had dealt
with a minx who cribbed off her neighbour. Ceaselessly, they
discussed the girls, and the chances in the lacrosse match, and
the amount of sweets that should be issued each day after
lunch : until, suddenly, one of them would remember that
outside the gates was a roar of traffic, and people, and another,

less comfortable, world. Then : " What's the news to-day ? "
or, " I suppose Dorothy Round is certain for the finals ? " would
suddenly cut across order marks and inferiority complexes.

Only Miss Tree kept aloof, crumbling bread between blood-
less fingers as she gazed sardonically from High Table on to
the chattering multitude below them. She had thin legs
encased in ribbed stockings and rouged her cheeks unnecessarily.
She tended to asthma.

She and Shirley became friends because their work brought
them so much together. At first her dry, almost contemptuous,
manner wounded. But in her rooms were French books that
could be borrowed, records of Josephine Baker, and a cupboard
of drinks. Without many words she smoothed difficulties, so
that a time-table which hadn't worked suddenly came to rights,
and the horrible Ida was removed to another form, and there
were cakes and coffee after tenuous suppers.

She encouraged Shirley to sit in her room, but always contrived to exclaim harshly, " Oh, *please* don't ruck up that
chair-cover," or, " Really, your nails ! Do you *never* clean
them ? " Sometimes she came up to Shirley's room at night
to borrow an aspirin or to say that she couldn't sleep. She
never slept well.

She was a Socialist, who said in a crowd : " The smell of
these people ! It really is disgusting," or, " I hate human
beings. In the mass they make me homicidal." She visited
the local prison, but never talked of what happened there.
Strangely the girls liked her.

One morning she lent Shirley a fountain-pen in the common-
room to correct exam papers with. It was an expensive pen,
massive, with a broad gold nib. " I don't mind your using
it," she said, " provided you don't press hard. But for heaven's
sake don't let anyone else touch it."

Later, after she had gone to read *Lettres de mon Moulin* with
the Upper Fifth, Miss Humber came in. She was a girl of

6

about twenty-five who taught science from behind thick glasses. The headmistress had once said, out of her hearing, that her figure was all over the place. She had worked hard from elementary to secondary school, and from secondary school to provincial university. Invariably in the summer her nose peeled and she took to going about in sandals, without socks or stockings. She was very keen to be a success, to be liked.

That morning the headmistress had pinned up a list for volunteers for the bathing-party : some girls had not been taken out at half-term ; a treat was to be arranged for them.

Miss Humber said : " Might I just borrow that pen for a moment ? I want to add my name here."

" Well—I'm awfully sorry. It's not mine, you see."

" I won't press, I promise. It's just to write my name. You can have it back in a second." She pleaded amiably, with flabby lips·that sagged in a grin and eyes that squinted. " Oh, please."

Shirley handed her the pen and she began to write : " D. Humber " in a round, unformed hand. Her tongue ran round her mouth as though she were doing something excessively difficult.

" Shirley ! " Miss Tree, entering at that moment, looked first at the astonished Humber, then at the girl, and then out of the window. Her sallow face was grey, she trembled with rage.

" I'm awfully sorry, Enid. It was just to write her name——"

In a harsh, loud voice she cut in : " I told you not to. I asked you not to. You betrayed me."

" But really——"

" Oh, don't try to excuse yourself. What does it matter ? What does it matter, anyway ? " She picked up the book that she had come back for. She spoke with incisive bitterness. " When you've finished with it, perhaps you would be good enough to put it back on my desk."

As she went out Shirley noticed the colour of her hand as it touched the door-knob. It was blue, as though with extreme cold.

Miss Humber seemed uncertain how to take all this. She cleared her throat, pushed back her glasses, grinned tentatively. " What was all that in aid of ? Was it her pen ? "

Shirley nodded.

" But what a fuss ! I haven't hurt it ! It was only to write my name. Why didn't you tell her ? "

She put the massive, gold-nibbed thing down before Shirley. The square point was flecked with ink.

Rain made a twanging noise, ceaselessly, on the corrugated-iron roof of the church hall. Outside were two six-foot posters. Shirley stood between them, in a green oil-cloth coat, her hands thrust deep into her pockets. She stared out at the blotched reflections of street-lamps in the road, *diminuendo*, circling into nothing. A car splashed by, holding, as though embalmed in amber, the curved figure of a woman in furs and evening dress. Shirley, stooping, ran a hand down her calf. The stocking lay like a poultice, water trickled into her shoes. Against her cheek stuck lank hair. In the distance, behind the door, was Miss Tree's voice talking of Embargoes and Ricardo's Law of Rent and Henry George, and Miss Tree herself, shivering a little in a tweed coat before a few rows of white faces. The electric light made it difficult for her to read her notes, and one of the boards creaked whenever she trod on it. Some-one said, in a high, piping voice : " Could you please read those figures again ? I didn't quite catch." And fumbling the pages she began once more on the interminable list.

Shirley looked at her watch. At least another ten minutes. She couldn't stand there for ever. Up to the war memorial and back : that should just cover it. And it would give her a chance to look in at Shine's window on the way. She moved off slowly, her shoes squelching at each stride.

Inside each brightly lit embrasure were waxen models, staring outwards in 'Six guineas, outsize' or 'Best quality Harris Tweed'. Their faces were curiously narrow, the features sharp. They looked like tribal gods. Next door were Kestos and Spirella in shiny pink satin, and some flowers made out of dyed leather. Then came Useful Gifts, a handkerchief satchet with a four-leaved clover embroidered on it, a triangular scarf, ostensibly 'home-spun', some belts, combs decorated with sealing-wax fruit, handbags with monograms. She looked at them all, thinking how warm and dry it must be there, behind the glass. No one else passed.

But suddenly : "Hullo ! What are you up to ? "

It was D. Humber, Call-me-Doris, with a man's umbrella and a pair of goloshes, making for the bus park. Under her arm, wrapped in brown paper, was John Buchan. Her fringe lay in six or seven separate prongs. She came from the "Luxor", the *de luxe* kinema, where in the back stalls she glared ferociously at the vices of *The Sign of the Cross*.

Shirley said : "I'm waiting for Tree. She promised to drive me back in her car. She doesn't finish till nine o'clock."

"Oh, I say ! Then you've missed her."

"Missed her ? "

"Well, I could have sworn I saw her at the toll bridge. She's probably got off early." Doris was notoriously short-sighted. "You'd better come along with me. The last bus goes in a jiffy."

"Oh, no. I really think I'd better go back to the hall—I mean to say——"

"There's no time for that. You'll miss the bus. And then where will you be ? I know it was her. She has that funny hooter. Come on ! "

"But she'll be——"

"Even if she hasn't gone, she'll know that in this rain no decent person can possibly be expected to wait. Oh, come on ! " A moist hand grabbed her.

Shirley hesitated, drew back, and then gave in. The rain was coming through at her shoulders.

In the jolting bus Doris said : " It's so difficult to teach some parts of biology. It's embarrassing, really." She did not specify to what parts she referred. Then she said : " You ought to go and see *The Sign of the Cross*, I think Tree would enjoy it. She's supposed to be interested in history and all that, isn't she ? " Then : " You're shivering ! Have my mack." She tucked Shirley in and wound a muffler round her neck. From her pocket she produced glacier mints.

Shirley hugged a hot-water bottle in bed. Her nose was blocked, she had to breathe through her mouth. Doris had made tea, and they had talked about cycling clubs and youth hostels. Now she had gone, leaving behind her some literature from the Oxford Group. In the darkness Shirley counted sheep, punched her pillow, tried to remember whether she had set French prep. to the Upper Fourths.

Suddenly the door was thrown open, the light flicked on. " Well, really ! " Miss Tree dripped water on to the frayed rug. She clasped her umbrella horizontally, in both hands.

Shirley sat up, blinking. " Oh, I'm awfully sorry," she began. " Oh, really I am. I thought you'd gone, you see. I waited until ten to nine——"

" But we said nine."

" Yes, I know. You see, I walked up to the war memorial to pass the time, and then I saw Humber——"

" Humber ! "

" Yes. And she said that you had passed at the toll bridge— and the bus was just going——"

" So she was behind it, was she ? I thought as much." Her lips snapped shut. For the first time Shirley smelled damp tweeds and spirits. " I'm sick of it," Miss Tree began again.

" I'm sick of being played up like this. I don't know why I stand it, I really don't. I don't know why I bother about you." She began to pace up and down the little room, still holding the umbrella as though she were about to break it across her knees. Shirley pressed the hot-water bottle hard to her breast. Her eyes began to prick with tears. " It's simply not good enough. Don't you see ? You expect too much. It's always want, want, want. You couldn't really have thought I'd believe such a story. Why not admit it ? You got cold—very well. You decided I wasn't worth waiting for."

" Oh, no," Shirley protested. " Oh, no, no. That's all wrong."

" Oh, Shirley, Shirley ! " She sat down on the end of the bed. " You *are* a little fool. Such a blind little fool. Do you see nothing ? "

" Nothing ? What do you mean ? "

" Do you never put yourself in the position of other people ? Do you never think of their feelings ? Have you no imagination ? "

Then, for no reason, Shirley found herself shouting. She was tense with rage, she clutched at the hot-water bottle. " I don't know what you mean," she shrilled. " I think you're making a lot of fuss over nothing. Just a lot of fuss——"

" Fuss ! "

" Get out ! Leave me alone ! Get out ! "

Miss Tree rose from the bed. " Very well," she said, breathless but calm. " Very well. This is the end. Very well."

Shirley heard her walking slowly downstairs. Throwing herself on to the pillow she burst into uncontrollable tears.

For the next two or three weeks they said nothing to each other except when they met in school. Miss Tree ceased to be Enid, Christian names were forgotten. It was now D. Humber who helped Shirley choose her winter suit at Shines, and added up her marks for her, and made drinks at bed-time. Miss Tree took out the car almost every evening. No one knew where she drove to.

Sometimes, at night, Shirley heard her walking about in the room below, or there was the sound of her Wagner records. For no reason, then, she found herself wishing that the door would open and the figure in the camel-hair dressing-gown would come in, and murmur : " I say, I can't sleep. Do you mind if we talk ? " But those days were over now. And Miss Humber slept ' like a top '—as she put it—her snores rattling aggressively beneath a widely flung window.

One afternoon there was a note on Shirley's desk. It said :
" It's silly for things to go on like this. Suggest you and Humber meet me and we talk the whole thing out. Reply by letter."

So Shirley wrote her agreement, and they all met in the Seventeenth-century Tea-rooms on a half-holiday.

The tea-rooms were not really seventeenth century, but like the station and the Boots Cash Chemists and the Crown Hotel had been erected in a sudden enthusiasm for Jacobean-Elizabethan. Some of the windows had stained glass in them, while others were leaded ; there was a minstrel's gallery where four ladies played selections from *The Desert Song* and *No, no, Nanette* ; there were beams, and alcoves where lovers were obligingly put, and ceilings villainously low. Here came the farming population of within a radius of twenty miles for tea on market-day. There were six different sorts of tea—Devonshire Tea, and Salad Tea, and Sandwich Tea, and so forth.

Miss Tree ordered for the three of them. " China tea, scones, cakes." Shirley noticed that her hand trembled on the menu. The rouge on her cheeks was like a round incision : it gave a Petrouchka effect. Her eyes were violet-lidded, but not with paint. She smoked while she ate, using a small ivory holder.

None of them talked. Doris sucked cream out of éclairs like ice-cream out of a cone. Sometimes she looked round at the other guests and smiled, not patronisingly, but as one would at friends. Shirley masticated slowly, staring in front of her. Then when the last éclair had been gobbled by Doris, and nothing could be coaxed out of the tea-pot but a yellowish fluid, Miss Tree put both elbows on the table, pushed aside her plate, and said : " Well ? "

Neither answered.

" We must get things straight," she began with a sort of weary indifference, her eyes roaming over stained-glass unicorns, a pre-Raphaelite girl with a basket of roses, and the illuminated crest of a firm of caterers. " We must talk it all out. At the moment we're all in the dark."

" But I don't really see what there *is* to discuss," Shirley said plaintively. " Is there anything ? "

Doris nodded her agreement. " To tell you the truth——" she began, about to embark on one of those speeches which contrived to make mistresses' meetings even more formidable than they would have been without her.

But Miss Tree had already risen to her feet, her eyes filling with tears. It was the first time that either of the others had seen her weep, and it shocked them profoundly. They gaped at her, the colour leaving their faces until they, too, were as white as she was. In a rasping voice she said : " Oh well, if you feel like that—then we're wasting our time. I mustn't keep you." She took up her bag and pulled out a ten-shilling note. " Here's some money for all this." She looked contemptuously at the plates congealed with butter that had been hot, and then at the silver dish, plundered of all its cakes, and finally at the bitter sediment within her own cup. Pushing her way between the closely packed tables she disappeared.

Doris said : " My hat ! Did you ever ? "

The next morning Shirley came into the common-room and found Miss Tree behind an old number of *Punch*. It was a room which tried to create a ' club ' atmosphere, but the attempt

was too conscious ; it lacked spontaneity. There were brown
leather chairs, with brass ash-trays fixed to their arms, a green
baize notice-board, and some rugs made by the handicrafts
class. Two mistresses had stuck a dart-board in one corner ;
and another mistress always contrived to litter the table with her
books. On the mantelpiece were plaster busts of Elizabeth Fry
and a later Roman emperor, the one a crude piece of work, the
other extraordinarily fine. Flanking a tumbler full of spills
they made an odd contrast.

Shirley went up to Miss Tree. " About yesterday," she
began. " I was awfully sorry to upset you so. I really didn't
mean——"

" But of course not," Miss Tree cut in, putting the magazine
down on the floor. She spoke without irony, in a flat tone.
" You were quite right."

" Right ? "

" One should never have things out. It doesn't work. Much
better to say nothing. . . . So you see—I apologise."

" But no," Shirley protested. " It's I who——"

" Let's say no more about it, shall we ? And we will remain friends ? I'm moody, I'm afraid. . . . But you do forgive
me ? "

Shirley nodded. " Oh, yes. Oh, yes, of course."

She was too bewildered to protest.

A note :

MY DEAREST SHIRLEY,—I always find it easier to write than
to say things.

In case you misunderstood me this morning, I meant only
that I was sorry for my behaviour and wished that we could be
friends once more.

May we ?   E. T.

As she read it Shirley found her face growing hot and cold.
Each of these incidents disquieted her profoundly. But she

6*

could not tell for what reason. Something was wrong, it was all jerking out of control. She knew this, but was powerless to stop it.

This life which had seemed so fertile in promise was a disappointment. She felt its emptiness each morning as she and two other mistresses wrangled over who should go into the bathroom first. In chapel she felt it, and when she sat at the top of a long table at meals, and heard, rising and ebbing around her, the chatter of twenty shrill voices. It was nothing, nothing; and she was nothing, a shell, a husk.

Each incident with Miss Tree intensified this feeling to an unbearable degree. We are damned, she thought, we are doomed. We hunger for life, but it evades us. We are gesticulating shadows. We are Homer's ghosts, who long to drink the blood of the living. But there is no blood to drink, and we wander, interminably.

One little happening, of no ostensible importance, disquieted her more than all others. It was customary for her and Miss Tree to change over their French classes half-way through the lesson, so that Shirley could do the oral training and Miss Tree could manage the literature.

One morning Miss Tree was late. Shirley, arriving at the classroom, could still hear her talking to the class. The voice rattled dryly, and for no reason, instead of going in she stood outside and listened, her mark-book under her arm.

Miss Tree was doing unseen translation. "Now, girls," she was saying. "What does this word mean? *Mamelon. Roland est venu au mamelon.* Who knows?" Someone said mammal, someone suggested house. "Wrong, wrong!" Miss Tree snapped. "Well—who knows the word *mamelle*?" No answer. "Oh, come, come! *Mamelle* means a breast. You must all know that. And from *mamelle* we get this word *mamelon.*" She went to the blackboard. "Look!" With a quick stroke of the chalk she drew in a breast, with nipple

" Now ! There's a breast. Well—what does it remind you of ? . . . A hill, of course ! A hill ! "

The duster erased the diagram. The class was over.

An intonation, an emphasis—what was it that made the whole scene intolerable ?

Part of the summer holidays were spent with Doris in Norfolk. Mrs. Humber had been the daughter of a country parson and had married a farmer. The farmer was now dead ; but with the help of a half-wit girl she still kept hens, some goats, and a small market-garden. Many of the fields had been let out ; others were derelict, a place to pick blackberries in. Once the land had been good ; but it had been overworked, nothing had been put back, and now it was sour and unproductive. The house itself leaked upstairs ; the top landing had been closed and there were damp patches on the walls. Grass pressed between the paving of the drive ; many of the stones were cracked.

Mrs. Humber was as upright as when she had first ridden to hounds as a girl. But her whole life, all that lay behind that splendid carriage, had been devoured by one grievance. After her marriage the gentry had ceased to ' know ' her : and even now, with her husband buried, she was still ignored. This was an intolerable burden, a cruel infliction of loneliness ; for she herself, in turn, refused to know the market-gardeners and small tradesmen who had been her husband's friends.

But Doris fraternised with all of them. When her mother said of one young man : " Isn't he rather C.O.M. ? " (which was her way of saying ' common '), Doris flashed back : " He's as good as father ever was." This made Mrs. Humber's eyes fill with tears—of rage, rather than repentance.

Shirley was no more of a snob than Doris. But from lack of practice she found it difficult to make conversation to the country-folk. Mrs. Humber took this disability as a form of breeding. Shirley, she privately noted, was a ' lady '. So dinner was substituted for high-tea, and the boiler was lit for baths nightly instead of once a week, and the Crown Derby tea-service, which she had brought with her from the vicarage over thirty years ago and had hardly used since, was now taken out for the half-wit girl to chip when she washed it up.

She never tired of asking Shirley about her English relations : and when she was not doing this she talked of her own. In the house were a few ' pieces ' left to her by an aunt. It was plain, solid Victorian furniture : but Mrs. Humber would say : " Yes, Aunt Sophie had some lovely things. You can tell from those few heirlooms of mine. Sad to think of it all broken up among a dozen of us. In her big house . . ."

For a long time she would brood in this manner on a remote, and perhaps non-existent, past. Then the hens would have to be fed or the goats would have to be milked, and with a gesture that said, " And now look what I've come to ", she would stride out, her lean arms clasped under her breast.

They were waiting for the bus that was to take them to a cinema, and the shops, and tea at the " Copper Kettle ". Shirley stood out on the road while Doris, who had a stone in her shoe, had retreated behind a tree to remove it. Perhaps her sense of decorum was too much developed ; perhaps she was ashamed of her feet, which were large and had bunions from squeezing them into narrow fittings.

The bus was late, as it always was on Saturday. " Is it coming ? " Doris asked, dusting her foot with the palm of her hand. " Oh, do stop it if it is. Ask them to wait."

" No sign yet."

A mile away the bus had stopped while the driver got off his seat and collected fares. But they were not to know that.

At the brow of the hill before them something moved, there was a distant rumble. " Oh, look ! " Shirley exclaimed, expecting the familiar green and red to appear.

Now it so happened that at the moment she said, " Oh,

look ! " a man was passing on a bicycle. Doris being screened by her tree he imagined that he was being addressed. " Yes ? " he said, braking sharply. " Yes ? "

Shirley shook her head. " Nothing," she murmured. " Nothing. Just that." A lorry drove past them.

He went on ; but half-way down the hill he got off his bicycle and began to wheel it back. " I'm sure you said something," he protested. " I could have sworn——" He grinned at her, a man of about forty-five, swarthy, with light-blue eyes and an open-necked shirt.

At that moment Doris appeared, hopping, with her bare foot raised in the air. " My friend was talking to me," she cut in. " Please go away. You know it was not to you she was speaking."

The man coloured, mounted his bicycle, and rode off, his alpaca coat flapping behind him.

" Oh, Doris ! " Shirley protested.

" That's the way to deal with them," Doris said, in high spirits. " Upon my soul ! Thought he was going to get off with you ! "

But : " Oh, Doris ! " Shirley protested again.

Shirley took the goats out to pasture. They were aristocratic, blue-lipped creatures ; white Saanens, whose muzzles tapered delicately into a point. As they moved forward their udders swung from side to side between bow-legs. Their bellies were distended with clover hay, giving them an appearance of pregnancy. Shirley had two of them with her, and, not being used to their management, her progress was slow. When she pulled they decided to stop, their teeth wrenching at nettles, thistles, and elder. But as soon as she stood still they dragged her sideways, across the road, to some more succulent pasture. She cursed them silently.

They were Mrs. Humber's pets, to whom fresh white bread was given and apples and dough-cakes. They must not be hurried or bullied or in any way crossed. She talked to them as one would to an infant. When one of them butted, she said : " Oh, darling, that wasn't at all nice. No, really. . . ." But if the person who had been butted attempted to punish the animal, she protested : " Oh, don't do that. You'll hurt her. Oh, please don't."

The turquoise eyes seemed to glint at Shirley maliciously ; the horns arched back ; delicate white hooves stepped between horse-dung. Shirley pulled breathlessly. " Oh, come on ! " she pleaded aloud. " Oh, do come on ! " Her hands were red with tugging at the heavy chains. Then : " Oh, very well." She gave in, she abdicated. They could move when they wished to. She stood by them as they gobbled cow-parsley. As though the Day of Judgment were upon them, she thought ; not a moment lost. One of them choked, coughed, and broke wind. Shirley tried to pull them on, away from the aroma. But it could not be done. In their own time. . . .

Moonily, she looked about her. In one of the fields that Mrs. Humber let out they had already cut the oats and were now carting them away. The horse stamped dust upwards into the still air. Two men were working, not very expertly, stripped to the waist. Could it be . . . ? She screwed up her eyes, staring. Could it ? But, before she could decide, with one accord both goats jerked forward : the chains were tugged from her hands ; they were loose and away. With the sagacity of their species they made immediately for an uncut field of corn on their right and began to plough through it, tugging at random at the heavy ears. " Come back ! " Shirley shouted. " Come back ! Betty ! Phyllis ! Come back ! " She ran after them. But the animals veered away, with lowered horns and cries of rage or triumph. She was trampling the corn and they were trampling it. " Oh, dear," she said aloud. " Oh dear, oh dear."

" Don't worry. I'll catch them."

She shot round to find herself facing the man she had encountered when waiting for the bus. She had been right. It was he who was working with the cart in the other field. He again grinned, impressing her with that strange contrast of dark hair and light-blue eyes. He was badly sunburned, his shoulders peeling and white with calamine lotion. The hair on his chest gleamed with sweat.

Then began a lengthy pursuit, a series of ambushes, stealthy tracking. Shirley helped as best she could. But the sight of Mrs. Humber's corn filled her with fatalistic pessimism. Another hour—and what would have become of it? Would it all be trampled to nothing?

A yell of triumph, a boyish "Hoorah!" greeted her. The animals were trapped against a wall of brambles. With lowered heads they charged, but neatly he caught one and then the other by the horns. Though in actual practice an easy enough task, this final piece of bravado filled Shirley with admiration. She clapped her hands. "Oh, splendid!" she cried. "Oh, splendid!"

He brought the animals back to her. "They haven't done much damage. But goodness—what a chase! I'm not used to all that exercise." Down his face poured sweat.

She took the animals from him. "Thank you. Thank you so much. It really was most good of you."

"I'm afraid I didn't have a chance of introducing myself before. My name's Petrel—Claude Petrel." He spoke with the unnatural bluffness of so many schoolmasters. One can almost hear them saying: "Now come on, boys! This is fun. Wake up, all of you." His voice had the same ring, as though a coin were being thrown down defiantly.

"I'm Shirley Forsdike."

"Yes, Miss Forsdike. We've met once before, I think." Was he being malicious? The light-blue eyes turned innocently on her. "I am afraid—rather a *faux pas* on my part. . . . I thought . . ."

"My friend was very rude."

"She was protecting your honour."

She moved on a little with the goats to a clump of nettles. As she did so she scrutinised him, wondering who he was and where he had come from. He was certainly not a farmer, she decided. His corduroys were too sleek ; his hands, though dirty at the nails, too well kept.

" I'm staying here on holiday," she said.

" So am I—with my brood."

" Your brood ? "

" My children. I have five of them. Quite a handful. I'm sure you must have seen them—or heard them—already. We're at Ash Farm. . . . Do you like children ? "

" Very much."

" Then you must come and see mine. I think they're perfect."

" I should love to."

" Good." He scratched his chest with a dry, scraping sound. " Where do you live ? "

" Opposite. With Mrs. Humber. Just over there."

" May I ring you up ? "

" We have no telephone. Mrs. Humber hates them."

" No telephone ! " He seemed shocked, as though at some indecency. " Oh, never mind. I'll send one of the children round with a note."

" Thank you."

He returned to the cart and began once more to toss up the sheaves. From a gap in the hedge where she could not be seen she watched him for a long time, her eyes aching in the glare. The white animals cropped grass around her with sudden tugs. He worked with extraordinary zest—frenzy it seemed— tossing one sheaf after another ;. but there was no co-ordination. Then he stopped and wiped the sweat off his forehead. His body gleamed.

Outside the village store five children took it in turns to ride on a bicycle. The bicycle was too big : they had to stand up, the bar between their legs. Shirley passed them with a bag of apples she had just bought, and then turned back. The dark complexion and the light-blue eyes—she could not mistake the features.

" Hullo," she said.

" Hullo." With the absorption of children they took little notice of her. They were squabbling over whose turn it was to ride the bicycle. Their voices were shrill and clear ; the arms with which they snatched at it, sinewy.

" What are your names ? " she asked.

Visibly they drew into an arrogant little phalanx. " We're all Petrels," one of them said.

" I'm Miss Forsdike."

The eldest boy stared at her and then came forward. " I think I've got a note for you."

" For me ? Oh, thank you."

" Do you want to see it ? It's days old. Father gave it to me, and I forgot."

Shirley bridled. " Certainly I should like to see it."

The boy began to fumble in his trousers pockets, producing string, sweet-papers, nuts, and eventually a soiled scrap of paper.

It was an invitation to tea—four days ago.

Ash Farm had been taken over by a young man from Cambridge and 'renovated'. This meant that the old fireplaces had been bricked in and tiles replaced them ; a flush-closet was now used instead of the shed behind the kitchen ; and the walls were distempered a hygienic white. Similar changes were perceptible on the farm itself—tractors instead of horses, laundered smocks for milking, a battery for the hens.

The young man whose money had made all this possible answered Shirley's knock. Perpetually, there was a dewdrop on the end of his pointed nose ; a lock of hair hung limply on his forehead : he wore tweeds baggy at the knees, with a slit up the back.

" Yes ? " he asked.

" Is Mr. Petrel in ? "

" Claude ! I say—Claude ! "

Mr. Petrel appeared, pen in hand. " Ah, Miss Forsdike ! And how are the *lascivae capellae*. Your goats," he translated hurriedly. " Very Theocritean animals." Now that he was no longer stripped and ostensibly dressed as a labourer, but wore instead a white drill suit and a spotted bow-tie, he relapsed into the pomposity that was natural to him.

As so often happens when one has prepared a speech beforehand, word for word, Shirley took no notice of the question but rushed ahead : " You must think it awfully rude of me— the invitation, I mean. You see, it's only just been given to me. Your son forgot——"

" Invitation ? . . . Oh, that ! " Was it a pose, this bland dismissal ? She could not tell. " I gathered that you must be too busy—or otherwise engaged. Reggy is very forgetful. I shall have to speak to him."

" But I should have liked to come."

" Well—come now."

" Now ? "

" The tea is just made."

After half-hearted protestations he took her into a room where the young man was seated reading a book with a yellow Gollancz jacket. On a card-table were some small, round cakes, plain sponge, sprinkled with ' hundreds-and-thousands ', and six fingers of toast. The young man rose, pushing back the lock of hair.

" My cousin—Alex Penny. Miss Forsdike."

" Yerce," said the young man. " Pleased to meet you. Yerce." Their hands touched.

" Miss Forsdike keeps goats, Alex. Extraordinarily *classical*, really. The Greek Anthology. The Eclogues. That line, ' *Sed faciles Nymphae* . . .' You know the one." He chuckled richly to himself. But the young man was holding out a plate.

" Some toast ? " Apparently he took no notice of these erudite ramblings.

" You know, Miss Forsdike, I have a feeling that you're a school-mistress."

She blushed with chagrin. " Is it as obvious as all that ? "

" Oh, no. You mustn't take it as an insult. After all, I am myself—a compatriot—a colleague in misfortune, as they say. . . ."

" You teach ? " she queried.

He inclined his head. " You may call it that. Though whether I actually teach anybody anything . . . I lecture once a week to a class of a dozen or so men and women."

The young man cut in : " Claude is a professor. Some more toast ? " His boredom made Shirley think, " How rude he is ! " He had already handed her a cup of tea in which he had forgotten to put any milk. Being not entirely at her ease she did not mention the omission.

" Ah, yes," Mr. Petrel continued. " I'm a professor. The horrible truth is out. Which means that Miss Forsdike will now expect me to be absentminded and pedantic. 'Don dull, don brutish. . . .' How cruel that poem is ! Do you know, when I first read it, I thought : ' No, I can't go on. I simply can't go on. I shall have to throw the whole thing up. Let me become a porter—or a dock-hand. . . .' " Suddenly he broke off : Alex was about to take a third finger of toast. " I think that last piece is mine, isn't it ? . . . I *think* so." Alex withdrew.

All through tea he talked. Sometimes his conversation became merely a jumble of quotations ; few of his sentences were ever completed ; he had private jokes with himself, in Greek or Latin or Italian, at which he chuckled deeply. Alex lay supine in an armchair, his eyes on the ceiling, a pipe in his mouth. Sometimes he said " Yerce, yerce ", or began " The point is . . .". But the point was somehow lost in the heterodox forest of his cousin's learning.

Shirley was listening intently, her mouth slightly open,

as children's are before a peep-show. On occasions she nodded
her head. For a moment she was an audience ; and audiences
made Claud voluble. But then he wearied. No man can stand
his own success ; he was tired of impressing her. He abdicated
in favour of Cousin Alex, contenting himself with facetious
interjections—" That's it ! The dignity of labour ! " when
Alex said, " We must increase the birthrate ", and at the mention
of land taxes, " God for Harry, England, and St. George ! "

This last annoyed Alex particularly. A fanatical Georgist, he
snapped : " Oh, shut up, Claude ! " Georgism was his faith, as
Social Credit, Buchmanism, the Pyramids is the faith of others.
If only sufficient people accepted the taxation of land values, then,
with this one foundation, everything would fall into place, the
house of cards would cease to totter. This was the rock. . . .

Later the children came in with a governess to say good-night.
" Oh, *must* we go to bed ? " they protested. " It's still light."
Dutifully they kissed Claude's forehead and went grumblingly
upstairs. Later, they could be heard laughing, screaming, and
racing down the corridors. Claude rose : " That governess . . .
She lets them get out of hand. With my wife away . . . Do
please excuse me."

Shirley remained below with Alex, who talked of his plans
for the farm. " Of course, it doesn't pay yet. But it will.
It's been mismanaged for years and years, you know. . . ."
He had studied agriculture at Cambridge.

For the half-hour that Claude was away, the din of voices,
the thud of feet worked impetuously towards a *crescendo*. The
walls shook ; there was a crash of something falling over,
followed by howls of laughter. At intervals Alex raised his
eyebrows and said, " Really ! Those children ! "

Eventually Claude returned, re-tying his bow-tie and patting
the dust off his suit. His face was blotchy with perspiration :
he was out of breath. Chuckling, he exclaimed : " My word,
what a tussle ! What a rag ! Whew ! It makes me hot."

Shirley got up to go.

The lamps were lit, Mrs. Humber got out the old card-table whose baize was worn from green to grey, and they played cut-throat through the long evening. From next door came the clatter of china as the half-wit girl washed up. Round the glass funnel of the lamp beside them moths fluttered with a tick-tick of wings : there were smells of paraffin in the air, the atmosphere was dry and hot. In hands with bulging veins, whose cracks were grimed and rough, Mrs. Humber spread her cards. With two fingers she twisted her lower lip. Doris concentrated glumly. Shirley yawned through her nose, so that the nostrils dilated in tell-tale fashion.

Mrs. Humber said : " I meant to ask you where you went for your walk this afternoon. You were out a long time."

" I had an invitation to tea."

" To tea?" She looked up hungrily, almost with resentment. " But who with ? "

" Some people at Ash Farm."

Doris cut in : " Oh, Shirley ! That was the awful man who——"

" He isn't awful." She blushed, and in her confusion threw away a trump. " He's very nice, really. It was all a mistake——"

" How *could* you ? I know a pick-up——"

" Be quiet, Doris ! " Mrs. Humber clicked her cards together. " Why will you talk in this vulgar way ? . . . Go on, dear."

" Well—he caught the goats for me one day when they got loose—and—and he invited me to tea. That's all." It seemed a very lame story.

" Well, what's wrong in that ? " Mrs. Humber asked querulously, as though Shirley were not properly excited. " Very nice, too. . . . Who are the people ? "

Shirley explained, saying at intervals : " They're awfully kind. . . . He's a dear, really. . . . The children are quite sweet. . . . "

" Are they here for long ? " Mrs. Humber asked.

" Oh, no. Just for the holidays. Mrs. Petrel is away in Germany with her mother."

" Oh, I see. I was going to say that if they were permanents I'd go and call on them." She liked to keep up this fiction of ' calling ', though in fact it was a practice which she had dropped years ago simply because her calls were never returned.

" I'd like you to meet them ! "

" Yes," said Mrs. Humber. " Yes, do bring them over. He's a professor, you say ? And his cousin was at Cambridge ? Perhaps tea on Sunday. . . ." Her hand trembled with excitement.

Doris looked at her sardonically from beside the lamp.

Shirley was sketching the old windmill. Everyone who could sketch in those parts had, at some time or other, sketched the old windmill. It was ' picturesque '. People also went for picnics there : their cars filled the country lane, and their waste-paper littered the fields. But to-day, perhaps because there was a certain autumnal sharpness in the air, the place was deserted except for the small group of children who surrounded her easel. Whenever one sketched the mill these children, or other children like them, miraculously appeared to suck fingers behind one's back with noisy absorption.

" Charming," a voice suddenly murmured.

Shirley turned round to discover Mr. Petrel leaning on a walking-stick. His plump face had the shiny, rather rubbed, look of someone who has just shaved. Under his arm was *Mr. Norris Changes Trains*.

" Hullo."

" Hullo." He fingered his buttonhole in which was a red carnation.

" Have you been there along ? "

" For a full five minutes." He stooped over to examine the picture. " Ah, yes. A talent—a decided talent. I had no idea you were so accomplished a young lady. But allow me—a suggestion. . . ." He took the paint-brush from her unresisting fingers. " Those clouds. Wouldn't it be more—more adventurous, if you took the brush this way—sharply ? So." He demonstrated on a discarded piece of paper. Then seeing that she was not entirely satisfied : " Ah, yes," he continued. " I know what you think. The effect is ragged. But certainly it is. And isn't that the very thing that you want ? This is a ragged day. Look at those clouds once more. They are tattered surely ; they are torn to pieces. If you will accept criticism from . . . I am no artist myself—no executant. But as a dilettante—I have given some time to the study of painting. . . ."

Clumsily she began to take his advice. But now that she knew that he was there, watching, everything began to go wrong. The colours ran into each other, she spilled her water. He smiled, in vanity, at these little accidents. It pleased him that he had the power to confuse her merely by his presence.

" You must be more adventurous, Miss Forsdike. You must make the High Bid. But yes . . . I think that you are too afraid."

" Perhaps I am."

A little crossly she began to pack up her things.

The invitation came as a surprise. Meeting her out, he said : " I am going up to town for a day—on Wednesday. There are one or two exhibitions—the National Gallery, the Tate. . . . Knowing your interest in painting, I thought that perhaps . . . It seemed to me that if you saw what can be done with paint— the excitement of the thing—then . . . Well, you remember what I said about the need for boldness ? I should like to show you Cézanne—Matisse—Picasso, perhaps . . ." Through all this she waited, nodding, for the invitation to be formulated in so many words. " The question is—would you like to accompany me ? "

"Oh, I should love to!"

He frowned a little, as though to discourage so obvious a show of enthusiasm. "Good. That's settled, then. Excellent. The only thing is . . ." He took her arm, confidentially. "I would rather . . . People talk so . . . Perhaps you had better not mention to your friends . . . A visit to the dentist, say . . . A sick relative. I leave it to you."

She nodded sagaciously. He was, she realised, afraid of scandal.

Shirley was accustomed to travel third-class. But on this occasion, without consulting her, he bought two first-class tickets. Putting one into her hand he said, "Thirteen-and-six". The hint was unmistakable. Apparently this was a 'Dutch' treat. She took the money from her bag and gave it to him.

When they were settled in an empty carriage, and he had chosen his place and crossed his legs and turned the heater from medium to full, he opened the portfolio which was the only luggage he had brought and took out the *Spectator* and the *New Statesman and Nation*. As he spread them on his knee he murmured : "Twin guardians of the Faith. So beautifully complementary. The *Statesman* is perhaps a little too—too *critical* for my tastes. While the *Spectator* . . . A certain dullness. But read together . . ." He put his glasses on his nose.

Shirley opened the *Strand Magazine*.

"No, no!" he exclaimed at the restaurant. "That's quite the wrong choice. You must have the Crêpe Suzette. Two Crêpe Suzette, waiter." Apparently he ignored the fact that Crêpe Suzette was three shillings more expensive.

At the end of the meal he said : "Let me see. Thirty-two shillings. That's sixteen each. Plus two shillings in tips. You owe me seventeen shillings." Dutifully she paid, wondering how soon she would find her purse empty. She dreaded the moment of having to say : "I'm afraid I've run out of money."

At the National Gallery he suddenly whispered to her, "Just run along for a minute." And because she looked at him in bewilderment he repeated, in a cross, high-pitched voice, "Oh, run along, do!" Then, as soon as she had left him, he turned smiling to a woman a few feet off: "My dear, what are you doing here?" Shirley stared, blushing, at an Old Master.

A few minutes later he tapped her on the shoulder. "I'm sorry I had to shoo you off like that. A friend. A friend of my wife's. . . . It would have been rather embarrassing to make introductions." As though to console her he took her arm.

After he had shown her all the things that he wanted to show her they sat down on a bench to rest. "You know," he said suddenly. "I don't believe you *really* liked any of those pictures. Did you?" He sounded petulant.

"Oh, but I did," she said, miserable at her failure. "But I did."

"Be truthful."

"I am being truthful."

He shrugged his shoulders and got up. "Now for the Tate," he said, as though he were faced with an ordeal. "Afterwards, we can have tea."

She had not been properly appreciative, she decided. From then on she exclaimed, "Oh, lovely!" at every picture that he made her stop at. She was determined to please him at any cost. But when he hurried her past a picture by Mancini she stopped dead, staring, saying nothing. "Oh, come on!" he protested. "You don't want to waste time on old Mancini. Here—look at this Derain." But she did not move.

He came back irritably. "Do you really like it?" he asked.

"Yes. Very much."

"All right," he murmured, as though he were giving her permission to indulge in so curious a taste. "Well, why not? I used to like him once. Of course, it's all rhetoric—bombast. . . . Would you like to paint like that?" She did not answer, and he continued: "He might be rather a good antidote to your artistic timidity. He's bold enough. The palette-knife being mightier than the brush . . ."

In silence they stood before the canvas. Then she said, half-bemused : " But it would take so much paint."

He laughed, not very pleasantly. " Good heavens ! One doesn't think of that."

" I've had very little practice in oils. Water-colours are so much cheaper. But I should like to try—like that. Yes, I should like to try."

" And so you shall," he exclaimed, hurrying her on to the Derain. Her whim had been indulged sufficiently he thought.

After they had ' done ' the whole Gallery he said : " I really wanted to go to Gunther's for tea. But there are sure to be a number of people I know there. Perhaps we had better go to the Corner House. I don't want to be seen. . . ."

In complete humility she replied : " If you like, you could go to Gunther's and I could go somewhere else. Then we could meet afterwards."

" Oh, no ! " he protested, as though shocked. " I wouldn't dream of such a thing. After all——"

" But why not ? " she pursued, at last seeing an opportunity for doing the right thing. " I have some shopping to do. I'll meet you on the platform at Liverpool Street."

" Oh. Very well." He acceded, as though he were making some concession to her. " If you like."

Alone, she sipped lukewarm tea over a smeared marble-top table.

Doris began to irritate her. She suddenly became aware that she was ungainly, and bit her nails, and showed absurd, childish enthusiasm. The sight of her in flannel pyjamas, sagging and cow-like, while her rump protruded and her ugly bare feet flopped as she walked, filled Shirley with a desire to hurt her at all costs. When she took Shirley's arm, Shirley now pulled away with : " It's far too hot." She became conscious of her foetid, animal smell and the purplish acne on her chin.

That afternoon they quarrelled. Shirley was painting a tray and Doris came and lent over her. Her hair tickled Shirley's neck, so that she moved her chair forwards and bent over the work with even greater absorption. The contact made her feel black and rather sick with revulsion. Then Doris straightened and sat down on the edge of the table. " You are clever," she said.

" Am I ? "

" Let me help you." She leant towards Shirley, intending to hold the tray. But clumsily, her thumb went into a lacquer rose, smudging it.

" Oh, look ! Oh, look what you've done ! "

" I'm sorry."

" You've spoiled the whole thing ! Oh, really, Doris ! "

" Couldn't you paint it in again ? Couldn't you ? "

She must control herself. With set lips she tried to mend the damage. But a moment later an arm rested on her shoulder, a cheek was pressed against hers. " I'm sorry, dear. Truly I am. I'm awfully clumsy, I know."

" Do leave me alone ! "

" Shirley ! "

" I'm sick—— "

Suddenly they were wrangling acrimoniously. Until, in a spasm of rage, Shirley struck out at Doris. Tears followed. Mrs. Humber ran in. " What *is* the matter ? . . . Oh, Doris, do control yourself. Go into the tool-shed, or something. This noise gets on my nerves. Control yourself, do ! "

Choking, Doris went up to her bedroom. Shirley went out for a walk. She knew that she had been in the wrong.

The house was said to be haunted. There was no reason why it should be so. Badly built at the end of the Victorian age, it had gradually begun to slip down the hill it had been intended to surmount ; the walls cracked ; parts of it fell in ; until, in irritation, the owner had gone off to the South of France and left it to wind, rain, and the curiosity of visitors. Facing squarely on to a drive that was now so overgrown that garden and path were simply one, a jungle of dock and bramble and willow-herb, it was crossed diagonally by a single great fissure. The windows were out ; locks had been removed by the thrifty villagers ; people had broken in and scrawled childish obscenities on the walls. There was a yellow patch beside the fireplace where someone had urinated.

Shirley passed the house, miserable at her behaviour towards Doris, and then turned back and went in. There were dry acrid smells ; a beetle was ticking in the woodwork ; she recoiled as a spider's web stuck to her face, and then brushed it away with frantic hands. Although she had heard it was dangerous to do so, she began to climb the stairs, making them creak at each footfall. On the first landing someone had carved in the woodwork : " Abandon hope all ye that . . ." Then it broke off, and there was a heart with initials in it. Farther on her eye was caught by a picture which had somehow survived the owner's removal and the depredations of visitors. It was the photograph of a Greek statue, a boy : the frame was smashed, and some wag had filled in dark patches of hair, making the whole thing seem somehow animal and depraved. For no reason Shirley thought : I shall take it away. But when she raised it on its nails a bat blundered out with a whirr of wings ; there was a moist smear beneath. She started back, letting the frame clatter into place.

Now the stairs became so dark that she had to fumble her way, lighting matches at intervals. She was terrified of falling into nothing. Her groping hand struck a door ; the knuckles were bruised at the impact. Opening it, timidly, she recoiled from a blaze of light. It was here that the roof had fallen in, leaving a jagged crater through which poured the rich afternoon sun. It was wonderful, this high room, over-arched by the sky.

Shirley stood in it for a long time, feeling, after the clammy touch of the passages, the warmth of the sunshine and the syrupy air. Looking out of one of the windows she could see far, far away the river curling through the flat Norfolk country ; while nearer, to her right, was Ash Farm and Mrs. Humber's and some children who were bowling an old tyre as a hoop. About her twittered larks, like fish swimming through an azure ocean. She sighed with pleasure and contentment.

Then she began to walk round the room, feeling the mouldy woodwork of the fireplace, and the walls whose plaster had peeled, and the jagged edges of bricks with oddly sensitive fingers. For once, she was using her sense of touch. The different roughnesses, surfaces now dry, now moist, filled her with extraordinary pleasure. Her nails picked at some loose cement.

In one corner of this room was a built-in cupboard, before which had fallen a girder and some bricks. She pushed them aside and opened it. Then she drew back with a brief shudder, a muffled "Oh !" Inside was a dead rat, lying on its belly, its eyes rheumy, its legs stuck out. She stared at it for a while, as her nostrils filled with the smells of putrefaction. Then, putting out a foot, she flicked it over with the point of her shoe. Disclosed, the belly was a mass of writhing maggots, crawling over each other. The smell became almost intolerable.

At the sight she screamed and rushed for the door. In sudden, inexplicable panic she tore down the stairs, as though pursued. She did not cease running until she reached the gate. There she pulled up and leant on the post, feeling an overmastering need to retch. Perhaps she would have retched if a voice had not said : "You look as if you'd seen the ghost. Have you ?" It was Mr. Petrel, with an empty sack on his back.

"Oh, no," she said. "The house was just rather eerie. That's all." For some reason she did not wish to tell him about her discovery. The carcase festering in that high, wonderful

room seemed more obscene to her than the crude markings of
the statue of the Greek boy or the yellow stain by the fireplace.

" Do you believe in ghosts ? "

She thought of her father, and shook her head. " I don't
think so. Do you ? "

" Sometimes. . . . But fancy your going into that place
alone ! That was rather brave of you."

She moved off beside him as he continued on his way.
" Where are you going ? " she asked.

" I'm going gleaning," he said. " Apparently, once a
field is cut and raked, we have the right to go in and collect
what we can. Extraordinarily Biblical, you know. Ruth and
so forth. . . . ' Amid the alien corn. . . .' Why don't you
come too ? "

" I should love to."

Later, they passed Doris, walking alone, her face puffy and
disfigured with tears. Sometimes she lunged outwards with
one hand to pull the tops off wayside flowers. She pretended
not to notice them. But Shirley, suddenly contrite, said,
" Hullo, Doris. We're going gleaning. Why don't you join
us ? "

For a moment she was determined to sulk. " No, thank
you," she snapped.

" Oh, do ! "

Shirley's pleading was sufficient to break her glum expression
into smiles. " Very well," she concurred, falling in beside
them. Soon she was laughing gaily.

Claude arranged everything. " We must have a rota,"
he said. " We must do the thing methodically." So while one
of them did the actual gleaning, another severed the heads
from the stalks, and a third sat out. Every ten minutes they
changed round. Claude also said : " Let's see who can collect
most heads in the ten minutes." He had a natural liking for
competition.

He was wearing a large straw hat which he had bought from a peasant in the south of France ; it was one of the small eccentricities that he allowed himself. Over the field the sun blazed hotly ; Doris had been bitten by harvest bugs and stopped at intervals to scratch herself. Soon she began to flag ; after the scene with Shirley she had had a nervous headache, which the glare now revived. Eventually she said : " I think I'm going to give up now. This sun is so hot. . . ." On her nose were minute bubbles of sweat, like small ulcers. There was straw in her hair. Under each arm spread great damp circles.

Alone, Claude and Shirley worked on for nearly an hour more. He had taken off his shirt, and she noticed that he was no longer sunburned in raw patches but had turned a violet-brown. He was rather proud of this achievement, and of his physique as a whole—not unnaturally, considering his age.

Then, when the early autumn evening began to draw around them, and bicycles passed along the lane bound for ' cooked tea ' and Saturday variety, he said : " Let's sit down for a bit ". Together, they placed themselves on the coat he had taken off, in a corner of the field. For once, he was silent ; until, suddenly, he murmured : " Shirley ! Funny little Shirley ! " He slipped an arm round her waist and drew her towards him : then they both lay back, their eyes fixed on the garlands of cloud above them. As he lay like this, with her so close to him, his stomach receded, falling inwards, so that in the gap between it and his trousers she could look down and see, with curiosity, the place where his pubic hair touched his navel. He began to caress her, without much intimacy, her face pressed against his bare ribs. Then he got up, and again said, with a smile : " Shirley ! Funny little Shirley ! " She did not rise, but looked up at him with a hungry gaze.

He put on his straw hat and threw the shirt that he had removed over his arm and the sack over his shoulder. Then he said : " Good-bye, Shirley ", and she murmured, " Good-bye ". At the end of the field he stopped to wave to her before he disappeared.

It seemed, then, as she lay there, her heart pumping blood into her face and hands and feet until they tingled, that at last her father's photograph had spoken and the sign had been given. She could not explain this. But she felt it to be so. And because for so long it had been withheld, and because she had despaired of it, the miracle brought tears to her eyes. She stretched out on the grass, and touched the earth, and thought, at that moment, that it was good.

In the late evening how beautiful the countryside seemed ! The sky, curving immeasurably like a chalice, was rinsed with amber light, while on the still air eddies of smoke swam upwards for it to cense. In the valley the leaves were turning, so that it seemed as if each tree had been gilded, as a benediction, by the great sun before it dipped beneath the horizon. From the river rose a pink flush of mist through which wandered lovers and noisy boys. There were rooks circling, and gulls from the estuary ; and birds chattered and fluttered from bush to bush with a crepitation of wings, uncertain where to rest finally, before night-fall. In the fields that undulated downwards they had sown spring cabbages : in vertical lines of green, the small shoots marked the dun soil. Bicycles whirred past, and dogs barked in the distance, and from the cottages came sounds of voices. Smells there were too, priming the dying air, of elder and wild mint and wood-smoke.

All this she apprehended with her five senses : and it filled her with exaltation. She discovered then what she had so long sought for and would never discover again. She realised at that moment that life was no more than this ; that to live, as she had so longed to live, was not to be visited by special miracles ; that it was no more than this recurring miracle ' I exist '. The secret of life was in those two words, and not in her father or her religion or in General Weigh. ' I exist ' : for all things this should be sufficient.

Contentment fell about her like a cloak. Nothing could shatter the crystal ; at that moment it was flawless. Only for a second she thought of the carcase in that high, wonderful room, her tower. But even this memory was as nothing before the reposing landscape, in which blended all sounds, all smells, all people. She walked slowly homewards : nor did she see Mrs. Humber lurching as she carried vast steaming pails of mash to the hens.

All that week it had rained. Prematurely, the year was waning, as the eaves dripped, and the goats pulled morosely at hay in their stalls, and Mrs. Humber marched to and fro in an old army greatcoat with a sou'wester on her head. Everything became suddenly damp ; the walls sweated, there was mildew on the bread. Clothes hung perpetually on the line in the kitchen, brushing one's face if one tried to cross without raising them. The water-meadows, where a week ago there had been picnics and bathers, were now flooded. Over the house hung a warm mist through which fell the rain.

They were sitting together after supper in the drawing-room. Mrs. Humber played patience at a small table on which she had set a lamp. Doris and Shirley read before the first fire of the autumn ; the wood was still green and it sizzled. As it was Sunday their supper had been cold and unappetising : in their mouths was the sour taste of pickles and cheese.

Doris got up, stretched, and went across to her mother. Leaning over her with that peculiar persuasiveness which always infuriated Shirley she murmured, "Red knave on black queen."

" Oh, Doris, don't ! It makes the game absolutely pointless if you help me. If you're really interested, take these cards and begin on your own." But already Doris had moved away sulkily and gone to the window. Turning back the blind she stared into the humid twilight. " It's still raining," she sighed.

7

" Does it *ever* do anything else ? Rain, rain, rain. I'm sick of it." She yawned and stretched, in so exaggerated a fashion that her blouse came away from her skirt and showed beneath the pink vest which she herself had knitted. " This time next week we'll be back in the old hole again."

Shirley looked up. " Oh, don't ! Must you be so gloomy ? "

" I don't know that I shall be so sorry. It gives one something to do."

" There's plenty to do here," said Mrs. Humber grimly.

Doris took no notice of her. " If it goes on raining like this for the rest of the time God knows how we shall amuse ourselves. I'm sick of reading, and knitting bores me stiff."

" It doesn't really worry me."

" Of course, it doesn't—at the moment. Not while you've got the Petrels. But after to-morrow——"

" After to-morrow ? "

Something in Shirley's manner made Doris hesitate. " Haven't you heard ? " she asked. " Didn't he tell you ? "

" Tell me ? Tell me what ? "

" Well, it may just be hearsay," Doris said hurriedly. " Mrs. Nibbs, who does for them, told me when I was down in the village. Apparently Mr. Petrel had a row with his cousin last night, and they've decided to leave."

" But it can't be true. Why, I—I saw him only this morning. We went for a walk together."

" Then, in that case——" Doris shrugged her shoulders.

Mrs. Humber looked up crossly. " Really, Doris, I don't know how you get hold of half these stories. You're becoming an awful little gossip."

But Shirley was thinking, a nausea filling her until she could hardly bear it. Somehow, she had known all along that he was leaving. Even this morning she had known it. But the idea had been dismissed by her as fanciful. So he had decided to go without telling her. It was the only conclusion she could come to. He had decided to sneak off.

In sudden decision she rose to her feet and went into the hall.
Mrs. Humber called after her : " Where are you off to, dear ? "
" I'm just going for a stroll." No one said anything further.
Turning up the collar of her mackintosh she walked into the
rain.

It was dark, and at first she lost her way. But eventually
she succeeded in blundering up the drive of Ash Farm and
knocking on the door. Everything was silent except for the
monotonous hush-hushing of the rain and the scrape of her
shoes. She stood under an ornamental porch from which ivy
dripped water with the sound of invisible kissing. She was
shivering, but whether with cold or anticipation she could not
tell.

There was no answer, and again she knocked, so that the
sound reverberated dully. A window opened above and a
head appeared. " Who's that ? " a voice asked crossly. It was
Claude Petrel.

" Me—Shirley Forsdike."

" Shirley Forsdike ! "

The rain trickled down her face as she turned it up to look
at him. " Could you please come down ? " she asked. " I
must see you."

" No, really," he protested. " We're all in bed. We were
all asleep. I really can't come down at this hour. Can't you
wait till to-morrow ? "

" Oh, please come down ! "

The window slammed shut ; there was the sound of someone descending. Then the door was unbolted and he stood
before her in pyjamas and dressing-gown. His hair was dishevelled, he rubbed his eyes and yawned. " What is it ? " he
asked.

" I had to see you," she said. " I simply had to see you.
They told me you were going away—to-morrow."

He did not ask her in. From the lighted hall he spoke to

her as she stood out in the rain. "Yes," he said. "My cousin and I—a final flare-up. . . . We've been getting on each other's nerves quite a lot recently."

"But why didn't you tell me?"

"Tell you?" He looked at her with surprise. Then he changed rapidly: "But what would have been the use?" he asked. "What would have been the use? I hate good-byes. They're horrible. Far better to behave as if nothing were going to happen. Don't you see, it's so much easier for all concerned." He took her moist hand in his own. "Believe me when I say that I was thinking of you in this. I shouldn't like to see you unhappy. As it is, we had such a lovely last walk. . . . It'll make a much better memory than if we had both been lachrymose."

"Where are you going?"

"Back to the university. My wife will be home to-morrow."

"You'll write?"

Drawing her into the hall he said: "Now look, Shirley, my dear. This has been an idyll. I'm going to be sentimental and call it that. It *has* been an idyll, in this lovely spot, away from it all. But like most idylls it must be brief. It must finish now. If it dragged on it would lose its idyllic quality. It would merely become a sordid *affaire*. Let's keep it as it is."

Tearfully she protested: "But I *must* see you again. I can't bear it if——"

"Shirley! Shirley please! Try to see it as I see it. You wouldn't like a hole-in-the-corner *affaire*——?"

"Anything! Anything! I can't lose you! I can't!" She clutched on to his arm, desperately, while a pool of water widened at her feet.

"Steady, Shirley! . . . If you don't mind my saying it, it's rather different for you. You see, I've got my children—my career——"

In sudden contempt she shouted: "If that's all you think about——!"

" Sh ! " He gripped her wrist, his patience at an end. Then with deliberate restraint he countered : " My children and my career may not seem awfully important to you. But to me . . . I'm sorry, but they are. I love my children. . . . And my wife. . . . I'm very attached to her. I'm too old now and too settled to think of breaking loose."

" Not to break loose ! " she protested. " But couldn't we see each other—sometimes. . . ."

" No," he said firmly. " No. That's exactly what we mustn't do. That would be worse than if we lived together. Then the whole thing would peter out, horribly. No. We must make an end now. I shall always be grateful to you : I shall always remember you. But——" Her head had fallen on to his arm ; she was weeping loudly, without restraint. For a while he let her be : then gently, decisively, he made her straighten up. " I think you'll see in the end that this way is best. Really it is."

" I—can't—bear—it ! " she sobbed again.

" Good-bye, Shirley."

She stiffened, choked, was silent. " Good-bye."

Stooping down he kissed her wet face, on the forehead, cupping it in both hands. Then he turned away, with a gesture of resignation, and began to mount the stairs. Without his knowing it she watched him. At the landing, before going into his room, he did something which filled her with a grim and devouring nausea : he yawned and stretched.

Doris met her at the door. " You do look done in, dear. Come up to bed." She helped her off with her things and then, arm-in-arm, they ascended together. Without mentioning the matter Doris had guessed what had happened. " Do you feel very bad ? " she asked, when Shirley had thrown herself on to her bed. " Do you ? " There was no answer but a muffled sob. Outside the rain still swished downwards. " Here—I'll get you something to put you right." She went out to her own

room and returned with a pill : she collected patent medicines.
" Swallow this, dear," she said, stooping over Shirley, a tumbler
of water in her hand. " You'll feel much better afterwards."

Shirley drew away. But Doris put an arm round her and
drew her up to a sitting posture, and turned the red and tear-
stained face to the light. " Do swallow it," she pleaded. And
Shirley, simply because it seemed the best way to get rid of her,
took what she offered and swallowed it.

Then a strange thing happened. At the touch of the pill on
her tongue she was transferred, backwards, into childhood ;
and she was in Barbizon ; and Cousin Maurice had given her a
menthol tablet ; and her father was just dead.

PART IV

TO THE DARK TOWER

To be a tutor is to be something between a family friend and a domestic servant. As soon as Frank Cauldwell had seated himself at the table Mrs. Maccabae called out : " Frank ! I say, Frank ! Could you come here a moment ? " She stood in the doorway of her room in a pink shift, out of which protruded her thin, bluish arms. Behind, was her personal maid, holding a chiffon tea-gown, an absurd affair of frills and ribbons.

" Yes ? "

" I wonder—*could* you—would you be an angel and bicycle over to Mrs. Trent for me ? Cook's gone and smashed the percolator. And coffee's so horrid made any other way. If you *could* borrow Mrs. Trent's——" Then, seeing his sulky expression : " Yes, I know it's Sunday, my dear. I'd send one of the maids, if the woman weren't so damnably fussy. I thought that you might be able to charm her into letting us have it. She won't be able to resist you."

This was sheer flattery, and Frank knew it. He stared for a moment at the pretty, cajoling face, whose eyebrows were pencilled lines above glistening mascara-ed eyes, before he said : " Oh, very well," in a voice intended to show that he was cross. But no sooner had he reached the hall than she shouted to him once more. " Frank ! Frank, dear ! One other thing. If Captain Carbo doesn't turn up—could you—*could* you possibly make a fourth at bridge ? The usual agreement." The usual agreement was that whatever he lost to her guests she paid. At first his pride had rebelled against this ; but playing at five shillings a hundred on a salary of three pounds a week he had learnt wisdom.

" Oh, all right." Hastily he slammed the door before she had time to impose any further on him. Was it worth it ? he wondered, bicycling through what Mrs. Maccabae called ' the demesne ' after a brief visit to Ireland : it was really little more than two or three paddocks, on which she had had planted tufts of spruce and laurel because they grew so quickly. Dinner would be as dull as the guests. He would eat food which cook had somehow depersonalised out of the most exciting ingredients. He would meet the usual guests. There would be the minor official from a foreign embassy ; two débutantes of the kind whose parents wonder if they can possibly do it on three hundred pounds ; an artist whose sole claim to notice would be either that he had illustrated a book for children or was going to do a mural for the third-class saloon of the newest luxury liner ; some City friends of Mr. Maccabae ; a writer whose work had been privately printed and had otherwise only appeared in university magazines ; and a heterogeneous collection of women who told you that they ran things, or were on things, or simply : " I'm still at home."

Was it worthwhile ? His predecessor had thought not. Was it worth enduring these hours of limitless boredom, merely for the sake of a room to oneself, and physical comfort, and regular meals ? The conversational " Have-you-read's ", and " Have-you-seen's " ; the " Of-course,-he's-extraordinarily-brilliant " ; the reminiscences of " When-I-saw-Isadora-Duncan ", and " It-really-was-rather-sordid " ; the recurring Leavis-Eliot-Sitwell theme which might even become Coward-Maugham-Gershwin : was it really better than the bank, and the boy's club that he had worked at, and starving among the gentilities of Edith Villas ? Then there was Mrs. Maccabae herself. For how long would he tolerate that girlish archness ? It was her habit to make sudden confessions which would throw her guests into paroxysms of " Did-you-ever ", " Oh-isn't-Gugs-too-quaint ". For example, when they were discussing Mr. Macarthy's last article in the *Sunday Times*

Mrs. Maccabae exclaimed : " Now I'm going to tell you all a secret—a rather shameful one ", and everyone, in expectation of another of her notorious pieces of ' wit ', followed the lead of her husband and cried : " What is it, Gugs ? Oh, *do* tell us ! *Do* tell us ! " Coyly she looked round at the assembled guests. " Well, you mustn't think me very silly. But the person whose novels I'm simply crazy about at the moment is—Ruby M. Ayres ! " " How *could* you ? Oh, you *can't*, Gugs. No, really, Gugs. . . ." Amid shrieks of laughter they savoured to the full this cultural impropriety. " But I do," she insisted. " The last one I read was *utterly* divine. It was called *Rose's Secret*." (In actual fact she had never opened any of Miss Ayres' books. She had seen *Rose's Secret* on the housemaid's chest of drawers.)

On another occasion it would be : " George's friend, Lord Tavenham, sent us this salmon from Scotland." " And very good it is, too," murmured some appreciative guest. " Yes, I suppose it is. But, do you know—it's awful to say this—but really, *I prefer tinned salmon*." And again there would be the exclamations of laughter, an atmosphere of " What-will-she-do-next ? "

Was it worth while ? Was it really easier to write his book among these vulgarities than in discomfort? He often wondered.

Returning to his room he found his thread lost, he could not continue. In anger he looked about him, at the disordered table on which lay notes, letters from the General, the cheque which the General had surprisingly sent when he was ill and penniless in Glasgow and which something, some scruple, had prevented him cashing. Then he stood at the photograph beside his bed, the woman whom someone else had married, her head severed from her neck where he and the General had torn it, so long ago, at Dartmouth. Finally he gazed out of the window. His charges, the two sickly, flaxen-haired boys played their tranquil, adult games on the lawn. Did even they make it worth while ?

Oh, damn, damn !

7*

All that afternoon it had rained : she had taught the girls how to make raffia paper-rings, and later the headmistress had read from *The Wind in the Willows*. The net-ball match had had to be cancelled. But now, as she walked from Earl's Court Underground station towards the Cromwell Road, a suit-case of exam papers in her hand, the sun was oozing thinly through a sieve of smoke, the pavements glistened, and a few birds chirped on blackened boughs in the gardens of squares. The air, too, was strangely sweet and fresh.

She lived in one of the many boarding-houses that flank the Cromwell Road. Three tall, Italianate houses had been knocked into one : and then, as though to bind them together, there had been fixed over their front, in round gold letters, " Bristol Hotel ". The proprietress had been the wife of a tea-planter in Burma ; but he had died or somehow got mislaid ; and now she sat in her basement sitting-room, among brass ornaments, photographs of big-game parties, and Egyptian mats that were nailed to the walls. Her clients were young couples home on leave from the colonies, travellers, clerks, and professional women : there were also old ladies, retired Army officers, and a German student whom they all disliked.

As Shirley climbed the stairs she passed a bust of His Majesty King George the Fifth, which remained perpetually grey in spite of innumerable housemaids and innumerable feather dusters following each other through the years. On the landing Captain Timpson, coming out of the lavatory, winked at her broadly : but she hurried on, not so much from disapproval as from boredom at a manœuvre which was repeated again and again without sequel. The lavatory had a stained-glass window and a notice : " Guests are asked not to put hair or tea-leaves down the closet."

Her room was at the top of the house, with a view into somebody else's room in an adjoining hotel. The net curtains were always kept drawn. She sat down on the bed, took off her shoes, and wriggled her toes. Then she yawned and stretched out at full length, forgetting that she was crumpling the bed-spread. The proprietress had had to speak about this before.

At that moment the gong went, reverberating dismally down a whole scale as the maid thumped one of the dangling pipes and then another. She was about to begin again when the proprietress passed and said, " That will do, Ellen ", in the same voice that she said " That will do " when Ellen made the helpings too big. Shirley sat up and then sank back again. Down the corridor she could hear a patter of feet, an opening and closing of doors. " It's the early bird . . ." as Captain Timpson was in the habit of remarking : and acting on this advice he was always seated in the dining-hall at least five minutes before time. He read the *Star*, drank water, and tried to break his roll. But for once Shirley did not join the genteel scurry, with polite " After you's " and insidious short-cuts through the bedrooms of friends. She thought of descending, and how at each step the aroma of cabbage became stronger and stronger ; and how, when she entered, Captain Timpson winked, from force of habit, and the proprietress fished into the casserole for a portion of rabbit, and one of the two old ladies with whom she had made friends patted a chair and chirruped : " This is my friend's seat ! This is my friend's seat ! " Oh, no, it was horrible ; she could not face it. She put on her shoes again, and soaped the ladder which was lengthening in her stocking, and took a violet cachou ; then she powdered her nose, pulled on a hat which had now been remodelled three times, and went out. She had no idea where she was going.

If one goes out in London after eight o'clock without any idea of where one is going, it is likely that the force of gravity will drag one to the West End. Shirley stood on the escalator and watched the theatre notices ; interspersed with them were advertisements for restaurants ; and these reminded her that she had eaten nothing since that welsh rabbit at the A.B.C. She set off for Soho, hungry and rather depressed.

Before she had gone very far she felt so faint that she had to

lean against a wall ; the wall being the wall of a pub she decided
to go in for some brandy. What she saw inside surprised her.
Six months ago this pub had been ' discovered ' ; no doubt
in another six months it would be abandoned ; but at the
moment it was enjoying a hey-day. The old customers had
dwindled to two of three taciturn cab-drivers, wedged between
groups of art students, writers, and ' characters '. Like a
common plant which has been crossed with a rarity the pub was
producing its exotic blooms ; later, no doubt, it would revert.

While she was waiting to be served she began to feel better :
so that when, at last, she was asked for her order she said not
brandy but beer. Beer was cheap. At the far end of the room
six tables had been half screened off by two velvet curtains
which were clasped in dusty festoons. Here other little groups
had congregated ; there was a woman with a writing-tablet
and pencil ; an Indian did tricks with a pack of cards ; two
elderly men read a paper together. Shirley made for one of the
tables which appeared to be vacant ; but as she pulled out a
chair she noticed that a youth was already seated there, concealed
by the curtain. Blushing, she apologised, and went to another.

She began to sip the frothy, bitter concoction ; she had never
liked beer. Feeling, among these chatting cliques, that she
was hopelessly out of it, forsaken, unwanted, she adopted the
attitude of most people in such circumstances ; consciously she
set about despising them. The young man concealed by the
curtain : how odd he looked with the crop of pimples round his
mouth and the ring which was shaped as a skull ! He was
reading a book by someone whom she took to be German—
Hölderlin : she spelled out the word on the cover ; and as he
read he jingled the coins in his trousers pocket. Further on,
there was a girl in slacks talking to an elderly woman with a
moustache : the conversation was entirely of the " I-said-to
him-he-said-to-me " variety. And the sad, thin man with the
dyspeptic face who sipped sherry wryly. Out of his coat
pocket stuck a child's doll.

But she couldn't do it ; instead of despising she began to envy them. They all seemed so self-possessed ; even the sad, elderly man seemed to know his destination. While she . . . She belched. The beer was going to her head. In a stupor she sat for a long time, turning and turning her glass, while the dusty curtains seemed to close in like an impenetrable wall, and a young man with a bracelet on his wrist crossed and recrossed her vision, and the tears began to prick at the corner of her eyes. She felt slightly sick, and empty. But she could not go out and eat ; she had not the will. The atmosphere of smoke and talk thickened ; the man who was reading Hölderlin suddenly snapped the book shut and began to squeeze one of his pimples into a black-and-white check handkerchief ; a girl went round with a tray and collected glasses. There were many voices, many faces, and yet she was lonely.

But her loneliness was changing, imperceptibly, even as she thought how lonely she was. For no reason she was becoming curiously excited. Perhaps it was only the effect of the alcohol, but she had the feeling that she was waiting here for something decisive to happen. It seemed as if all life had been a preparation, a fumbling ; but now the key would turn, the door would open, there would be singing ; the dove would break the turgid air ; the curtain would put on leaves. Now, soon : the hour was moving to its climax ; and all things would be transfigured ; and all things would be new.

This sensation of inexorable climax was too much. She could not sit here and wait ; she must go out. As she walked to the door she tripped over the feet of the young man with Hölderlin ; but she did not notice it, and he only scowled. Out in the street, in the violet twilight, she stood, swaying a little ; and far away there scurried a furtive chime of bells ; and again bells chimed, nearer, with broad-shouldered chords ; and she thought : " Now, now."

On the other side of the street a man in uniform came from under the awning of a restaurant and walked away, his back to her. Dizzily she ran forward, the tears trickling down her cheeks; she made no attempt to staunch them. The clock in the hollow tower had struck. It was General Weigh, she was certain of it.

She clutched at his sleeve with: "Oh, stop. Oh, please stop. I had to . . ." But a young lieutenant was staring at her with a pink, clean-shaven face on which were stuck two shreds of cotton-wool where he had cut himself. He was very drunk. "All right," he said thickly. "All right." She tried to break away, but he caught her against the wall, his knee stuck grotesquely between her legs, pinioning her. She screamed, high and clear, and struck out at him; struggling, her hat fell off. "Let me go! Let me go!" But already he had taken fright; she was free.

People were collecting. She pushed her way through them and began to run, on, on, till she reached Green Park, and then Hyde Park, and at last Kensington Gardens. At Kensington Gardens she was sick outside the gates; she could not get in.

So again she found herself climbing the stairs, as she had climbed them once before that evening; but fortunately this time neither Captain Timpson nor any other of the residents passed her. Coming to her room she once more stretched on the bed and closed her eyes, and thought: How long? How long? It seemed then as if she only were doomed; as if she only were that wanderer between two worlds, the one dead, the other powerless to be born. She saw herself as an ambitious phantom, moving restlessly between the ranks of the living. What was the miracle that would give her life? What was the oblation, the ritual.

She thought: Why did I scream then? Why did I run away? If only she knew what she wanted! If she knew that, she might be able to achieve it. But she wandered through dark corridors; she climbed interminable stairs; and there was nothing but the darkness, the endless journeying. Oh, would she

never reach the high wonderful room, into which poured sunlight and bird-song ? Oh, would she never ascend the hollow
tower ? The dusty, velvet curtains dulled all sounds ; they
closed impenetrably ; and the sediment in her glass left a sour
taste in the mouth ; and though she talked, they did not talk to
her ; and the violet twilight was meaningless.

She thought : I must be dreaming. Images had crowded
into her brain and she could not understand them. One hand
pressed to the wall she dragged herself from the bed, feeling
dizzy and hungry and sick with fatigue. She went to the chest
of drawers and took out a square tin with a Scottie painted on
top of it ; inside were damp, crumbling shortbread biscuits
which she gnawed voraciously. In the room opposite there
was a light on, and shadows against the blinds. How intolerable
those shadows seemed. They hinted, but would not reveal ;
they eluded ; they belonged to a world not hers. Far away
there was the mournful jingle of a fire-engine ; elsewhere,
a house was burning, men were hurrying to it. And the electric
trains. . . . They made a lurid lightning, a laceration on the
sky's cheek ; and within each carriage, like microbes in a test-
tube, were set the living generations. . . . But she sat in a high,
unlighted room, her eyes fixed on the stain where she had
crushed a moth against the wall.

Her fingers groped for the light-switch ; she sat down at the
table, pulled out a sheet of paper, and took up her pen. " My
dearest," she wrote. " My own dearest one. If you do not
answer this . . ."

Everything was forgotten now, even the ache and smart
of her loneliness. Tears splashed on to her white hands. She
was performing the only ritual that she could perform ; she
was making the only obeisance possible to her.

The General sat alone. The bow-windows were open on
the spring night ; the curtains flapped noisily. Beside him was
a table on which were a number of books, a reading-lamp, and

a watch. One o'clock. Far away a clock sprinkled the hour. He looked up for a moment from his work, frowned, and then continued.

He was wearing a dressing-gown of camel hair, striped pyjamas, and thick woollen socks. The close-cropped head was bent over *Strabo*.

Suddenly, there was the sound of a key turning in the front door. He hurried to his feet, crossed the room, and turned on a light in the hall. "Judith !" he called.

But already she was hurrying up the stairs, her taffeta skirt raised in one hand. She did not answer. "Judith !" he called again. "I'll make some tea. Hi, Judith !" Then, for the first time, he noticed the mud-stains on the carpet—thick cakes of mud. Her door slammed.

Again he frowned, at a loss what to do. Going back to the study he picked up *Strabo* and then put it down. He seemed to be listening for something ; but no sound came except the gusty flapping of the curtain and the drip-drip of the rain-water butt outside. Later, he climbed the stairs and knocked on her door. "Judith ! Judith, old girl ! May I come in ?"

At the silence he reflected a moment, his hands deep in his dressing-gown pockets. Then he turned the handle. Judith lay, still dressed, on her bed, with Lucy's old doll, Hetty of the shoe-button eyes, clasped against her. She was weeping ; her gold shoes were covered in mud. She resembled Lucy hardly at all, at that or at any time. Big-boned like her father, she had a brown tomboy face and hands that were strong and competent, with nails clipped close in a horizontal line. Lucy had ridden to hounds, side-saddle ; Judith had captained the lacrosse team. Both might have been created for these activities, and for these alone. Impossible to forget Lucy, graceful, arrogant on a grey mare ; impossible, too, to forget Judith as she yelled, " Come on, St. Jocelyn's ", and flicked with sinewy wrist the ball towards the goal.

As the General came in she turned away with a sort of gasp

and buried her face in the pillow. The taffeta, stretched un-
prettily tight, showed the cleft of her buttocks. He went up
to her and turned her towards him, easing her round until her
eyes flickered at the light and gleamed with the tears she had
shed. " What is it ? " he asked. " What's the matter ? Didn't
you have a good time ? " Stubbornly she did not answer,
and he continued : " Why are your shoes so dirty ? Did you
have to walk home ? "

She nodded.

" But why ? "

" Part of the way. From the Long Road."

" But why ? Why ? "

" Oh, don't go on asking me why ! " She pulled away from
him, once more weeping uncontrollably.

" Did Eric Anwood bring you home ? "

A muffled " Yes."

" I see. And did you quarrel ? Was that it ? " Eric Anwood
was the naval cadet, now a lieutenant, whom they had met
bathing.

" Oh, do leave me alone ! Oh, please leave me alone ! "
Goodness knows what eighty-odd girls at St. Jocelyn's would
have thought of their former school captain at that moment.
Choking, staunching her tears with her fists, she repeated :
" Oh-leave-me-alone ! " on a gradual descent of the scale.

" But, my dear Judith—naturally . . ." Then, meeting
with no response, he took a more vehement attitude. " If that
little beggar has made you miserable—or been fooling around—
I'll wring his neck. Horrible, conceited——"

" Oh, no, no ! It's not his fault. Oh, please go away. You
don't understand. I didn't expect you to. Oh, leave me ! "

" But, Judith——" he protested.

She cut in : " Go away ! Can't you see I want to be left
alone ? Why must you always ask so many questions ? Something must be private——"

Already he had gone. I've spoiled her, he thought, as so

many parents think when their children behave unsatisfactorily. I've spoiled her.

Judith, meanwhile, clutched Hetty and howled, amidst tennis rackets, pictures of dogs, and gym-shoes. On her bedside table lay *A Hundred Things that a Modern Girl should know*.

Mark Croft and the General had been together to one of those 'little' revues at which the mention of either Beverly Nichols or Godfrey Wynn is sufficient to send the audience into derisive peals of laughter. They had been bored, as one is bored when one finds oneself, a stranger, among a party of old friends. Now they walked together across Hampstead Heath to Mark's flat, where the General had been asked to spend the night.

They moved briskly, the General striding as he always did, his chin raised with a touch of arrogance. Mark Croft was less set, less disciplined; he tended to move aside erratically to kick a stone, or examine a tree, or pat a dog. The General did none of these things. They did not talk; they knew each other sufficiently well not to; but sometimes the General whistled a Mozart aria and Mark Croft joined in. Then, a little later, the older man began to hum a tune from *Trial by Jury*; long, long ago, out in India, he and Lucy had sung in it, in the chorus. But Mark said : " Oh, don't ! "

" Don't you like Gilbert and Sullivan ? "

" Gilbert, yes. Sullivan, no."

The General bridled. "I'm afraid I'm not very quick to follow the fashions in these things." But Mark Croft did not intend to argue with him. They walked on in silence.

Once in the flat the General said : " How are the plans going ? " They were drinking whisky and soda before a wood-fire. Mark's face was pleasantly flushed with the heat.

" Oh—shaping well. I'll show you." From the desk he took a map which had disintegrated into four separate parts and had then been stuck together with transparent paper. A pencil in his hand he leant over the General : "We sail up here—the waters are just navigable . . ." He began to describe the itinerary.

As he spoke the General felt a sudden shock of excitement, as though they were, at this very moment, embarking on the Amazon for some perilous destination. He related this sensation partly to Mark's imaginative description and partly— he could not understand why—to the clean, almost fussy, smell of carbolic soap that exuded from his presence. His skin was pink and healthy ; as he bent forward a small white bone appeared at the back of his neck.

Suddenly the General said : "You know—I've wanted to ask you for a long time. May I come with you ?"

The pencil stopped short. Mark stared at him, as though in incredulity. "To the Amazon ?"

"Yes."

"My plans are very sketchy as yet. I haven't thought about a party. Of course, I should be only too pleased. . . . It'll be hard going, you know."

"I'm used to that."

It sounded like a rebuke. "Oh, yes, I know. I didn't mean that you wouldn't be equal to it——"

The General cut in : "You young fellows always imagine that we're fogeys. We're not. My grandfather rode to hounds when he was over eighty. . . . Think about it, anyway. And let me know."

"Another drink ?" Mark switched the conversation without much deftness.

"Thanks." The General watched him as he took the glass, and began to pour whisky into it from a Victorian decanter. A lock of hair fell across his forehead, which he brushed back with a gesture of impatience. His hand was steady.

A moment later there was the sound of a key in the front door and Cynthia came in. She hesitated when she saw the General, with a subdued "Oh !" of surprise. Then she smiled

bleakly and held out a hand on which gleamed an opal, her
engagement ring. "I didn't expect to see you. Mark never
told me——"

"The General is staying the night."

"Oh, yes." She sat down on the arm of a chair. She wore
a dark-green skirt of some soft woollen material and a purple
jumper. Strange that a tranquil, dreamily idealistic girl who
believed in the perfectability of mankind should yet feel this
hostility towards someone who had never done her an injury.
She herself could not explain it ; and it worried her. It was
not simply that she was a pacifist, for many of her friends had
headstrong and violent characters. The antagonism was more
fundamental than any difference of opinion. When she was
with this man she wanted to score off him at any cost ; and
because she disliked scoring off anybody she contrived to be
with him as little as possible. Even now one cutting remark
after another came into her head and had to be suppressed :
until, unable to endure it longer, she said : "I think I'd like
some tea. Would anyone else ?"

"We're quite happy with our whisky, thank you. Shall
I get it ?" Mark rose to his feet.

"Oh, no, no. Don't be absurd." As she went out she had
to restrain herself from slamming the door.

Suddenly the General leant forward and said : "Tell me,
Mark : are you and Cynthia living together ?" He spoke in a
matter-of-fact voice.

"Since you ask—yes."

"I hope you don't mind the question. I feel that I know
you well enough. . . . To tell you the truth, I'd already
guessed——"

"You'd—guessed ?" He stared at him, flushing.

"Didn't you want anyone to know ? It seemed rather
obvious to me. I'm sorry. . . . I suppose Cynthia is already
married——"

"No."

" Then you——"

" Neither of us have any—commitments." He spoke with abrupt coldness. " As for your knowing—Cynthia certainly won't mind. You see, she doesn't believe in just rushing into marriage without a trial."

The General interposed : " But you do ? "

" I don't think an unmarried relationship can ever be really satisfactory." He was becoming a little pompous as he kicked at the fire-dogs. "If I had had my way we should have been married six months ago. But, of course, I respect her principles. She's terribly idealistic. We're going to give it a trial for a year."

" And you'd like it to be a secret ? "

" Y-yes. I don't exactly want it shouted from the house-tops. Of course Cynthia's very proud of it, and says there's nothing to hide. I admire that. But it's an attitude which I simply can't share. Perhaps I'm inherently conventional. . . . Not that I haven't told all my closest friends. I have. But with acquaintances——"

The General winced at this not too tactful suggestion that his relationship with Croft might be anything less than intimate. " Did you imagine I should be shocked ? " he asked.

" Frankly—yes."

" But why ? "

" Oh, your generation——"

" My generation is a good deal less prudish than yours. Good heavens—of course, it doesn't shock me." He was being unconvincingly emancipated. " What do you take me for ? My own wife and I . . ." But he found it impossible to talk of that day when he and Lucy had found themselves alone in the clearing in the jungle and Lucy had thrown her arms about him. He went to the sideboard and poured himself another drink.

Later, Cynthia came in with a tray, and they sat, making forced conversation. She herself said little, but remained curled up in an armchair while she sipped tea from a china

beaker. Then, when she had finished : " I must go," she said,
" or I'll miss that last train. Good-night, General."

"Good-night."

"Good-night, darling."

"I'll see you out."

"No, don't bother." They kissed, almost ashamedly, and
she left them. The General watched Mark, expecting that this
was all a show and that she was going to spend the night with
him. But a moment later the front door slammed and feet
descended.

He was glad.

Montherlant's *Pitié pour les Femmes* first gave Shirley the idea.
As she wrote in one of her letters to the General, her mother
had lent it to her, and she had been struck by the similarity
between the love which three women bear for the libertine,
Costals, and her own devotion to someone who seemed so
much more worthy.

She had read in that book of how Andrée Haquebaut, the
little provincial, offers herself to Costals for a week, a night
even ; the happiness of such an encounter will be sufficient for
a lifetime. At first Shirley had dismissed the notion as ' im-
probable ', ' untrue to life ', as so many people dismiss what they
cannot see themselves experiencing. But the seed was to
germinate.

She had sat down in a cinema, with her shoes off, while next
to her two lovers huddled together, and on the screen two other,
gigantic lovers met in a less ungainly embrace. The girl on her
right was stiff as though with some intolerable ache, her eyes
staring moonily ; while the sinuously voluptuous lady, balanced
above the craning necks in the ' ninepennies ', seemed almost
nonchalant. Somehow, the conjunction of these two beatitudes,
the shadow and the substance, made her feel sick and empty.
It was then that she decided on a last desperate step ; propriety
and pride and self-respect were to be forgotten.

Sitting in her room, on that airless afternoon, she wrote frantically :

MY OWN DEAREST ONE,—Two weeks have passed now since I sent you the last of my three letters, and still there is no answer. You are tired of all this ; you would like to be rid of me ; you do not wish to hear from me again. I know that you feel all these things without your saying them. And I only wish that I could satisfy you—that I could say " No more letters " and that were an end of it. But I *must* write. Perhaps I should go mad if I didn't. It is as necessary to me as food and drink and sleep—no, more necessary, much more necessary.

But I should be sorry to become a nuisance to you. I should be sorry if even my love were to prove a burden—a greater burden, perhaps, than the hostility of your enemies. I wish to act only as you would like me to act. But to cease to write these letters—Oh, no, no, no !

As I turn all this over in my mind—over and over, in trains, at school, at night—it seems that there can be only one way out, and only one solution. Otherwise I shall always be a prisoner ; I shall always burn in this flame. Take me—take me, I beg of you—even if it be for only one night. One night would be sufficient. After that annunciation, that seal on my faith, I think I should learn resignation and patience. I think I should learn how to set aside all desire, complete in my love, in the consummation of my love. Without this seal, all life is meaningless. But with it—how full it then becomes. In your hands are the keys of the kingdom. Shall these dry bones live ?

. . . If you will have me once, then I shall not importune you again. You shall not hear from me again. *One night will be sufficient.* Is this so much to ask ? Is my whole life, my salvation, worth less than just one night with you ? I beg of you. . .

She wrote much in the same vein until exhausted, she put the five sheets into an envelope and posted them at Earl's Court post office. They were overweight, and the General, to his annoyance, had to pay one penny for them at the other end.

Mark Croft had a violent temper. It was many months before the General discovered this. When he did he felt as one does when the young stranger sitting next to one in the theatre suddenly throws an epileptic fit. One feels that there should have been some sign. But the youth appeared quite normal ; one suspected nothing.

Cynthia, who wore the badges and read the literature of many societies, was agitating for Indian freedom. On Sunday she stood at Marble Arch with a placard " Free India Now " and a dozen copies of *The Black Man's Burden*. On her right was a woman in a beltless mackintosh and a tam-o'-shanter whose placard proclaimed " The dead speak to us " ; on her left was a cloth cap and the *Matrimonial Post*. She thought : I *am* being crucified in bad company. But then she blushed, feeling she had been irreverent. Many people stopped to stare at her, as one does at a model in a shop window ; a few held out two coppers, the price of the pamphlet. An old woman passed and said " Disgraceful ". " I beg your pardon ? " But it appeared that she was referring to the *Matrimonial Post*.

Later, Mark and the General came up to her and the General offered to buy a pamphlet.

" Oh, no," she said, with a dry little laugh. " I've no hopes of converting you. My pamphlets are scarce."

" You might give me a chance."

But she shook her head, " I only sell where I think there's a chance of success. I don't expect you to believe in Indian freedom."

" Why not ? "

But before she could answer Mark had eased a copy out of her hand and handed it to the General. " It's never too late," he murmured pacifically, smiling. Cynthia scowled.

They stood by her for several minutes during which the

General, who was in high spirits, bought a copy of the *Matrimonial Post* and read the advertisements aloud to them. " Single woman, C. of E., thirty-seven, simple tastes . . ." But suddenly he stopped short, thinking for no reason of Shirley Forsdike. He found himself pitying her.

" Let's move on," Mark said at last. Turning to Cynthia he queried : " You won't mind if we leave you ? "

" Of course, not. I haven't sold a single pamphlet while you've been with me. You don't look serious enough. People think we're having a joke."

As they boarded their bus Mark happened to glance back over his shoulder. " Oh, Lord ! " he exclaimed. " It looks as if there were going to be trouble." Cynthia was in conversation with a red-faced man in a bowler hat. There was a high-pitched, indignant torrent : " You young girls . . . Bolshie . . . traitors to your country . . . ought to be locked up . . ." The man had a mean little snout, eyes with long, white eyelashes, and a blue shirt against which he wore a tie whose spots were the size of billiard balls.

" What's the matter, darling ? "

" Nothing much, really. Just this creature being particularly offensive."

" Offensive ! Me offensive ! Well—didn't she call me a Blimp ? Didn't she——" He began to appeal to the beltless spiritualist who rubbed a damp nose on the back of her hand. " Didn't she——"

" That's enough," Mark cut in sharply. " Just apologise to this lady. Or there'll be trouble."

" Apologise ! Me apologise ! I like that ! You won't catch me bloody well apologising. Ought to be locked up——"

" Apologise ! " Mark caught the man's arm and thrust him towards Cynthia. But squirming, he evaded this grip and punched Mark timidly in the stomach. " Let me go ! " he squealed. " Don't you touch me ! "

But Mark, white with rage, advanced on him inexorably.

Taking the rim of his bowler hat in either hand he began to force it downwards with successive jerks, until it touched the man's nose. His ears stuck out, grotesquely crumpled. Then as the man floundered Mark caught the lapels of his check suit and hurled him against a lamp-post.

Afterwards, he said to the General ashamedly : " I'm afraid I just saw red."

" Do you often do that sort of thing ? "

" Far too often. I have an infernal temper. And when I lose it—well—anything may happen. . . . Cynthia's marvellous about it. I think she'll probably cure me in the end."

The General smiled sardonically.

From the Diary of General Sir HUGH WEIGH

May 8th 1938

Frank Cauldwell is in town for the day. He tells me that he is looking for another job, and asks if I can meet him. I am afraid that he is just another drifter. The tutoring post I got for him with the Maccabaes should have suited him pretty well.

Our rendezvous is outside Tottenham Court Road Underground station, at eleven o'clock. He is seeing some publishers there. Of course he is late, arriving breathless with a portfolio in his hand. " Oh, I *am* sorry," he says. " This really is awful of me. I must have kept you here for nearly twenty minutes. And now I can only spare half an hour. I've just been told of someone who wants a secretary : I'm going off to see him at twelve." I grunt my indignation.

" Let's go in here," he says, and without waiting for an answer disappears into a milk bar. I should have chosen a pub.

We push our way to the far end, and both perch on stools covered with imitation leather. The counter is of smeared marble, flecked with pieces of egg from someone's sandwich. In glass cases there are curling pieces of bread with mauve ham between them and shiny pork-pies. Frank gives the order and a nonchalant girl pulls at a lever from which gushes a frothy,

bright pink concoction. She takes two straws, sticks them into
the tumblers, and slaps them down before us. I suck gingerly ;
my front teeth ache.

We talk for a while in the inconclusive, self-conscious fashion
of people who know that they are being overheard. The
waitress takes a cloth and swabs over the place before us, her
head inclined. Then she says, " Excuse me," crossly, and Frank
has to remove his portfolio. I notice that, for once, he is dressed
in an almost dandified fashion—bow-tie, brown suède shoes,
and so forth. I suppose that he has never had the money to
dress well before. I remember him at Dartmouth in indescrib-
ably stained flannels, a Fair Isle sweater, and gym-shoes.

Suddenly he opens the portfolio and takes out seven or eight
typed sheets of paper. " I wanted to show these to you. They're
from the novel." As he pushed them across his hand catches
my glass and spills some of the sickly liquid on to them. This
he mops up with a silk handkerchief. The sheets are now moist
and pink in one corner.

Feeling that he will want some critical opinion from me
I try to concentrate on the illegibly dim typing. The passage is
about a young girl in a hotel in France. But someone jolts me;
and two women on my right are reciting to each other the names
of most of the cinemas in Greater London with their current
attractions. It is difficult.

What disappoints me at first is the discovery that in these
sheets I do not appear. So I was right ! I am merely to be
introduced for comic relief. I read through twice and then
hand them back to him.

" Well ? " he queries.

" I like it."

" But you must say more than that. That doesn't help me
at all."

" You know, Frank—it seems to me that you haven't begun
to discover people yet ; you've only discovered their genital
organs."

Then, seeing the look of resentment on his face, I hurriedly add : " You mustn't take that seriously. It was intended as a witticism rather than a criticism."

I begin on a detailed but dull examination of his prose style.

Judith, in tweeds, lay curled up beside the General, running the fingers of one unmanicured hand through his close-cropped hair. " Fibsy, darling ? "

" Yes ? "

" What would you say if Eric Anwood and I got engaged to each other ? "

The General started. " Engaged ! But don't you think he ought to see me first ? I mean——" He put a hand on her knee as though to restrain her.

" Oh, don't be so old-fashioned ! " She laughed, not very satisfactorily. " In any case, he hasn't asked me yet. . . . But he might."

" Judith—promise me something. Don't commit yourself until I've——"

She pulled away angrily, pouting. " Why must you be so mercenary ? I know what you're thinking. Eric's only a lieutenant. He hasn't any money. Hadn't we better wait. Those sort of considerations don't count if one is in love."

" And you're in love with Eric ? "

" You say it in such a contemptuous way. I know you don't like him——"

" I never said that."

" Oh, yes, you did ! That evening—you said he was horrible —and mean——"

" Judith ! You know I was only distressed because——"

" Oh, don't pretend. I've seen it all along. He's not much of a catch—no money, no position. In any case I think you'd like me tied to you all my life. I don't believe you *want* me to get married—to anyone."

Conciliatory, he put an arm round her, but she wrenched

herself free. "Please don't treat me as if I were a child, to be cuddled and mauled about ! Oh, don't you see—Eric may be my only chance. I'm not the sort of girl whom people fall in love with easily. And he does love me—he loves me so very much." For the first time she was giving away to him her morbid fear of spinsterhood.

"Well—that's all right, then," he said, not without irony. "That's fine."

He took up *The Times* once more. But a moment later the door slammed.

At lunch, Judith came and kissed him and said she was sorry ; and he took her on one knee and kissed her and said : "I just don't want you to do anything rash." At the words she seemed to stiffen with resistance, but he went on : "I want nothing so much in the world as my little Pynx's happiness." And again she embraced him : "Fibsy, darling. I've been horrid to Fibsy." Then they both sat down to veal cutlets.

The scene was reminiscent of others with Lucy.

S. N. G.'s chair had been set in the afternoon sunshine. But the sun had moved, the shadows had lengthened ; and now he felt cold and a little querulous. He had called many times, but no one seemed to hear him ; far away the maids giggled and rattled crockery, and cars pushed along the by-pass, and an errand-boy whistled. He drew his rug up to his chin, yawning. On his knees was the latest detective story by Agatha Christie and a leather knitting-bag. All that morning he had knitted ; he was making a scarf for his nephew, and already it was so long that it dangled on the grass. But he did not like visitors to see him at this pastime. As soon as the bell rang he bundled it away and pretended to be reading. Hence the bag ; hence the book.

At the moment he was doing nothing. His scholarly face, the cheeks caving in and raddled, was turned to the orchard in front of him. The trees had been planted by his mother shortly before her death ; but they had suffered a pest, a beetle with saw-like jaws, and had never grown. They should have been pulled up long ago, before they infected the apricot tree and the quince. But something prevented this step. Sentimentality, perhaps.

On this lawn, he pondered, he had written *The Effigy* ; here he had given tea to generations of undergraduates ; it was here, too, that his mother had asked to be wheeled, dying, breathless in purple silk. But why here ? The view was so much better on the other side of the house, where one could see the rose-garden, and the Downs, and the sea. Here there was nothing but a wall of brambles, and the curve of the by-pass, droning with cars.

The house was one of the oldest in those parts. He could remember a time when the by-pass had been a lane, and instead of the vistas of bungalows there had only been the Hall and the church and some cottages. But the countryside was now ruled symmetrically by threads of concrete, pinioning it, holding it down. In the valley were the electric trains, bringing each evening bowler-hatted multitudes to " Chay-Noo ", " Dun-romin' ", " St. Leonards ". The Hall had become an anachronism.

He meditated on all this, his white hair sticking up in astonished tufts, his hands crossed over his stomach. He remembered how, as a boy, he had leant out of his bedroom window, and the nightingales had sung ceaselessly for him from the bramble thickets. But the children and the lovers and the noise of cars had silenced them long ago. Only a few sparrows now splashed in the bird-bath that his mother had had erected.

In this way he tended more and more to savour with wry satisfaction the deterioration which he saw about him. He was out of it, thank God. He had just escaped the lean years. . . .

"Hullo, S. N. You seem to be in a brown study." The General appeared round the house, followed by the patient Simpson, who had been gardener's boy, chauffeur, and now sick-nurse.

S. N. George smiled wanly : "Hullo !" Then he turned to Simpson : "Please move me into the sun. I've been calling for hours and hours."

"Sorry, sir." Tenderly, he wheeled the chair out into the open. "Anything else, sir ?"

"Get the General something to sit on."

"And how's the patient ?"

"The patient's in excellent spirits. The patient has knitted over six inches." He pulled out the scarf. "Look ! How would you like to wear that round your neck."

Simpson came out with a deck-chair. "Shall I get the tea, sir ?"

"Oh, yes, yes. Good gracious, yes. It's nearly five."

The General sat down, taking the book from his friend's lap. "Agatha Christie ! Well, I never expected you——"

"Oh, yes. I read little else now. . . . This is an extraordinary refreshing existence, you know. I mean, the whole cultural racket—the strain of being clever, of knowing the right people—the need, my dear, of keeping up—well, it all just vanishes. I sit here, and see nobody, and do exactly what I want."

"I think it's a pity."

"Reading Agatha Christie ?"

"No—not only that. I think the whole thing is a pity. You seem to have made a sort of premature exit from the world."

"Considering the circumstances, is that exactly kind ? When one is crippled——"

"Oh, yes. But I didn't mean that. You seem to have rejected life——"

"Life ! Ah, that's the word. It all depends on what you

mean by life. For you life is bathing, and buccaneering, and writing newspaper articles. For me parties and lectures and week-ends in country houses. But there is something else, you know. One day you will have to discover it. Life isn't simply doing. It's also being. . . . Just to sit here, in the sun, while that wretched bird picks the buds off the peach tree—that has its importance also." The General was smiling, and he continued : " A truism, perhaps. You're laughing at me. But when you, too, are old, and everything seems flat and rather worthless—then perhaps . . ."

He did not complete his sentence.

Simpson had dressed him for dinner ; he always dressed when possible. He himself tied the tie, for this was one thing which Simpson could never do. " Easier to buy it made-up," Simpson grumbled as he laced S. N. George's shoes. Then he held up a mirror, after the fashion of hairdressers, and the invalid peered into it. " Do I look very pale to-night, Simpson ? " " A bit off colour, sir. It's that asparagus you ate." With relish they discussed the symptoms until the gong sounded.

Seated at either end of the mahogany table course after course was brought them : but only the General ate with any appetite. S. N. G. had a prescribed diet ; delicately, like a bird, he picked his way over boiled fish while Simpson stood behind him. From the cellar some excellent wines had been produced. When S. N. G. wasn't eating he sipped at some hock and watched the General with grave eyes. They neither of them spoke much. The polished mahogany table held the reflection of S. N. G.'s aureole of white hair, the glitter of diamond cuff-links, and a steady glow from the lights. This mirrored effulgence burned up at them, making them seem somehow drab by comparison.

After the meal S. N. G. was wheeled into the study, and Simpson was told he could go. The General was offered a

fat Romeo and Julietta which at first he declined ; but S. N. G.
urged him : " Oh, do, my dear. I like to see you smoke."

" Do you ? Why ? "

He shrugged his shoulders.

On the desk was an accumulation of unanswered correspond-
ence, among which could be perceived the yellow of many
telegrams. These were the congratulations sent by friends and
admirers at the news of the success of the operation. " An
internal operation ", *The Times* discreetly put it. On the wall
was his mother, painted by Sargent in a blaze of emeralds :
she had been young then, thin-lipped, ugly. But elsewhere
there was a de László portrait of a lined but magnificent
matriarch.

S. N. G. stretched his hands to the fire, scratching the palms
as the heat made them tingle. Again he watched the General,
seeming to brood upon him as though upon a mystery. " Well ?
What news of yourself ? "

The General told him about Judith, and the meeting with
Frank Cauldwell, and how he had asked if he might accompany
Croft to the Amazon. Then suddenly, on an impulse, he took
from his wallet the letter from Shirley Forsdike which he had
received a few days ago and passed it across. " What do you
make of that ? "

The flames seemed to corrode each of the five sheets of
paper as S. N. G. read them in turn. Then, when he had
finished, he put his head back in the chair and smiled. It was
not the usual sickly, fragile twitching of the lips. This was a
full-blooded grin.

" Well ? "

" What are you going to do about it ? "

" Do about it ? What is there to do about it ? This is the
fourth letter this month."

" But you must see her."

" My dear S. N. G.——"

" You *must*." A thin, blue hand with pointed nails closed

8

on the General's wrist. "It's the sort of thing one must accept.
You must live up to your myth."

"Do you mean that I'm to do what she asks—— ? "

"Of course—grotesque though it sounds. This is a symbol,
a gesture. You can't reject it."

"I don't understand you."

"You should. Gods are magnanimous creatures. They
like to make these sudden descents——"

The General stared at him in incredulity. "Do you really
think I should write to this girl——? "

"You *must* ! You must promise me——"

"Certainly not."

"Please, H. W. ! You can't reject——"

"No."

"Please ! "

Again he caught his wrist, but the General drew it away.
"You must be mad. . . . Do you know—I think this is the
first time you have ever shocked me." And indeed he was
shocked—not so much by what had been said as by his friend's
importunity.

"So I shock you ? Well—I don't mind that. Perhaps all
my life I've been too afraid of shocking people. All I ask is
that you shouldn't be traitor to your myth. Reveal yourself."
He smiled : "Otherwise people may forget that you are
a god."

The General stared into the fire. There was sweat on his
forehead.

Judith was staying with her friend Mabel in a mews flat
off Russell Square, while the General stayed at his Club. They
were spending a week in London. It is Mabel who must really
be held responsible for what followed. Without her it is
doubtful whether either Judith or Eric would have taken the
step.

Mabel had spent three or four terms at St. Jocelyn's, during

which she and Judith struck up a romantic friendship. Mabel
was fat and rather jolly, and the girls looked up to her ; she
seemed so securely adult. She brought back to school a copy
of *The Well of Loneliness* which she said she had stolen from
her mother, and a souvenir programme of the Folies Bergères.
She swore vehemently. The mistresses soon decided that she
was ' a bad influence ' and the head took to having long talks
with her on Sunday, after prayers ; she emerged from these
flushed and giggling.

Eventually she left, but whether from choice or compulsion,
it never became quite clear. She took up art ; and stories
circulated that she was living in sin, had had a baby, and so
forth. Little of this was true. Perhaps if she had had the
opportunity it might have been. But no one could be found
willing to face that greyish countenance, plump and like suet-
pudding, in which were embedded currant eyes, day after day, at
breakfast. So although Mabel had ' boys ', none of them ever
shared the flat.

On the night after Judith arrived Mabel gave a party, during
which a number of people were sick ; and someone threw a
bottle up at the ceiling so that it splintered and cut Mabel's
arm ; and Mabel, grinning and always a good sort, bled pro-
fusely on to the carpet. But Eric and Judith sat apart, huddled
together on a corner of Mabel's bed. Judith was shocked but
fascinated by Mabel's friends, who appeared at all hours with
bottles bulging in their overcoat pockets. Many of them kissed
Mabel ; some were now petting in corners.

After the party Judith and Mabel began to clear up. " Leave
the messes to me," said Mabel. " I'm used to them." Judith
emptied ash-trays. Round Mabel's arm was tied someone
else's handkerchief, soggy with blood. It slipped, and she
asked Judith to tighten it. " I'd like to know the bloody bastard
who did that. Christ ! that was a bloody thing to do." She
finished what was left in the bottom of a tumbler with a wry
face.

Then, when everything was tidy once more, they both sat down on the divan bed and drank tea.

"Tell me, honey," Mabel said. "You and that lieutenant seem pretty mad about each other."

"Yes, we are."

"Going to get married?"

"I don't know." And because it was late, and two o'clock is the hour for confidences, she told Mabel about her father and all her difficulties.

At the end Mabel said: "You must elope! You must get married secretly! It's the only thing."

"Oh, no," Judith protested.

But Mabel usually had her way.

The next morning there was a telegram for Frank Cauldwell. It was brought into him as he was hearing his two charges recite *mensa* in the schoolroom. He read: "Am marrying Judith Weigh to-morrow. Can you be witness. Eric."

"Any answer?" queried the maid.

"I'll telephone one later."

All through the lesson his mind was absorbed with plans—the journey, where he was to stay, permission from Mrs. Maccabae. He thought, also, in incredulity, of those far-away days at Dartmouth, when Eric and Judith bathed together and he and the General talked. And now they were to be married. "The accusative of *aquila*?" he said to one of his charges.

"*Aquilam*," came the grave reply. "You've asked that one already."

"Have I? I must be dreaming." He spoke crossly.

As soon as his watch showed eleven o'clock he left them to find Mrs. Maccabae. She sat in the garden, sipping coffee, among copies of *Vogue* and *The Lady*. When she heard his footsteps behind her she said: "Is that you, Roe? Do go and tell Cook to hurry. Really, I can't wait all day . . ."

" It's me."

" Oh." She swung petulantly in her chair. " I've been trying to give my orders for hours. But Cook simply——"

He cut in to tell her what he had come for. " You see, he's a great friend," he explained. " We were brought up together. I should like so much to be present at his wedding."

" But it's such short notice," she grumbled. " And it's only a week since your last holiday. You must realise, Frank——"

They bickered aimlessly for many minutes, until at last she gave in to him. " Oh, very well, then. But you must get back to-morrow night. And I won't be able to send the car to the station. You'll have to walk. It's too much to ask Perkins——"

" I'll walk," he interjected. " You needn't bother."

" It's so inconvenient ! " she sighed. " But still— ! There it is. If you must go, you must go. I'm only afraid that my two babies are getting no education at all." She knew that he was set on going ; it wouldn't do to lose him ; but she wanted him to feel as uncomfortable as possible.

" Thank you," he said grudgingly at the end of their interview.

" That's all right. Just ferret Cook out of the kitchen, will you ? " She took pleasure in sending him on the errand.

At lunch that day Mr. Maccabae suddenly looked up half-way through the meal and said : " Good heavens ! Where's Frank ? " He was not observant.

Mrs. Maccabae explained. " It's too bad," she said at the end. " We're far too kind, that's the whole trouble. We just let people impose on us. They ride over us—rough-shod. Grab, grab, grab ! Always out for what they can get ! We *must* take a firm line."

It was raining, and he was late. They had arranged to meet at the Apple-tree Tea-rooms for a cup of coffee before going on to the registry office. Frank sat back in the taxi, while the window streamed with rain and about him a mushroom rash of umbrellas covered the pavement. Sometimes he glanced at his watch. He was incapable of being punctual. Partly, of course, it was due to selfishness : there was always the chance that the person one was meeting might also be late ; and one hated waiting. Far better to arrive ten minutes after the time arranged.

The taxi suddenly swished to a standstill, a draught gathering about his legs. He got out and paid, and then for the first time noticed the three figures huddled pathetically together under a small, silk umbrella. They were in a tight bunch, a little circle, all facing inwards, while this ridiculous affair of red and white stripes hung above them.

" I'm terribly sorry to be so late. Why on earth didn't you go in ? "

" We couldn't. It's closed. There's a notice here." Eric, dripping from nose, fingers, and ears, pointed to the white piece of cardboard in the window : " Closed for the week. Staff on holiday."

At that moment Judith exclaimed petulantly : " Oh, do let's move on. The rain's got into my shoes."

Mabel, the wise virgin, was unable to resist saying : " I warned you to bring an umbrella."

" A lot of use it is, saying that now ! "

" Now, now, girls ! " Eric was cheerfully stoical. " What we all need is a cup of coffee."

" Let's get on then ! " Judith moaned. " Why are we standing here."

But the district was surprisingly poor in restaurants. At some they said, " Full up " ; at others, " Luncheons only ". Even Mabel began to flag. " This is bloody awful," she said. " Let's give the whole thing up and go to the registry office."

" But I *must* have something to drink. I *must* have something hot ! I shall get the most awful chill." Clinging to Eric's arm Judith squelched and whined.

At last a coffee-stall was found, with an awning under which sheltered far too many people. Mabel rubbed her hands and said, " This is cheery," and talked to the man in charge. The others drank in glum silence a liquid which tasted of chicory and methylated spirits.

" You might have turned up on time," Judith suddenly said to Frank. But Eric intervened : " Oh, stow it ! Oh, let's forget about it ! " Mabel began to whistle. Later, she bought some cakes and gave one to each of them. They were small and dry, with a chasm in the centre from which exuded a pus-like lemon-curd. The whole stall smelled of cat.

Mabel turned to Frank : " Have I met you before ? "

" No, I don't think so. Introductions were somehow forgotten——"

" That's all right, son. I'm Mabel Ruster."

" I'm Frank Cauldwell."

" Right ho, Frank." She slapped him across the belly with the back of her hand.

Over her arm was a heart-shaped bag of red leather with the initials M. R. in one corner. Her lips and nails were conflicting shades of purple, her cheeks mauve. She wore her hair untidily in a bang over her eyes, and there was a circular hat at the back of her head. On her middle finger was an enormous ring, an intaglio in a gold setting.

During the ceremony she caught Frank's eye and began to giggle ; but Judith turned round and said " Sh ! " with such emphasis that she stopped at once. At the end Eric kissed Judith ; and Mabel said : " What about me ? " " May I ? " Eric asked ; and when Judith nodded, Mabel was kissed also. " Mmm," she said. " Oh, boy ! That was a kiss." Judith and Eric walked out arm-in-arm.

In the street Mabel said : " Can you wait a minute ? I must go and shed a tear for old England." She disappeared into a latrine from which she appeared with her lips several shades darker. They got into a Tube, and went to Piccadilly.

At the Chinese restaurant Frank ordered the dinner while Mabel talked, giggled, and knocked over a water carafe. Judith and Eric pressed hands under the table ; and Eric, by mistake, rubbed his knee against Frank's. Frank found this curiously stimulating.

Afterwards, Frank was somehow left with the bill while the others all contrived to be engrossed in conversation, and they made their way out into the watery sunshine.

" Now what ? " asked Mabel.

Judith said timidly : " Eric and I are going off now. Do you mind ? "

" Good Lord, no ! Go off and enjoy yourselves ! "

Eric and Judith looked at each other in tacit understanding : Mabel was quite unspeakable. Then they both said : " Good-bye, Mabel. Good-bye, Frank. It's been so sweet of you. Thank you so much." Hand-in-hand they walked to Cambridge Circus and then up the Charing Cross Road. At a shop which advertised " Damarrhoids : The Great Rejuvenator " Eric bought a copy of *Ideal Marriage*. Then they both returned to Trafalgar Square and sat among the pigeons and read it.

Meanwhile, Frank, and Mabel watched a revival of *The Private Life of King Henry the Eighth*. Mabel had said, " Oh, do buy me an orange drink." The drink was now finished but she still pulled at the straw, the suction making a gurgle against the tumbler.

It so happened that at one o'clock on the day of the wedding Shirley Forsdike was, as usual, walking from school to lunch at the Bristol Hotel. She passed the registry office, as she always passed it ; and at the same time a car drew up and four people got out. She could not see their faces or she would have known that one of them was Judith, her old pupil and daughter of General Weigh. But being one of those people

who always stay to see a wedding she thought : They'll be
out soon. I'm a bit early to-day—and took up her stand beside
two other women who had appeared from nowhere. " Bad
luck to be married in rain," said one, whose straw hat was
flagging visibly. She wore rubber goloshes which zipped up
the front, and carried a shopping-basket. The other said :
" Your hat, dear ! I should get home before it's ruined."
" But I must see them come out. They'll be out in a minute."

This estimate proved to be wrong. Ten minutes passed ;
and first one woman, and then the other, hurried away ; until,
at last, even Shirley gave up and made for the Cromwell Road.

" You're late to-day," said one of the two old ladies, her
friends.

" Am I ? Yes, I was kept."

It seemed silly to tell them about the wedding.

Lying on her stomach, Mabel read *Eyeless in Gaza*, and
polished her nails on a well-worn buff. The telephone rang.
It was green, and lay on the floor beside her. " The colour is
ten shillings extra," she told her visitors. " But it's rather
jolly, isn't it ? It just doesn't match the green of the walls."

" Hullo," she said, her mind still occupied with Huxley.
Then she swung her legs off the bed and sat up with a jerk.
" Oh, it's you, is it, General ? "

" Where's Judith ? "

" Judith ? "

" She was meant to meet me here this morning. We were
going to travel back together. Is she with you ? "

Mabel's face was expressive in the mirror opposite : she
watched herself, eyes wide open, lips smiling. " Oh, no. She
left here the day before yesterday."

" Day before yesterday ! "

" Do you mean she hasn't told you yet ? "

" Told me ? What *is* all this ? " He began to bluster.
" What are you talking about ? "

8*

"Her marriage."

There was a long silence, during which Mabel began to wonder whether he might not have rung off. Eventually she said : "Are you still there, General ? "

"Yes. . . . It's come as rather a shock. . . . I'd no idea——"

"She's quite all right—and quite happy." Mabel, warm-hearted creature, suddenly felt sorry for him. A moment ago she had been gleefully triumphant. "I expect you'll hear from her soon. She's so incurably romantic—an elopement and all that. . . . I suppose it *does* make it rather more exciting."

But this time he really had rung off. Poor dear, she thought. Poor, poor dear. Regretfully she replaced the receiver and took up her book.

In his first grief he had imagined that it would be intolerable to return home, alone. He viewed with horror the prospect of an empty house ; the meals during which he would sit silent ; climbing the stairs to bed without the friendly good-nights, the kiss, Judith's arm round his waist. He would bathe alone, and eat alone, and go for walks alone. And there would be no early morning sounds of Judith grooming the dogs, Judith curled beside him, Judith asleep over a book. Judith was gone, and the loss seemed irrevocable. Lying on the beach he would think of her coarse, healthy hair between his fingers ; and working he would think of her leaning over his shoulder with : "Fibsy, do leave all this nonsense ! Do come out ! " All the time in the train he brooded bleakly on the future : he couldn't stand it.

But, of course, he did. In actual fact he almost preferred being alone. There was still his resentment, and his anger at being betrayed, and his wounded pride ; but all this apart, and setting aside sudden pangs of love, sudden longings, he was perfectly happy. If he wanted company, there were

plenty of friends in Dartmouth ; and if he didn't, at least he
was rid of Judith's pestering. She always wanted to help with
his work ; but this meant finger-marks on old books, and
upsetting the inkpot, and facetious jokes. He was glad to be
free of it.

And yet, and yet. . . . He felt he ought to feel lonely ; he
felt he ought to be stricken with grief. Which probably
explains why, at times, he was. There were nights when he
could not sleep, and moments, in conversation with friends, at
work, sailing, when suddenly there was this ache, this emptiness
within, like a physical hunger ; and he could do nothing,
could say nothing until it passed.

One day he was shaving in the bathroom when Clark
knocked.

"Yes, Clark. What is it ? "

"It's—Miss Judith, sir," Clark gulped. "She's just arrived."

The General had learnt that one should never betray oneself
before one's subordinates. He continued shaving. "Tell her
I shall be down in a minute."

"Yes, sir."

As soon as Clark had closed the door he hurriedly splashed
the soap off his face, snatched for a towel, and began to dry.
But already someone was mounting the stairs.

"Father ? " She tried desperately to be matter-of-fact.
"Do you mind if I come in ? "

Without answering he opened the door. Throwing her
arms round his neck she kissed him, soapy and wet as he was.
He still held the razor in his hand. "Have you forgiven me,
darling ? You got my letter ? "

Suddenly unable to contain himself he burst out : " You
might have told me. It's not as if I would have stopped you
getting married."

"Not stopped us—no. But the fuss——"

"Do try to understand——"

" I understand perfectly."

" It was so callous——"

" Oh, very well ! If that's all you think. If that's all you have to say to your daughter. I came here quite prepared to be friends. I thought everything could go on as it always used to. But if you're not prepared to bury the hatchet—if that's how you feel——"

" Well, naturally—I'm glad to see you—but I'm not going to pretend——"

" Oh, you make me sick ! "

As she ran out he called after her. " Where are you going ? " But there was no reply. Going to the bathroom window, he saw her climb into an open two-seater car in which Eric Anwood waited. For a while the two of them seemed to argue ; then they drove off.

He dipped one hand into the warm, soapy water and pulled out the plug. There was a loud, guggling sound. It was only then that he realised that half of his face was still unshaved.

Croft and the General went to the New Forest to watch birds. Between them they had a rucksack, some binoculars, and a car. It was the first of May, spring, with the promise of bluebells and anemones. The promise is always more satisfactory than the fulfilment. There had been a hint of last night's frost in the morning air : but now the warmth was expanding, was mellowing ; it was possible to walk without a coat, without a shirt even. Everything was sappy, sticky, green. The trees made bowery arcades through which the sun sauntered. There was a twitter of birds, a scurry in the undergrowth. A pleasant, sylvan scene. But no dryads, no Pan—only Southampton matrons opening portable gramophones and picnic baskets at the end of each vista. Children jumped on to logs, screeched at each other, played hide-and-seek. And every now and then voices called to them : " Not too far, dears. Don't get lost."

Not too far : that was the great thing. Keep to the paths and picnic where others had left their picnic paper. And in case the solitude and the silence should suddenly become intolerable and one had to escape, two or three hundred yards away were parked the Morrises and the Austins and the Hillmans.

Croft and the General passed many such little groups, set in a circle round thermos flasks, sandwiches, beer bottles. The women wore fur coats, and felt hot in them. The men smoked pipes and clasped their knees as they leant against tree trunks. The children yelped. Sometimes there was a wireless ; more often a gramophone. In such cases, no birds sang.

Not far off ran the arterial road, loud with traffic and hedged with dust. Beside it, at intervals, were stands with brooms in them for putting out fires. There were also picnickers, in cars. Not too far. Don't get lost.

But Croft and the General cut away from this worn aorta. There were brambles now, to tear silk stockings. And if one was not careful one might find oneself up to the ankles in squelching mud. They were alone. The only intruder was a distant voice from a distant wireless. They both sighed. And then, with the irresponsibility which afflicts one when one knows that there is no one looking, Croft ran forward and swung himself on to a tree trunk. For a few seconds he stayed there, straining, his muscles tense, then the whole thing cracked and came away in his hands. He was on the ground, on his stomach. They laughed.

Later, Croft exclaimed : " Oh, look ! Gypsies ! " In a dell stood a caravan, with a horse cropping grass beside it.

" Not on your life ! Nothing so romantic."

Coming closer, they examined the yellow and green paint, the frilled curtains, the bunches of flowers daubed round the door. " Week-enders," the General murmured.

Bacon sizzled. Outside, a girl whose hair was tied into a scarf, whose buttocks protruded from slacks, cooked over a spirit

stove. Some hot fat spat on to her hand and she exclaimed :
" Oh, hell ! " Then she saw the General and Croft and scowled.

On the other side a fat, elderly man with a beard was washing
under the arms. He looked up and grinned, without friendli-
ness. " Good morning." The nipples on his chest were blue
with cold.

" Good morning. . . . That's a nice way of spending a
holiday."

" No holiday. I'm here to paint." He took up his towel
and disappeared into the privacy of the caravan. From the
other side the girl could be heard bawling : " Leo. Oh, do
hurry up, for Christ's sake ! This bacon's burnt to a cinder ! . . .
Ow ! "

" What's the matter ? "

" It spits so bloody much."

Croft and the General moved on. Behind them they could
hear the man's voice : " No privacy ! "

" You've said it. And me looking such a sight. Thank
goodness I wasn't washing."

Farther on they suddenly came to a slope. At the bottom
were alders and sallows and tufts of rush. And a stream which
here made a small, circular pool. The grass was long, and
intensely green, and lush.

" What about a bathe ? " the General queried.

" A bathe ? "

" Why not ? "

" It'll be horribly cold."

" Nonsense. I've been bathing since February. I'm going
in anyway." He began to strip off his clothes, throwing them
into a heap. Then naked, he splashed his way into the centre
and began to kick about. " It's lovely," he spluttered. " Beautifully watm. Why don't you come in ? "

Croft hesitated and then undressed with his back to the
General. His pants he turned back to front and fastened with
his tie. Then he walked slowly, shiveringly, downwards.

" Oh, come on ! " the General encouraged. Catching him by the shoulders he ducked him twice. They began to scuffle. Horribly hearty, Croft thought. I might be back at Rugby. But he enjoyed it, without wishing to.

" Race you to that log and back."

" But I say—you've got a start."

More splashings, laughter, shouts. For a long time it continued, while their bodies changed from blue to pink and then to a glowing red. They began panting.

At last the General said : " Oh, well ! All good things must end. I'm getting out."

As Croft followed him the General looked around, and immediately sniggered.

" What's the matter ? "

" Your pants ! "

Blushing angrily Croft looked downwards. The tie had run, staining the pants red, white, and blue, in patches. " Goodness ! " Then he, too, began laughing. But he was feeling cold now, and as the wind dried him his flesh seemed to become hard and scaly. " Wish I had a towel," he grumbled.

" Take some exercise ! " The General leapt from one tree trunk to another, slapping his thighs and whooping like a schoolboy. Oh, this is too much, Croft thought. This really is too much. But the cold and the prospect of getting into his clothes wet made him join in. He began to race round the pool, pursued by the General, who had broken off a sallow and was trying to belabour him. They both shrieked, whistled, and emitted terrible cat-calls.

Then suddenly, in the middle of this pursuit, they were conscious of being watched. They both drew up, breathless. Looked at each other. And with one accord whisked behind a bush.

It was the girl from the caravan, with a pail. She stood openmouthed, incredulous. Then, going down to the stream with a shrug of her shoulders she began to draw some water. She

had the bemused expression of one who has just woken from
a vivid dream. Eventually, looking about her, she disappeared.

" Oh, I say ! How frightful ! " Croft hurriedly began to
put on clothes.

" Why frightful ? What does it matter ? " The General
lay down on the grass. " My dear Mark, one worries far too
much about the sort of impression one is likely to make on
people. In this case it's unnecessary. You'll never see that
woman again. And anyway, this is the way one *should* bathe."
Getting to his feet, he began to dress slowly.

One couldn't help admiring him, Mark thought. With
anyone else the whole business would have been too self-
consciously back-to-nature. But apart from his first reactions
he had really enjoyed it. It had been worth while. He suddenly
felt a great affection for the General.

Eating a sandwich he said : " About the Amazon business.
I've been thinking. If you're still game, I should awfully like
you to come."

The General looked up. " Thanks. I'm still keen." Then
he stared outwards, towards the crests of a mound of chestnuts,
smiling.

" Good."

" I hope you're not going to have a lot of newspaper
publicity."

" Good God, no. That's the one thing I don't want. Of
course, my publishers want to make a big thing of it. Inter-
views. Headlines. All that sort of thing. But it's more than
just a stunt. I'm not going just so that I can come back and
write a book about it. If I write a book, it will be incidental
to the main business of finding that tributary we're looking
for."

The General nodded his head in tacit approval.

It was late when they returned home, and cold. Croft
drove through a faint, clinging mist which made him want

to cough. The General sat beside him. They felt satisfied, as grown-ups seldom are. It is usually only children who feel this sense of fulfilment at the end of a day. Lovers too. One is wonderfully replete. Nothing is lacking.

Croft broke the silence. "Cynthia must be getting rather worried. I said that we'd be back for tea. She had a meeting to-day. I wish she could have come." Then he thought : No. I'm glad she didn't. It would have spoiled everything. And immediately he felt guilty.

The General frowned. "I suppose you're going to get married soon."

"Not till I return from the expedition." Suddenly, he turned to the figure in the twilight beside him : "You disapprove ?"

"What of ? Certainly not of Cynthia. I think she's very charming." (Liar, liar, he accused himself.) "Of course, I sense—a certain hostility—my feelings not exactly reciprocated——"

"Oh, nonsense !"

"Oh, yes."

Croft let it pass, knowing that denials were useless. "But Cynthia apart——?"

"I don't think any artist should get married. It seems to me a mistake. Marriage incessantly gets between one and one's work. Of course, one may surmount the obstacle. But if one succeeds it's in spite, rather than because——"

Surprised, Croft cut in. "An artist, perhaps. But I'm hardly——"

"I'm using the term in its widest sense. Your occupation—like mine—like the artist's—demands a complete singleness of purpose. A wife distracts."

"Oh, no. Not always. Quite the reverse. A wife helps. And later when one is old——"

"Ah, yes. When one is old. One wants companionship and someone to keep one out of draughts. Marry then by all means. By then your work will be finished."

For a while Croft said nothing, his eyes fixed on the curve of the road.   Then at last : " You speak from experience ? "

" Perhaps."   The General took a rug from the back seat and put it, first of all over Croft's knees and then over his own. " You see, either one allows the obstacle to remain—and one's work suffers.   Or one rides over it."

" And the obstacle suffers ? "

" Yes."   Closing his fingers round Croft's wrist he asked : " Do you really think you would make a good husband ? "

" Probably not."   He laughed, without humour.   " But you see—I shall make a very good father.   I'm certain of that."

" You !   A good father ! "   The conversation had heaved upwards :   they were now being flippant.   " But my dear Mark—with your temper——"

" I don't think my temper really matters."

" But surely patience is the one thing one must have.   Without it——"

" It's important, certainly.   Oh, yes.   But it's not as important as all that.   The really important thing is—well—sympathy. I can think of no better word.   Sympathy for the essential pathos of childhood."

" The pathos of childhood ! "

" Yes.   The pathos of childhood.   That's the whole secret. One must acknowledge it.   One mustn't pretend it doesn't exist.   Of course, there's nothing one can do about it.   Nothing. But one must see that it's there."

" Well, really—I've brought up two children——" the General began.   Then he stopped, and said nothing more. I've brought up two children and I don't know what you're talking about.   A lot of nonsense.   The pathos of childhood ! You're using words which Cynthia has used.   You don't really think that.

Suddenly, and for no reason, he felt very tired and cold.   He drew the rug up to his chin, stretched out his legs, yawned. As he moved, he could hear the leather of his seat creak noisily.

And each time they met another car its headlamps made his
eyes ache and prick. Eventually, he closed them, became
drowsy, slept. Far away, he could hear Croft's voice :
" I think I'll ring Cynthia from here. I don't want her to
worry."

She was in the train, and she was feeling sick. It was years
since she had got over that. The last time had been when she
was travelling to Aunt Mathilde in Lyons, and in the lavatory
she had found the cutting about the General. And now she was
making another journey, perhaps equally momentous, and she
was a child once more, counting, counting ceaselessly, and
saying, " Oh, God, don't let me be sick ! Don't let me be
sick ! " Nothing changed, or changed very little. If one
looked for them, one found endless repetitions. Life going
over the same theme again and again, with variations. The
excitement lay in the variations. Last time she had stood in the
corridor and clutched a brass rail with gloved hands. This
time she sat in a crowded third-class carriage, reading the *Daily
Sketch*. The same, but different. A variation on the old theme.
A woman had taken a leather bag from under the seat, and
produced a cardboard plate, an orange, and a small silver knife.
She made a careful incision in the orange, so that the skin was
divided into four quarters. Then she tugged at each in turn.
There was a pungent, sickly smell, which filled one's mouth
with saliva. Piece by piece she devoured the orange, spitting
the pips into the palm of her hand. Then she took out a
crumpled handkerchief and wiped her fingers on it. She
sighed.
Shirley's nostrils were full of the sharp, pricking stench.
She wondered if she would have to go out to be sick. A child
leant across her and said : " Marmee ! Marmee ! Look !
The sea ! " And the mother said : " Oh, leave off, do ! Sit
straight ! " She had seen how Shirley had recoiled.
Out in the corridor it was unpleasantly windy : sweet papers

scraped along the floor, like dead leaves ; and her hair kept on
blowing into her mouth and eyes. A soldier, passing, pressed
unnecessarily close against her. She could not see his face, but
his neck was mauve with acne. She tried to think of other
things. What shall I say ? What shall I do ? Shall I say :
" Here I am ? " Letters were so much easier. Somehow, it
was possible to say those things in letters. But face to face. I
might dry up. Or faint. Anything.

He might not even be there, she suddenly thought. I
may arrive at an empty house. Or Judith. That would be really
awful. A nice fool I'd look. Eighteen-and-six wasted, thrown
away. Then she felt angry. Fancy thinking about the rail-
fare at a time like this. Isn't that typical ? When to-day I shall
see the General. Or will I ? Perhaps he'll have me thrown out.

The train was running beside a river. The river broadened
and became an estuary, green with conifers, flecked with buoys
and sails. Small ships were moored on it, gulls flapped. And
now on either side rose hills, on which were piled houses and
narrow streets, like sugar confectionery. Oh, well, thank God
for that. This must be Dartmouth. I won't be sick now.

But in the ferry she wasn't quite so certain. It pitched, and
churned out thick, sulphurous clouds of smoke. The engine
made a continuous plop-plop-plop. They were all crowded
together ; the sea was yellowy green. Sickly.

But I shall see the General, she thought. This was her
charm against the elements, her nausea, the never-ending
pushing. I shall see the General. And all shall be well. Oh,
yes, all shall be well. It must be. She felt, then, an overmastering, exquisite optimism. She was completely certain
there would be no mistake.

A boy in stained dungarees, with a light-coloured fur on his
upper lip, leapt out on to the landing-stage and began to moor
them. One by one the women stepped out, helped by their
consorts. Shirley gave a jump, disdaining the platform, and
almost caught her ankle on a winch. If she had she would have

been in the water. But she did not seem to realise the danger she had escaped.

As she climbed briskly up the hill a voice called : " You've left your suit-case, miss."

That was a silly thing to do. Blushing, she had to go back.

The house stood at the top of a creek. It was square and white, like a box, with a drive too steep and narrow for cars. In any case the General did not possess one. Along the front ran a veranda with hanging pots of ferns and rose-trellises. The black tiles gleamed in the morning sunshine.

She thought : Well, here I am. I'm for it. But strangely, she no longer felt nervous or apprehensive. She was still buoyed up by an incredible optimism. She began to crunch up the drive, her suit-case in her hand. Primroses were out, and a few daffodils. For no reason she stopped to pick a primrose and put it in her buttonhole. She did not realise that it clashed violently with the red of her coat.

One had to pass the back door before reaching the front. And as she did so two dogs leapt out at her, barking and wagging their tails. She started back, dropping her case. But they were chained, she realised. She walked on. Hanging upon a line were a pair of bathing-trunks of a dull magenta colour, caked with salt. She noticed the triangular piece of white cloth at the fork, thinking : Those must be his.

Clark answered the door. He was bald except for two tufts of white hair above each ear, and wore a green baize apron. His hands were twisted with arthritis. For a while he stared at her, as if in suspicion, before he asked : " Yes ? "

" May I see the General, please ? "

" What name ? "

" Miss Forsdike."

She thought : How dark it is in here. He had left her standing in a cupboard-like hall. Almost as soon as one crossed the threshold the stairs began steeply. There were old framed

maps on the wall, the head of an antelope, and two crossed oars.
On a table which had a top of engraved brass stood a pot with
a cactus in it, a Bradshaw, and some fishing-flies. The light had
a plain white porcelain shade.

She must have waited a long time. She felt nothing now,
not even optimism. She sat down on a wicker chair, and crossed
one leg over the other, and powdered her nose. After that there
seemed little left to do. She examined the brass top of the
table. It's Indian, she thought. There were peacocks on it,
and tigers, and rosettes. With one finger she traced the pattern.

Clark came back. " The Master's in the garden. Would
you mind going out there ? " He opened a door behind which
iron steps descended.

" Thank you."

As she climbed down her nostrils were filled with smells of
herbs. There was a lawn, two beehives, a seat painted white,
a shed painted green, a herbaceous border, and a gravel path.
" Where is he ? " she asked.

" At the end, Miss Forster."

" Miss Forsdike," she corrected.

He looked puzzled, and left her. With deliberation, not
hurrying, she made her way down the path, expecting at any
moment to see him, on a seat, beside a tree, gardening perhaps.
But all that she found was a wooden contraption, like a crow's-
nest, about twenty feet high. At the top was a boxed-in platform ; steps led up to it. This was the end of the garden ;
before her was a wall, with a pear tree against it, and nothing
else. But where was the General ?

Suddenly a voice said : " Do come up. This is my eyrie—my
tower. I sunbathe here. Can you manage the steps ? " He now
stood upright, fastening a dressing-gown about him. " I suppose
it's that little B.B.C. matter. Do come up. It's quite safe. I had
it built so that I could sunbathe in privacy."

She had been hesitating at the bottom. But now, clasping
the rail, she began to climb. For some reason the little effort

required made her extraordinarily breathless, so that she stopped twice, at the fifth and at the ninth step. At last she emerged; he faced her. On the floor was a towel, on which he had presumably been lying, and a copy of *The Times*. He put out a hand: "How d'you do, Miss Forster?" At that moment a gust of wind plucked at the newspaper and almost sent it over the rail. The General lunged outwards and grabbed it. "How d'you do, Miss Forster?" he repeated.

There could be no mistake. "Not Miss Forster," she corrected in a dry, harsh voice. "Miss Forsdike."

"But you're from the B.B.C.?"

"No."

He tightened the cord of his dressing-gown, staring at her. "Then who the hell are you?" She saw the question, unspoken as yet. "I'm Shirley Forsdike," she said, feeling suddenly giddy on that high platform.

"Shirley Forsdike! Then you're——"

She cut in loudly, fiercely. "I'm the person who wrote you those letters."

For some time neither of them said anything. They were both conscious that the newspaper had again been blown against the railing. But they did not attempt to rescue it. They simply watched its progress as it was torn, stage by stage, between the bars. Then it got free and fluttered downwards like a bird.

"I see," he said.

And almost at the same time she began to explain. "I had to come here. I had to. I've tried so long to forget about—— Oh, it's madness, I know. But, don't you see—this is the only way that I can hope to get cured. It's like an illness, don't you see. I had to see you. Oh, it's been awful—I've been so miserable. . . ."

She felt she was going to burst into tears. The nights when she could not sleep in her room in the hotel. And the way food nauseated her. "You eat nothing," said the two old

ladies, her friends. And beside her bed the sleeping-tablets.
" Only one, remember." But one was nothing. It made her
drowsy, incapable of action : that was all. He must see all
this, she thought. He must realise. He must see how thin
I've become, and my hair is so brittle. And these awful rings
round my eyes. He *must* see.

" Could you wait, please ? " He took up the towel. " I
must go and get some clothes on. You know your way to the
house. I'll be down in a minute. Then we must talk. We
must try and get all this clear."

He waited for her, ironically, to descend before he did. As
she passed she noticed that he was wearing red-leather slippers.
And nothing else, she thought. Slippers and a dressing-
gown.

She was shown into a darkened room. Clark, grumbling
under his breath, began to tug at heavy curtains. Apparently,
the room was seldom used. There was damp in it, so that one
could readily believe that if one took up the carpet there would
be cockroaches beneath. But everything was beautifully
polished : the fire-dogs shone.

She sat down, feeling sick again and strangely hungry.
Taking out the mirror from her bag she thought : Oh, I do
looks a sight. Dreadful. The rims of her eyes were red,
inflamed, the pores of her skin enlarged. Tears started to prick
at either side of her nose, her throat ached. Oh, damn !

This was Lucy's room. It was her portrait that hung above
the mantelpiece. She smiled blandly, in green silk, her hair in
a snood. Consciously pre-Raphaelite. The furniture, too, was
hers. It had been left to her by a rich aunt. The·General had
always hated it. There was a Queen Anne escritoire, a set of
occasional tables which fitted into each other, another table
inlaid with birds, an ivory musical-box, and a hideous Edwardian
lamp—Truth, bearing a torch to which was fitted a pink electric
light bulb. Lucy had never lived in this house ; she had never

been into this room. But it was hers, all hers. A dedication to
her memory. The General never sat there.

Shirley began to wander, aimlessly, round and round the
room. The curtains were faded William Morris, with lilies
on them. The stuff was thin. Next, she tried the musical-box,
but it only whirred, without tune. Beside it was a silver frame
with a photograph of two borzois in it, and a horse's hoof,
rimmed with silver. " Clara, 1901–1918." It was intended to be
used as an ash-tray.

Suddenly she saw a mantilla comb, its handle set with
brilliants. The teeth were very sharp. She took it in her hands
and turned it over, over and over, thinking : I suppose she
wore it. All that red hair. I'd look absurd in it. For a moment
she stuck it into her bun. Then, in exasperation, she pulled it
out again. It was of delicate tortoise-shell.

Footsteps descending. In alarm, she swung round. As she
did so the comb snapped in two. A nervous reaction. Quickly
she put it back on the piano, in such a way that the break could
not be seen. Then she waited.

But no one came in.

Upstairs in his room the General slipped into his clothes,
slowly, meditatively. He thought : Now what am I to do ?
What on earth am I to do ? He felt peevish, irritable. Sitting
on his bed he began to scratch himself—his shin and then the
inside of his thigh. The sensation was not unpleasant.

Odd that she should have arrived at just that moment. Lying
up there in the sun he had suddenly felt an appalling loneliness.
Partly, of course, it was Judith's letter. It had arrived that
morning, the first since her brief visit. The writing was round,
unformed, childish ; there were misspellings and horrible blots.
But as far as she could express herself on paper, the tone was
bleak.

I've lost her, he had thought. Irrevocable. For the first
time he saw the magnitude of the thing. Lying on a towel,

his back to the sun, he brooded blackly. She's the only soul
I've ever really loved. The relationship was perfect. Quite
perfect. It was perfect because it was set perfectly within its
limits. Neither of us ever trespassed. There were privacies.
We had our privacies which we mutually respected. That
seldom happens. You love a person, and the person demands
more. And you demand more. And there's dissatisfaction
all round.

It was my fault of course. I did trespass. I suddenly walked
into her territory. Jealous, I suppose. And the whole thing
was immediately ruined. Finished.

It was unusual for him to be so depressed. The solitude,
on which only a few hours ago he had been congratulating
himself, now irked him. I'm completely alone, he thought.
Completely independent. I thought it would be fun, but it
isn't. Croft hasn't answered either of my two letters. God
knows what has become of Frank. There's S. N. G., of course.
A troublesome ghost. As dead as Lucy. No, even he is lost,
lost utterly.

He thought of his conversation in the car with Croft after
their jaunt to the New Forest. Marriage is an obstacle. No
artist should get married. And Croft had said : " But when
you're old . . ." Am I old ? I suppose I am. When you're
old, and your work is done. Ah, that's the time.

He had sat up moodily on the towel. Why am I thinking
all this ? What's the matter with me ? I'll write Judith a
conciliatory letter with a cheque. That'll bring her round.
And in two months it will be the Amazon, with Croft.
The thought of the expedition made him feel strangely
excited.

All this was passing through his mind when she had appeared.
She was worse than he had ever imagined. Far, far worse.
Her hands were raw and red, her neck sinewy. But—yes—he
had welcomed her. At that moment he had welcomed her.
After one of Lucy's flirtations, when he had taken her to task,

she had sighed : " Yes, I know, darling. It was very naughty of
me. But one does like to be loved." He had thought it a
particularly vain and inept remark at the time. But now he
saw what she meant.

He stopped scratching and pulled on a pair of socks. Then
he methodically tucked his shirt between his legs and reached
for his trousers. As he took them, Judith's letter fell out of one
of the pockets. He left it, on the floor.

At the bottom of the stairs, instead of going into the drawing-
room immediately, he went out into the garden and cut a
rose for his buttonhole. Then he felt angry. It was a long time
since he had done that.

She rose to her feet, but sat down again at his brief gesture.
She waited. Hitching up his trousers below the knees he
lowered himself into a chair covered in pink satin. The chair
creaked. There was something ridiculous in the sight of him
in it.

" Well ? " he said.

" I'm afraid you must be angry with me. I ought never to
have come, I know. You must think me mad. If only I could
explain. . . . It seemed the only way out, you see. You never
answered my letters. I was desperate, I felt I had to see you."
She began biting her handkerchief. The spectacle nauseated
him.

" I'm not angry," he said. " A little surprised, perhaps.
What do you want ? What on earth can I do for you ? I
simply don't——"

" I told you in my last letter."

For a moment he looked puzzled. Then quietly, but with
great emphasis : " No. That's impossible. You must see
it is."

" But why ? Oh, please. For one night——"

" No."

" But why not ? "

" The whole idea is grotesque, horrible."

" It would cost you very little.   And if it meant my life—my whole life——"

He looked profoundly shocked ; he was shocked.   Stiffly he replied :   " One has a certain integrity."

" Oh, integrity ! "   She sat back in the chair, her lips trembling. Her fingers wrenched at the damp handkerchief.

" But don't you see—surely you see—it simply wouldn't work.   Grotesque.   Utterly grotesque."   He repeated the word to impress it on her.

" Oh, yes !   Perhaps ! "   Her voice jarring, grating, jerking out of control, she went to the window.   Outside she could see the river with sails on it—calm, green, distant.   " Grotesque. Oh, yes—it would be that.   But wonderful—wonderful also."

" Grotesque *and* wonderful ? "

She swung round.   " Why not ?   From the sublime to the ridiculous—it's not as far as you think.   They lie side by side. They mix.   At any moment the sublime may tip suddenly downwards into the pit.   And then you begin to laugh."   She spoke hurriedly, quoting from her last letter, which had never been posted.   She, herself, had come instead.   " I think you're too ready to see the ridiculous in the sublime—too ready to laugh.   That's the trouble with so many people.   And as for looking for the sublime in the ridiculous—oh, no—never ! Oh, can't you see—can't you see how wonderful it would be— the gesture—the magnanimity of the thing——"

Strange, he thought.   That's S. N. G.   Uncanny.   His voice, his words.   But he only shook his head.   " I still say— no.   Never.   Never, never, never."

She sank into the chair her eyes slowly filling with tears. " Then I've made this journey for nothing," she said.

Suddenly he found himself pitying her.   " I'm sorry," he said.   " You must understand.   I only wish there was some other way of helping you.   Oh, don't cry."

Clutching the arms of the chair she suddenly broke down.

Her body shook. The words jerked out of her : " It's-so-hopeless. I-don't-know-what-to-do. I'm-so-unhappy."

He went across to her chair, but could not bring himself to touch her. " Is there anything ? Is there any way ? I mean——"

For a long time she was inarticulate with grief. He waited, walking sometimes to the window, patting her shoulder, trying to comfort her. Then, wiping her eyes on the moist, frayed handkerchief, she said : " There ! I'm sorry. I don't know why I did that. It just happened. I've never done that sort of thing before. I'm sorry."

He took a cigarette and lit it. Thinking : Of course I should never have consented to this talk. I might have known. How plain she looked ! Her face blotchy, eyes red. He could not stop gazing at her, fascinated. The raw hands were horrible.

" Don't make me go yet," she pleaded, misinterpreting his movement for a cigarette. " Let me stay. Let me see you for a little. A week. Five days. Three. Oh, please. Three days of your company. Please."

For a while he thought, staring past her, out of the window. Then he said : " I'll make a bargain with you."

" A bargain ? "

" You shall have your three days. But afterwards—you must promise never to badger me again. No letters. No visits. You understand ? "

" I understand."

" Well ? "

" I accept, of course."

" Where are you staying ? Perhaps you would like to go to your hotel. Then you can come back here for lunch."

" I have no hotel, yet. I just grabbed a suit-case and came. It was the impulse of a moment. But I'll find somewhere."

" I doubt if you will. This is the week of the regatta. The hotels are full. Perhaps you'd better stay here. I'll get Clark to make up a bed."

" Oh, thank you, thank you ! "

She clutched at his hand, smiling, trembling. But he drew away and rang the bell.

Clark disapproved, of course. His presence alone was sufficient to make dinner a fiasco. He moved about sourly, while they sat in silence. The meal was fastidious, but sparse, the room cold. The General had dressed. He noticed how blue her shoulders were, how bony ; her nails were brittle ; she had rouged her cheeks inexpertly. All this, and Clark's unspoken disapproval, irritated him. He found he could not eat. Instead, he watched her every movement in impotent disgust.

She ate well. It was the first time that she had had an appetite for many months. When he said : " Will you have some more ? " pointing to the joint with the carving-knife, she said : " Yes, please," and passed her plate. This mere act, her hand pushing the plate towards him, made him furious. He piled her plate with meat to see if she could get through it. She did.

As she ate he listened to the slow click-click of her jaw, the methodical chumping. Once she put her napkin to her mouth and hiccoughed behind it. Later, eating an orange, she let the juice run down her chin in a manner which sickened him. Her fingers became soppy with it.

It was not a good beginning. And when, as he rose from the table, he saw her undignified scramble to find the shoe which she must have taken off during the meal, then he all but told her to go.

In the drawing-room he suggested some music. " Oh, yes," she exclaimed in delight. " Oh, please. Do play."

" I hadn't meant that. I was thinking of the gramophone." He was politely cold.

" But you can play. Oh, please." She went to the piano and opened it. " Mozart. I know he's your favourite composer. Please play some Mozart."

My vanity, he thought. Why do I do it ? Granados.

Someone worthless.   At least, I shall deny her Mozart.   He
began to play one of the Goyescas, without interest.   She stood
beside him.

At the end she said : " Oh, lovely ! I do love Mozart ! "

He slammed down the lid.   " Let's have the gramophone."

" I sleep on the terrace.   You mustn't be frightened if you
see me prowling about."

" Of course not.   But on the terrace—in May !   How could
you ? "

They were talking at the bottom of the stairs.   Her room
was on the ground floor, his upstairs.   Clark had just passed with
a hot-water bottle for her.

" Well—good-night."

" Good-night."

She put up her face at him, oddly, as though expecting to be
kissed.   The eyes were bright, feverish ; the lips trembled apart,
disclosing small, discoloured teeth.   She gripped the banister.

" Good-night," he repeated.

Later, lying out on the terrace, while one by one the lights
on the opposite hillside went out, and a ship hooted, and a car
moved along the road below with a swivel of headlamps, he
felt strangely replete.   He was not certain whether this sensation
came from the conjunction of stars and sound and fragrances, or
from her presence.   For a long time he lay there, wondering.
It was very late ; something scurried in a bed of ferns ; a chill
breeze blew across his face with a tang of salt.   Drawing his
blanket up to his chin he yawned.   Oh, Lord, Lord ! Lying
in the sun that morning everything had seemed finished.   And
now lying in the moon . . .

Suddenly turning his head towards the house he noticed that
her light still burned.

The second day.   In the cove he bathed while she watched
him.   Far away, the ferry bumped across the river, children

called, a ship glided slowly, slowly towards the sea. She lay
on the warm sand. Spreading five fingers. A moment ago
he had sat where her fingers were spread. She looked out to
the figure climbing the slippery rock, the Tower. Oh, the
implacable ache of love. The lust of the eye. Watching,
watching incessantly. That the image may be sealed, that the
negative be made positive. Hoarding a few careless postures,
flex of elbows, a twirl of the wrist. The lingering, unending
hunger.

Afterwards they walked into the town for ices. Sitting
in the crowded restaurant Shirley plunged her spoon into the
mound of strawberry and then put it to her mouth. And
immediately, even as her teeth began to ache at the impact,
she was filled with an immeasurable nostalgia, a thirst for the
past. She was a child, and this was a café in Fontainebleau,
with a red-and-white striped awning and tables out in the street,
and the General was her father. And with this transfiguration
came all the certainty and faith of childhood : life ceased to be
an endless variation on a worn-out theme ; but life itself was
many themes, many recurring themes. And the past was here,
now, not a tyrant, but an ally. The past was in the flavour of
the ice-cream, and in the quality of the light, and in the ache
of her teeth. And slowly, slowly, her eyes began to fill with
tears.

" What is it ? " the General asked. " What's the matter ? "
" Nothing," she said. " Nothing. It's so cold."

That evening they sat out on the terrace. A breeze was
blowing and she found it chill. Her teeth chattered ; she
shivered in her overcoat. But the General appeared not to feel
it. He sat back in a wicker-chair, smoking. The moon had not
yet risen, so that it was impossible to see him except as a dark
shadow from which erupted at intervals a shower of sparks.
The air was laden with the smell of his tobacco ; she could hear
his teeth bite on the stem of his pipe.

She, herself, did not smoke. She crouched, rather than sat, her back against the wall. It was only in this way that she could avoid the wind. Her eyes were watering with it ; her lips felt chapped. But she did not dare to suggest that they should go in. In any case it was very beautiful on that hillside, the white house a ghost behind them, lights flaring up opposite like matches struck at random in the dark, and the water coiled, sinuous, shot with its random reflections. Later, the river would sparkle. But now, without the moon, it only gleamed. The silence was heavy, falling about them, dulling the twitter of birds, the sound of cars. They were lapped in it, rocked in it, gently, gently.

In spite of physical discomfort, the cold, the wind, she felt immeasurably happy. It seemed as if at last some conclusion had been reached. Like an intricate pattern which one cannot grasp till the last arabesque is put in, like the rounding off of a sentence with some gracious period, some dying fall, so now what had seemed haphazard, trivial, formless, suddenly crystallised into a rhythm, a beautiful order. She tried to put this into words. Somehow it was easier to talk when she could not see his face and he could not see hers. " It's extraordinary how happy I feel. For that I must thank you. To-night—oh, it seems as if everything had been a preparation for me here, and you there, and this terrace, and the lights. An inevitable sequence, steps of a ladder. Entirely inevitable. It had to happen. Imagine reading a detective story—clue after clue baffling one—and then the solution, making all that has gone before suddenly intelligible—making it fall into place. That's how I feel."

But she would not really express what she meant. In her mind was the image of those unquiet spirits, maimed, sundered, who wander through the world seeking each other ; they bleed while they are apart, they mourn, they pine ; but when they find each other, then all their wandering becomes as nothing, then all that matters is that the two should have at last become

9

one, and that the halves should have been united. Behind her
she saw the immeasurable days of seeking ; each day was a
step, a clue ; and now the halves were no longer sundered,
they no longer bled.

Pushing back his chair he said : " It's getting cold. Let's
go in."

He, too, was succumbing to the magic.

The third day. A letter from Croft :

MY DEAR GENERAL,—I have now made four copies of this
letter ; and each time it seems more difficult to say what I have
to say. I am writing to tell you of a certain change in my plans
which will, I am afraid, disappoint you. As you have probably
inferred already, it concerns our projected trip together. Briefly,
my news is this : Cynthia and I (for reasons which I need not
go into) have decided to get married within the next month or
so, instead of after my return from South America. This, in
itself, will mean a delay of several weeks. But when I do go,
Cynthia, not unnaturally, wishes to accompany me. I have told
her of all the hardships and dangers involved, but she is quite
willing to accept them. She is a person of great resourcefulness
and courage. Now of course there was nothing in all this to
prevent our original agreement standing ; Cynthia would have
been delighted to have you as a third, and so should I. It is my
publishers who have forced on me a change of plan. Their
contention is that the selling value of the book will be greatly
enhanced if my wife and I make the journey together *alone*.
Naturally, I would not, in normal cases, care two hoots about
how the book sells. But in view of the marriage and so forth
one has, unfortunately, to consider these things. In any case
my publishers are willing to give me many more facilities if
I accept this one condition.

. . . Well, there it is, H. W. I know you'll think me quite
despicable. Lord knows how I hate the thought of all the
mawkish publicity that will now be put around. But, frankly,

we do need the money. And if the book is a success, then at least it will put us out of reach of that sort of thing for a long while. You see, I do have to consider Cynthia now, and not solely myself. I do hope you will understand.

What makes it so difficult to say all this is that I know how disappointed you will be. I really am most deeply sorry. . . .

The General, eating breakfast out on the terrace, tore the letter into four pieces which he left beside his place. His face was grey and strained.

"Excuse me," he murmured. Getting up, he crossed the lawn and disappeared. His feet made dark imprints on the wet grass.

Later, he returned. "What do you want to do to-day?" he asked with forced cheerfulness. Picking up the pieces of the letter he dropped them into his coffee-cup.

The General was making a model yacht. He took her into his carpentry shed to show her.

"It's wonderful," she said.

"Oh, no, it's not. Look at that. And that." He pointed out various defects in the wood. "I only hope she'll be sea-worthy."

"And the sails?"

"I'm sewing them myself. The only thing she really needs now is a figurehead. But I'm a pretty poor carver." He held up a grotesque figure. "Obviously that won't do."

"Let me try."

"Do you carve?"

"Oh, yes. It's one of the things I do with my girls. They much prefer it to basket-work." She took up a piece of wood and a penknife. "May I?"

"Go ahead."

"Let's go out on to the terrace."

As they worked, they talked together. For the first time

that morning he ceased to think about Croft's letter, cursing him for what he regarded as a betrayal. The intolerable bitterness that had weighed him down like a disease, his hatred for Cynthia, coming thus between him and his dream of the Amazon, his disappointment were all somehow assuaged. He began to think : What does it matter anyhow ? I'm too old for that sort of thing. Perhaps she'll die out there. That'll teach her. Perhaps they'll both die. No, not Croft. Let him return chastened.

This morose but not unpleasant brooding was interrupted by an exclamation from Shirley. The knife, slipping, had cut her palm. She put it to her mouth, but the blood trickled down her chin and on to the figurehead, staining it like some barbaric idol. She smiled, apparently not in pain.

"Here ! Let me." He took the hand and pressed it, to stop the flow of blood. Pulling a handkerchief from his pocket, he dabbed. The blood had already flowed on to his own fingers. It was warm and sticky.

"That's better," he said. "It'll stop in a moment. Then I'll get some iodine."

Their eyes met. "Thanks," she said. They both smiled.

Thinking : Obviously Cynthia persuaded him to get rid of me. I don't believe a word of all that talk about needing money. She's behind it all. Took a dislike to me right from the beginning. How I hate that type. And after all that he said about no publicity. Falling for a stunt like this. No doubt the women's papers will have pictures of her in a sola topi. Oh, blast, blast !

He felt suddenly weak, doubled-up. He couldn't walk any farther, the road jerked. "Let's sit down," he said.

"All right."

But it was no better. He felt sick with disgust and anger. His hands trembled. Funny, he thought. I imagined I was over it. Congratulating myself on not caring. But I do, I do.

The whole bay seemed to wither, to shrink. The light went livid. On the pretext of tying his shoe he put his head between his knees. Thinking: Strange. The physical disturbance. Perhaps if I could weep or throw a rage—if I could show it in some way—then all this wouldn't happen. Christ, I feel ill!

He clutched the back of the bench on which they sat, and gazed outwards at the gulls. They whirled down the wind, with thin shrieks of pleasure: or motionless, they poised on the waves' hands. The pleasure steamer from Totnes veered inwards, lurching with its crowds. The sea caved into black hollows.

Putting out a hand he touched her. To steady myself. At first she recoiled with a muffled " Oh ! " Then she remained perfectly still. His face averted, unable to look, he began to caress her body, while far off a sail jerked slowly, slowly outwards like a fan. He watched it, absorbed.

" Good-night."
" Good-night."
They parted at the bottom of the stairs, and she went to her room. Switching on the electric lamp she sat for a long time, thinking. The light was fluted, rosy, like a shell, as it fanned outwards from the parchment shade. Twice she yawned, stretching out with strange voluptuousness on the chill eiderdown. She looked at her arms, white and downed with blonde hair, and then round about her, at the room. There were the bold eye-tones of the brass warming-pan, the twin lustre jugs, a Dutch snow-scene, two chairs with lace over their arms : and then, beyond, shadows, darkness.

This was the end of the three days. The thought filled her with conflicting emotions. It was difficult to know what to feel. She rubbed the fingers of one hand across her cheek. What she had, she had. But was one ever satisfied ?

Going to the windows : she pulled back the heavy curtains. The curd-like moon was yellow on the terrace ; it was bright

and warm. Click. Her hand, extinguishing the lamp, turned
the room into an aquarium. It was flooded with a saffron tide
in which quivered algae, delicate objects, shadows. The carpet
seemed to curl, the chairs to bob upwards. The bed swung
soundlessly round and round. Then the water went static ;
everything was seen distorted, tall, immovable. It was a little
frightening.

She began to undress slowly, humming to herself and
dropping her clothes on to the floor. When she was naked she
stared for a moment at her reflection in the glass ; and then, as
though dissatisfied, she pulled on a nightdress. How cold the
sheets were, swishing as she scissored her legs downwards. The
pillows seemed mountainous. But at the centre was her own
heart, radiating warmth and life.

For a long time she lay there, her head resting on her arms,
while the moon seeped over the carpet and began to be drawn
up the edge of the counterpane. The yellow liquid mounted
as though on blotting-paper. She could not sleep. For no
reason, her heart thumped, her wrists trembled, her eyes refused
to shut. She wished to prolong for as long as possible the last
few hours that she spent in his house. If one could only stop
the hurrying feet, drawing one inevitably into the future. If
one could only stop the passage of time, corroding the hours
as the moonlight corroded the counterpane. Time would make
all this history. Time drew everything away, greedily. . . .

Eventually she became drowsy, she dreamed. She was
being shown over a great dusty palace whose rooms were
labyrinthine ; echoes rumbled down empty corridors ; the
walls seeped damp or gaped in jagged fissures. The corners were
furred with cobwebs. And someone was saying, incessantly :
" This is yours. This is all yours. This belongs to you." But
she took no pleasure in her possession. Rather, she wandered
on, hoping always to come upon a room which was not vast
like this, nor empty, nor desolated by neglect. At last, at the
end of a long flight of stairs which spiralled upwards she found

a door, much smaller than the rest, which she opened; and as she did so she exclaimed with pleasure, " Oh ! How wonderful ! " The tower-room was narrow; a fire was lit; brasses gleamed; and because all the rest of the house was old and crumbling into ruin, this seemed the end of the quest. But the voice that had said : " This is yours," now said, over and over again : " Not here. You may have everything else. You may have all the other rooms. But not this room. This is the housekeeper's room." And with those words in her ears she woke.

Someone's nails were tapping lightly on the window. She lay for a moment sick with apprehension. Then she said, weakly, " Who's that ? " Her voice seemed to come up from a pool of ice, sharp and wintry. Then again she said : " Who is it ? "

The french windows opened and the General came in. He did not close them after him, so that the curtain shot outwards and then deflated in the wind, and eddies of draught crossed her face. Her tongue seemed paralysed, enormous; she could not speak. Slowly he came to her; and for no reason, she found herself listening to the creak-creak of his slippers. Then she gripped him, as though in terror. " You've come," she said.

" I've come." His voice seemed very distant.

She drew him downwards, turning her face so that on her cheek she felt the touch of his hair. Pains teased her joints; suddenly she went rigid. But he murmured : " No, no. You must do nothing. Relax." Relax. And she was falling into circles and cycles of peace. She was falling. . . .

Dawn appeared as a pink smear over the estuary. Birds were twittering; a ship's hooter reverberated in a glum *decrescendo*; the light was grey and cold. She woke up with a start, her eyes blinking open. She had been breathing through her mouth, so that it now tasted dry and acid. Suddenly, she remembered. As she did so, she began to smile with extraordinary pleasure, drawing her fingers down her cheeks. Then she put out a hand and touched the part of the bed where she herself had not lain. Thinking : It's all complete now. All things are well. A circle. Nothing more is necessary. She sighed, pulling the bedclothes up to her chin.

For a long time she lay there ; until on an impulse she suddenly leapt out of bed and put on a pair of slippers. Opening one door of the french windows she went out. It was very cold. The air was sharp with frost, and where last night she had spilled her coffee on the terrace there was now a grey-brown wedge of ice. The grass was crisp and shiny. She began to wish that she had put on a dressing-gown, for already her teeth were chattering and her hands were blue. Two sparrows startled her, whirring noisily out of the ivy as she passed. They curveted over the lawn in sudden, excited swoops and then disappeared. A dog rattled its chain.

It was strange how sharp everything became. The trees stood out boldly, with an almost fussy precision ; the clop-clop of a distant milk-float sounded close and very distinct ; and each of the houses on the opposite side of the river resembled wooden models on a shelf. If one put out a hand one could touch them.

The pink fissure in the sky widened and seemed to clot. The light went suddenly gauzy and unreal, as though one were looking through tinted glass. A tree began to drip on to the terrace with a lisping sound ; the lawn darkened, so that each blade of grass ceased to be distinct ; sun gleamed zig-zag in the puddle of coffee. It was thawing.

She found his bed at the other end of the house. He slept on his side, with one hand under his cheek. He breathed deeply, and as he did so his chest rose. Only a sheet covered him, and his pyjama jacket was open. On the floor beside him lay a fragment of paper resting on a book, and a pencil. She knelt down to read. But the only words were : ' Of course I was disappointed '.

She remained kneeling thus for a long time, watching him,

while her eyes began to fill with tears. There is always pathos in the sight of a person asleep; perhaps one is too easily reminded of the resemblance between sleep and death; when one sees someone sleeping, one sees too that last inevitable dissolution. All this she felt, and also the impossibility of his ever realising how much he had done for her, and she had done for him. For the miracle belonged to them equally. She believed that. If she had thirsted, so had he, without knowing it. In a sudden uprush of tenderness, she put a hand to his cheek, running the fingers downwards so that they scraped on the unshaven flesh. He woke with a start.

As though not knowing where he was, he looked about him wildly. Then he saw her. " Lucy ! " he exclaimed. " Lucy, my dearest ! "

" Lucy ? Why do you call me that ? "

With one hand he covered his eyes, a gesture of illness or fatigue. Looking up, he said with odd distinctness : " I'm sorry. I've been dreaming. It's you, is it ? I'm sorry."

She repeated : " Why did you call me Lucy ? " And because he did not answer, she pursued : " Was she your wife ? Was Lucy your wife ? "

He nodded.

" And you called me—— ! Oh, I'm glad. I'm glad. I'm so happy."

But he only said crossly : " Get back to bed. You'll catch cold. You've no dressing-gown. Get back to bed."

Clark knocked and, without waiting for an answer, came in with a breakfast-tray. His face was sallow and lumpy, like a potato : when he had put down the tray, he wiped swollen, red-veined hands on his apron and went to the windows. It was swinging, unlatched. With an abrupt gesture of pique he slammed it to and grated the lock.

Shirley woke with a start. " Good heavens ! What time is it ? "

Ignoring the question he made for the door. " The master said I was to bring you your breakfast."

" But did I over-sleep ? " She had not breakfasted in bed on any other morning. " What time is it ? Has the master had his breakfast ? "

He pulled out a watch on a chain, from which dangled coins and a locket. As he pressed the winder, it opened with a metallic ' ping ! ' " Ten o'clock. The master had his eight o'clock. Gone out. Gone sailing. Told me to see about your bags. Told me to order a taxi for you." The raw hands continued to dry themselves needlessly on the apron.

" Very well. I'll let you know about the taxi—and the luggage. Thank you."

He drew in his breath sharply, like an asthmatic, and then went out. The joints of his knees creaked. In sudden desolation, she turned over in bed, breathless, choking. The bed seemed large and cold, the light brutish. Her hands shot up to her mouth, from which came a series of moans. The sheets twisted round her legs, like grey bandages. Then, in a spasm of anguish, she flung out an arm. The tray of neatly ordered crockery crashed to the floor.

On the table of her room in London stood a shaving mirror in a mahogany frame. It had belonged to her father ; it magnified. She looked into it now with suppressed disgust. It showed each pore of her skin, distended, rough, like a loosely woven fabric ; it showed distinct hairs, on chin and upper-lip, blemishes on the nose, scarlet filaments round the bulging eye-balls ; there were particles of scurf where her hair was brushed away from her forehead. For a long time she stared at this caricature, glumly, her chin on her hands ; she stared into her own eyes, flecked with light blue and green like oysters ; she stared at the inflamed lids, which seemed to have been skinned, so raw were they. She had not slept for three nights.

Then she took up a pen. Thinking : This is the last letter

I shall ever write. This is the last time I shall sit here, before this mirror. The end. Words formed in her mind, confused, haphazard, a torrent of words : she had never composed with such facility, nor such carelessness. As she wrote she turned the mirror face downwards, obliterating the pop-eyed gargoyle. It was easier when one was not looking at it.

MY DEAREST,—For the last time I write to you, for the very last time. By the time you get this letter, I shall be dead. One has read that last sentence so often before—in novels, in films, in newspaper reports ; one does not expect that one shall ever write it oneself. But now death seems the only conclusion possible. All that should have happened, has happened. Anything more would be superfluous.

I read somewhere that all or nearly all suicides are caused by the wish for revenge. ' You'll care now. This'll teach you.' You must not think that I have any such thoughts. There is no anger in my heart, no bitterness. I simply feel that I have accomplished all that I was sent into the world to accomplish. And now there is nothing more.

I doubt if I can ever explain this to you. I do not understand myself, completely. But I am certain that all my life before was nothing more than a preparation for those three days I spent with you. Why ? I simply do not know ; perhaps you will, one day. This was my act of service to you. Service—I am convinced of that. Those three days were a crisis for you as well as for me. More I do not know. But of that I am certain. And now my part is over.

To do what one was destined to to—there is nothing more that one can ask for. That is enough. Our lives momentarily converged. In some way—I do not know how—I have been of help to you. It is sufficient. I think I am happy now, and at peace. That terrible inner restlessness—you have freed me from it.

I have no thoughts of the future. I do not know what will become of you. I still see you as a superman, the embodiment

of my own and perhaps this country's destiny. I still believe you
can do so much, if you will only awake to your power.

I am not afraid to die. In a sense, I feel that I am dying *for you*.
In some way, I feel that this too is necessary.

Now and at all moments—now and at the hour of death—I
am yours, yours only.   SHIRLEY.

She pushed the sheets into an envelope and licked the flap
with a greyish tongue. The pen seemed to scratch intolerably
as she wrote the address in careful flourishes. Then for a while
she sat motionless, looking outwards at the plane trees, the
little square, the blotchy façade opposite. Suddenly it seemed to
her bitter and terrible that she should never see these things
again. If it had been raining or there had been a fog perhaps
she would have been able to leave them without regret. But
the spring sunshine was sad and autumnal as it flowed over the
window-sill ; it was lax with memories. She wanted to sit in
it, doing nothing, while far below people made random furrows
of shadows on the gleaming pavements, and a dog sniffed a
lamp-post, and a barrel-organ tinkled in the distance.

Oh, no. She must be resolute. She put on her coat with
its fur collar that stuck out in drab tufts, and then her hat, and
last of all some green woollen gloves embroidered with eidel-
weiss. But before she left the room she went on an impulse
to the head of her bed. Taking from the wall the framed photograph of her father she smashed it downwards on the brass
bedpost. Then, from the splintered glass, she extricated his
image and put it in her pocket.

As she walked downstairs she fingered it all the time.

From a letter :

MY DEAR GENERAL,—I am sending you this typescript of the
novel. I have called it *To the Dark Tower*. This is the third
draft. But it still is not you. . . .   FRANK CAULDWELL.

On the following pages are details of Arrow Books that will be of interest:

THE MAN ON THE ROCK
Francis King

Con man, petty thief, parasite – Sprio Polymerides is all of these and more. Like so many young men trapped in the poverty and unemployment of post-war Greece he has nothing to rely on but his own good looks and natural cunning.

Restlessly, he drifts from one victim to another: Irvine, the repressed homosexual who befriends him; Helen, the rich middle-class Englishwoman with whom he has an affair; Kiki, the Greek shipping heiress he eventually marries.

All these he exploits, betrays and destroys – only to find that the final victim is himself.

THE WAVES BEHIND THE BOAT
Francis King

In a remote corner of Japan an Englishwoman is drowned by a freak tidal wave. Bill, a young university lecturer, and his wife Mary are asked by the Consul to identify the body.

On their arrival in the seaside village they are met – and befriended – by Bibi Akulov, the immensely rich White Russian in whose house the dead woman was staying.

For the English couple it is the start of a complex and un-nerving relationship with Bibi and her mysterious brother Sasha – a relationship which reveals the darker side of the Akulov household, and involves Mary in an increasingly brutal exploration of her own secret nature.

A DOMESTIC ANIMAL
Francis King

'Italians are not really domestic animals . . .'

Antonio Valli, a brilliant Italian philosopher in his thirties, comes to a redbrick university for a year of research.

Handsome, impulsive and with an insatiable need for admiration and affection, Antonio captivates all who come into contact with him – including Dick Thompson, the successful middle-aged novelist in whose house he goes to live.

Soon Dick has fallen completely – and disastrously – in love with his flamboyantly heterosexual lodger. Out of this ill-fated relationship, Francis King has created a novel of bitter longing and painful complexities.